PANIC IN THE BALLPARK

Sam made a final review of his calculations and program settings before bringing back the omniview. Double, even triple, number and procedural checks were bursting from his head. He ran through one more mental checklist. Once started, he knew the auto-targeting program would run to completion. It had to be correct.

It was.

Sam took a deep breath and clicked "Go" on the menu.

The operation started with the UAV rising from the tower to its designated height.

Tiger headed north—away from the stadium—to gain the 5.2 seconds necessary to reach 60 mph.

This was huge and sure to turn Camden Yards from wonder to zoo to war zone in seconds.

The auto-fire control menu ticked down. . . .

TARGET ACQUIRED

JOEL NARLOCK

LEISURE BOOKS NEW YORK CITY

Leisure Entertainment Service Co., Inc. (LESCO Distribution Group)

www.leisureent.com

A LESCO Edition
LESCO
65 Richard Road
Ivyland, PA 18974

Published by special arrangement with Dorchester Publishing Co., Inc.

Printed in the United States of America.

ACKNOWLEDGMENTS

To all those who design, build, and operate the curious flying machines known as unmanned aerial vehicles—while the rest of us sit in wonder.

Special thanks to Commander Joe Beel, USN. If I live to be 100, I'll never understand the equation for probability of UAV damage from n penetrators.

And to my wife, Terri, for tolerating an imagination run wild.

TARGET ACQUIRED

Chapter One

Troy Wells Jr. stared through his Cessna's windshield at steam rising from the engine into the cool Maryland night. He could feel the first dull throbs of a tension headache: small and not yet painful, but rhythmic and building—like waves before a storm. Tonight they were early, compliments of the U.S. Secret Service.

A certified flight instructor moonlighting for extra cash, he'd worked for the FAA before and was used to false pretenses—a rookie logging night hours in unfamiliar surroundings, restricted airspace, zero permission. Most were harmless flights that tested air traffic controller reactions. Sometimes he even played with a military base—never the White House.

He rested his hand on a Bible on the passenger's seat. Chicken-soup nourishment for the low and slow. It was his father's. When he was alive, Troy Sr. had dusted crops in Virginia. He complained of headaches, too, but not from tension. After ten years, that book still smelled of ethylene insecticide.

Tonight's route was shaped like an elongated number six with a tiny toe loop that started out innocently enough on a westerly course to the Potomac River, turned not so innocently south toward Reagan National Airport, circled through the National Mall, then back to the Potomac for the exit home. Troy clicked the radio on, then off again. If he could only listen but not respond there was no point. Besides, quiet air would help him focus on the fact that in eight minutes he'd sneak into the heart of the nation's capital with no traffic control or tower communication, and break some of the strictest aviation laws on the books. He had already disconnected the transponder to mask the plane's identity. His father surely lurched in the grave at that. There'd be no pride for this juvenile delinquent of a pilot who was about to ring a major airport's doorbell, then run away through the backyard of the most famous house in America. No jail time, either. Not that it was a cakewalk. Even in calm weather with good visibility, flying mere feet over buildings in the middle of the night was never predictable. Troy had already beaten the biggest hassles by tying a video camera to the Cessna's airframe and putting his signature to a nondisclosure contract. A twenty-three-mile flight for five thousand dollars. Now that was chicken soup. Hassles aside, it was his largest fee and his most exciting assignment ever. Having it paid in advance also made it the sweetest.

Four minutes.

Troy unfolded a sectional map for one more look at the prohibited no-fly zone, or NFZ, surrounding DC's central monuments. One level higher than restricted, the airspace maintained a fragile truce with three overlapping radar patterns that looked strangely like the ears—Dulles and Baltimore—and face—National—of Mickey Mouse. It was a truce that was about to be shattered, as his flight path wouldn't simply nudge the zone's perimeter, but violate its inner sanctum.

He tucked the map into his jacket. Somebody obviously wanted movies, but why? he wondered. The feds had enough of their own planes and low-flying pilots to videotape every inch. He had a flawless flight record and could keep his mouth shut without a contract, but why use a civilian instruct—Damn! That was it. A training film. Collision-close with another aircraft, then a low-altitude escape through the middle of Washington on a path that just happened to cross over the White House. Simple enough. Jesus—what government genius had brainstormed this? An aircraft with passengers? No way—that'd be prison. It had to be cargo. Some hush-

hush arrangement with a major carrier. United's flight simulators always seemed to have uncanny realism. It made further sense because the path mirrored National's southbound approach, albeit several hundred feet lower. As for the Mall breach and north loop, aircraft regularly bumped DC's holiest of holy airspace dangerously close to the president's house no matter how many federal agencies denied it. Careless pilots at National did it *three times a month*. Nothing ever came of it except wrist slaps or brief suspensions. He wouldn't even get that. To his thinking, this was the first time any pilot would intentionally fly into airspace so hot Santa couldn't get flight permission at Christmas. The White House. *Man—what a rush!* And what a story, after the confidential-disclosure time limit expired. There'd be tabloid cash, but how could he prove it? Snatch a copy of the film? Maybe personalize it somehow or leave something behind on the grounds or even the roof. He could finally afford that engine overhaul.

Troy shook his head at the greedy face in the windshield. *Forget the money and do your job so the industry can set some real penalties*, he told himself. But this wasn't just a harmless bump—more like a frontal assault on the most highly guarded acreage on the planet. An assault that flew in the face of National's departure rules requiring outbound pilots to turn hard left—west—a few seconds after takeoff. Inbounds had that opposite but equally nasty juke over the Potomac before setting down.

Either way, a lapse in concentration meant buzzing the White House and taking a stinger missile up the ass. Crude, but so went the warning.

One minute.

Troy pressed the throttle and taxied onto the runway.

Marking the time, he started the video recorder and surveyed the buildings from the refueling pumps to the hangars. Too small for a control tower, College Park closed at ten P.M., along with the rental car station and restaurant. The airfield was deserted except for a raven-black sedan sitting quietly in the parking lot. He was glad there were observers. They brought some legitimacy to the assignment. Doubtful they'd even see the traditional gesture, much less acknowledge it, Troy raised his hand and flashed thumbs-up. Headlights blinked once.

The Cessna lifted into the air and turned southwest, down the six.

Ten minutes later, the plane dropped into the Potomac River's tree lane at Foggy Bottom. Light from private boat docks outlined the river's contour. Waterfalls and rapids helped muffle the propeller's whine. Ahead, Washington's night vista shimmered reddish gold, like a horizontal aurora borealis. Flying parallel with, but below National's glide slope, he was now naked to area radar—a lone blip of slow-moving metal that literally appeared out of nowhere with no identifying characteristics. There was no sign of another aircraft. So much for the training theory. Still, he wasn't about to putter around and let the next inbound jet roar up his tail at 170 knots.

Guided by lampposts dotting the George Washington Memorial Parkway and runway eighteen's blue landing lights at National, the Cessna whisked over Interstate 66 low enough to wave to the sparse but steady bridge traffic. No one cared. There was nothing extraordinary happening in the sky except a slight increase in turbulence from some tower controller's curses certainly pummeling his craft through the air.

As he banked, the plane's wheels missed the Lincoln Memorial by a scant eight feet. The nose challenged the Washington Monument, guardian of the Mall. The cadence of the obelisk's aircraft beacons now seemed to blink a stern but unheeded warning as the intruder split the reflecting pool. At center Mall, one more lazy turn framed a sleeping White House twenty-five hundred feet to the north. The altimeter dial read seventy-five.

As he approached the venerable south lawn, Troy's normally keen flying senses dulled. Sounds deadened. Scenery details blurred, and heat flushed into his face with the sensation that someone or something knew he was there, and that he had come upon extreme danger. The relaxed yet businesslike aura of a daytime White House was now unfriendly, even foreboding. There was no welcome ceremony, reception, or festivity. Those were ground-based and controllable. This was airspace, and its aura carried only anxiety. The temptation to throttle up and climb was strong—so was the urge to click the radio and start barking explanations, beg forgiveness from those surely listening. If that didn't work, he could always feign mental lapse or talk gibberish, ruses he'd used before. Wait—*not* a good idea. A suicidal nutcase would have no credibility here. He glanced at the Bible. *Great.* A religious suicidal nutcase.

He shielded his eyes from the glare of halogen lighting on the south portico. There was movement ahead on the ground. Shadows—no, they were figures. Black. The same outlines were on the roof. Running with . . . guitars? Why were they kneeling?

Troy closed his eyes. The lead guinea pig in an elaborate targeting scene had just won an Oscar for gullibility.

Shoulder-fired.

Get up and out now! Exercise or not, he wasn't about to let some gung-ho security rookie put his plane in crosshairs and make a firing mistake.

He jammed the throttle and twisted the yoke.

The Cessna, cruising near stall speed of fifty knots, bucked forward in a frantic turn to the west. To hell with low and slow—this was an air sprint. The starting gate was Pennsylvania Avenue, the track a brief stretch over a city thoroughfare into one last radar-free tree lane that skimmed the Potomac. He needed distance. He needed clutter.

A missile impact would come from behind, and once one was sent, there was nothing he could do to stop it. History and world headlines flashed through his mind in the form of collateral damage, debris, and some very unlucky victim guilty of nothing more than nocturnal pet walking.

Troy sensed a burst of light behind the plane, locked on and deadly, moving at blazing speed. In the cockpit, his back arched forward off the seat as though someone had run a knuckle down his spine. Braced, he held that position, paralyzed like a newborn fawn, frozen as though he felt the warm breath of a predator ready to kill on his neck. He had just become the epicenter. A gigantic shiver, the kind he had after finishing a long pee, spread through his torso and limbs like the energy released from a great quake, the largest he'd ever felt.

Preflight headache waves had reached tsunami levels and pounded in his temple almost as hard as the wheels pounded the runway.

He finished the six in record time—right over the complex.

No alarms, no missiles, no history. Nothing. Not even a checkered flag or a victory cheer. Just an empty parking lot and a night flight that never happened.

Troy cut the engine and pressed his hand onto the Bible. Moist with perspiration, it left an imprint on the cover that slowly disappeared into nothing, much like the White House security retaliation.

But there was another imprint. He had left it hanging in the air over Washington—proof that he'd been there. Not made of sweat but an energy imprint; a tiny buzz, faint and also disappearing. Not quite as intense or traceable as that which still hangs in all airspace, left eons ago by the Big Bang, discovered by Nobel Prize winners at absolute zero but a similar imprint just the same.

That shiver.

Chapter Two

The Pentagon
Department of Defense Advanced Technology Office
(ATO)
Post–9/11

Maj. Gen. Ken Blalock's ears were legendary in unmanned airborne reconnaissance; huge, they stuck out an inch from the sides of his head and turned shades of red whenever he got upset in sort of a temper barometer. Right now they were approaching the color of a chili pepper.

"Seven hundred ninety godblasted pounds. One and a half billion taxpayer dollars falling out of our wallet, and not one contractor can design anything more creative than the Pillsbury Doughboy." He lifted the one-sixth-scale plastic model of the IRS—International Robotic System, Inc.—UAV and hurled it the length of the conference table. For a moment, the model actually seemed to drift through the air under its own power until it hit the floor, its pieces mingling with those of four others that had met similar fates in the morning review session.

Blalock's current billet had been a relatively comfortable one until the world turned upside down on 9/11. Overnight, his team in the Defense Advanced Research Projects Agency, DARPA, and its objectives to specify, obtain, and deploy next-generation short-range tactical aerial drones to the U.S. service branches had become top priorities. Every commander with a terror defense directive and money was screaming for UAVs. In addition to a tenfold increase in funding, Blalock had been given broad, even rogue authority to bypass the DoD's snail-like acquisition process and award vendor contracts based on nothing more than a few pages of text and specifications, even a scribbled drawing or gut feeling, if he wanted.

"One point seven billion, sir," peeped Lt. Cmdr. Rob Glomb, officer in charge of financial management.

"Makes it even worse. Who's next?"

"Sikorsky Aircraft at sixteen hundred, sir."

Blalock glanced at his watch. "Lou, what's their story? If it's fat and round I will not be happy."

Test and evaluation manager Capt. Lou Tavella knew the answer but didn't want to speak it as he thumbed through a stack of proposals for the three-page overview. Sikorsky's machine was lightweight but unstable and had short range. It looked exactly like an inverted Frosty the Snowman. Thank God they hadn't included a model.

Blalock rolled a water glass over his forehead, trying to cool his propulsion frustration. He scanned the summary specifications, pausing at a color diagram of the Sikorsky unit. A propeller sat in place of a top hat.

"Right out of Beany and Cecil." He noticed the blank faces of his support staff. Book-smart officers with good operations and number skills, they had little experience working with savvy defense contractors—only one was over thirty.

The team's deputy director, Col. Dan LaCroix, poked his head into the conference room doorway. Blalock raised one finger.

"Beany was a dumpy cartoon kid who couldn't fly straight, and neither can any of these head-mounted contraptions. I want everyone hitting the books during break to tell me the shortcomings of vertical turboprops. Georgia Tech did some nice work on this for General Atomics. If private consultants know the answers, we should, too. Reconvene in an hour. Dismissed. Dan, c'mon in."

A veteran U.S. Army officer on loan for the past two years to the Defense Intelligence Agency, or DIA, LaCroix was the military's recognized father of remote-control systems. He had sponsored the *Pioneer*, the UAV that had flown targeting missions in the Gulf War while a worldwide CNN audience gazed at Earth from its video lens. A tireless—some considered him eccentric—campaigner for unmanned technology, LaCroix entertained proposals for amphibious and ground-based mine killers, robotic televiewers, and even miniature helicopters that could deliver medical supplies to wounded ground troops. Once he had given serious credence—and so had naval intelligence—to a West Coast civilian who claimed his remote-controlled submersible had, on the morning of Easter Sunday 1995, approached *two* docked U.S. aircraft carriers in San Diego Bay undetected. Timed high-energy explosives would have turned the propellers and shafts of those ships into shredded wheat, rendering both vessels helpless for months. Capable of unnerving even liberal military planners, most of LaCroix's wild-eyed notions ran headlong into department budget cuts that ultimately put those types of proposals out of their misery.

LaCroix sidestepped the plastic heap on the floor. "I see you're pleased with the vendor prototypes. Beany and Cecil? I thought all you did was play army."

Blalock's ear color had returned to pink. He rotated his neck, trying to loosen a muscle cramp. "God, I miss the old days. Simple requirements, honest contractors, and the *Hunter*. I loved that damn machine. Day or night, a reliable flying camera—period. Three years and we're no closer to a joint tactical UAV than we are to Mars. I'm rookie-staffed, overworked, and the Congressional Budget

Office is camped out in my office expecting me to clean up the mess DARO left." The Defense Airborne Reconnaissance Office had managed all DoD unmanned systems until Congress, frustrated that four military jackasses refused to pull in a common direction, disbanded DARO and transferred UAV functions back to the services.

"*Hunter* crashed three times in forty-five days," LaCroix reminded Blalock. "Not exactly a model of reliability. Smile. We've got decent machines in the air: *Pioneer*, *Predator*, *Hawk*, and *Outrider* all have good sorties under their belts. It's a great time to build UAVs now that we're finally able to shoot the bad guys. Long overdue in my humble opinion. We should've sent airmail to Hussein and Milosevic." He was referring to the *Predator* UAV and its in-flight ability to launch Hellfire missiles.

Blalock shrugged. "We never had clean authority until they lifted Executive Order 12333. Now we can target all the bin Ladens that come along. I personally think it's better if shooter and weapon remain a mystery, but then, what do I know? When I sleep, I dream about a small machine able to penetrate even the most highly guarded areas. Something maneuverable and quiet enough to secure a perfect vantage point. Hover in-range. Blend into the surroundings. Patiently wait for the optimum moment. An unknown, unseen assailant. Detect. Identify. Lock. A lethal shot on target. Exit. No one knows if it was friend or foe. Clean."

"Sometimes dreams come true," LaCroix said matter-of-factly.

"Stop it," Blalock ordered. "The last time somebody said that to me, I found myself in charge of the Aquilla project and lost the army's ass. Hell, I'm the general of practicality now. I'd retire before funding another billion-dollar lemon. Guess I'm jealous that I won't be here to see the next generation." He held up a magazine. "A Fort Worth contractor built a radio controlled jet in his garage that weighs thirty-eight pounds and flies two-hundred and eighty miles per hour. Do you know how hard it would be to defend troops against fifty of them with offensive minds? Someone could have a field day with civilian assets—buildings, bridges, aircraft, and even nuclear sites. Perhaps not the containment vessels, but aboveground cooling systems would be vulnerable. Name any radar system that can track thirty-eight pounds. These birds are small, fast, and look so real you'd swear they belong on an aircraft carrier. One club in Ohio even has an air show with a five-thousand-foot runway. Civilians are on the leading edge and we're launching snowmen across conference rooms. Machines *should* be small, fast, and simple; penetrate deeper into hostile territory; and collect better data, including positional coordinates, all without detection. But what good does it do to keep agreeing with ourselves? None of our contractors get it. They keep designing these complex lumber buckets because all they want are the maintenance payoffs. It still irks me that Runner commandeered *Predator* and hides his numbers whenever we come around. I swear he's getting kickbacks. I hate fat and complicated more than push-button wars." Blalock never was a big fan of what he termed "kissy-kissy firepower sharing" between platforms. This time it was the *Predator* versus the manned AH-64 Apache helicopter.

"Glad to see you don't carry vendettas." LaCroix laughed. "Are you trying to say it's out of control? What about *Predator*'s record in Afghanistan?"

"We threw the media a few bones about the surveillance, but we all knew it was too slow and too hard to fly. *Hunter* would've spotted that terrorist SOB five years ago." It wasn't true. *Predator* had double the endurance hours and better radar.

Blalock cleared a space on the table in front of him. "Enough venting. So where's the update on that secret project no one's supposed to know about? For a while I thought you retired. Or do you just want my rubber stamp?"

At a time when *joint* was the operative buzzword in the DoD, Blalock had willingly offered LaCroix for the DIA assignment and never pressed for details on the project. As a courtesy, Blalock was briefed on key milestones so DARPA felt comfortable with the funding.

LaCroix instinctively glanced over his shoulder. "I need a check cut after the first off-site test. We haven't seen the lethality yet, but if the reports are accurate, Aerotech's machine will do all we expect and more. The motor noise output level is phenomenal. Wescott says he's within range on lethality as well. The preliminary results are so stunning I can't wait to see it in person. We set the original levels so low that even if they doubled, we figured to have a damn quiet UAV. They're telling me twenty."

Blalock scoffed. "That's quieter than blowing in my wife's ear. There's no way a turbine engine produces just twenty decibels of sound."

"Tell Sharon hello. Who said anything about engines? Guess you do need updating." LaCroix opened his briefcase and produced a single sheet of paper. "Enjoy."

Specifications

Status:	prototype micro unmanned aerial vehicle
Country:	United States
Corporation:	Aerotech, Inc.
Mission:	stealth approach, target acquisition, elimination
Structure:	host transport, detachable cub
Max Ceiling:	8,000 feet
Exterior:	Kevlar/carbon fiber, bidirectional graphite
Wingspan:	host, 22 in.; cub, 12 in.
Propulsion:	rotating hover fan
Dash Speed:	vertical 0–60 mph 11.0 secs, horizontal 0–60 mph 5.0 secs
Max Speed:	100 mph
Range:	600 miles

Optics:	circle-vision omniview zoom 1.0 miles
Launch:	vertical takeoff and landing
Recovery:	memory origination module
Fuel:	autophageous lithium-ion structure-battery
Endurance:	32 hours
Sensors:	wide-angle electro-optical infrared
Navigation:	remote pilot, COMSAT aided
Lethality:	projectile targeting ultra-wideband-pulse reflective sighting
Munitions:	.223 ceron round, muzzle velo 3,100 fps, range 200 yards
Noise Range:	host, 20 decibels; cub, near-silent
Weight:	host, 7.6 pounds; cub 1.9 pounds
Security Level:	top secret

"My God, somebody finally made autophageous work. The airframe is the battery. You people don't fool around. I'm surprised it was Aerotech. They've been on a shoestring for years. There's no code name," Blalock observed.

"After they stole Wescott from Lockheed, their whole program took on new life. He's got their Board's undivided attention." LaCroix stretched over the table and wrote with a black felt pen, *T-I-G-E-R*.

"I heard you had a hand in that. Wescott's a good man. He worked for me on *Aquilla*. He was one of the few people who'd actually give me a straight answer." Blalock continued to study the document. "*Tiger* and detachable cub; that's original. What's a cub?"

"A disposable flying mailbox I designed myself. An ultramini drone that can break away from the host unit and attach itself to a target. Carries its own camera."

"Attach how?"

"Cyanoacrylate pellet heated by remote signal."

"Let's have it in English."

"Superglue. It even has its own flight program and joystick. The first time Wescott took the controls, he flew it through his driver's-side window and stuck it on his dashboard. It's that easy."

"I suppose it's got a compartment for carrying surprises?"

LaCroix smiled. "You could say that."

Blalock's ear color deepened mauve. "Who gave you access to wideband? We've been on our knees to the FCC for nine months. Won't even return calls anymore."

"Ross's people in Homeland came to us. Asked if there were any testing waivers that needed to be accelerated, so to speak."

Ultra-wideband technology would revolutionize traditional locator systems by sending and receiving timed radio waves over a wide swath of spectrum up to one billion pulses a second. Return signals could track the location of sending units and targets far more accurately than single frequency radar or satellites.

"I guess it pays to work on an intelligence team," Blalock sniped. "What's the time frame to initial operating capability?"

"Six weeks, give or take. We're getting our first paper look at the lethality at Bolling in four days. Wescott's working day and night to meet the testing deadline."

Blalock thumbed through a pocket notebook. "Dammit—I'm at the fort. Our crash ratio is a whopping ninety percent. The others managed to stumble back into the air for a few minutes. Technically, that's considered a pass."

LaCroix was thankful he wouldn't have to sit in the desert documenting maiden UAV flights at Fort Huachuca, Arizona, the U.S. Army's testing facility. "I heard we lost four *Predators* in as many months— one in Afghanistan and three in Iraq. That's twelve in reserve?"

"Ten," Blalock corrected. "One lost a wing yesterday and another one's missing somewhere over Lebanon. It just disappeared. Runner hasn't the faintest idea where it is. He holds his breath every time there's a breaking news alert. Talk about poetic justice."

LaCroix produced an inch-thick folder. "Let's see if we can't make some justice of our own. Here's a bootleg—"

"No—I won't do that," Blalock said firmly. "When *Tiger*'s ready, bring it through the normal chain. We'll do all reviews by the book. Floring still work for you?" LaCroix nodded. "Get him to figure out how to console the losers. Tell him I said knocking down snowmen is right up his . . ." Blalock snatched the specifications off the table.

LaCroix knew what was coming. He raised his hands palms out and brought together the tips of both thumbs, then his index fingers to form the *Tiger*'s elegant stingray shape.

Blalock smiled. "An eight-pound camera and two-pound assassin that can sneak into places they shouldn't without any godblasted Beany. I'll believe it when I see it in the air. If this machine tests out, we might have some credibility again—not to mention one hell of a lethal toy. We won't need to ask anybody for anything. That's the beauty of *my* team."

Chapter Three

Northern Wisconsin
Nicolet National Forest

Rambunctious teenagers had broken the fence—again. They lay drunk, sprawled across the railroad tracks, chewing.

The machine floated down through the darkness into the gang like some mechanical bird of prey returning to its nest—a bed of wood and stone nestled between steel rails. The fan blades slowed to a stop; the soft whirring of the electric motor fell silent. The only sound now was a dull vibration deep within the rails that seemed to strengthen with time.

The machine's forward video came into focus.

A freight train's headlight. Closing. Bearing down.

Bloodied limbs and hindquarters flying through the air.

My bulls!

Startled awake in his office recliner on the third floor of Aerotech Inc.'s UAV research and development center, *Tiger* project manager Peter Wescott felt something wet between his legs. Dreams had never made him do *that* before. His coffee mug, heavy and ceramic, imprinted with black-and-white Holstein cows, had tipped into his crotch. Liquid dripped onto papers on the floor. At least it was cold.

He set the mug on the windowsill and glanced outside at a crow squawking atop the company flagpole. Something was tormenting it, forcing the bird off its regal perch and into the spring fog.

Named for the European explorer, the Nicolet comprised millions of acres that were federal lands, although there were grandfathered tracts. Fifty miles south of the Wisconsin-Michigan border, Aerotech's R and D building sat on two thousand acres, secluded yet complete with on-site housing so a handful of employees could develop their tiny flying machine without a back-roads commute from Green Bay, or tents pitched in the forest.

The first UAVs were Nazi-built Vengeance rockets used against Britain in World War II. Precursors to the high-altitude spy planes, small, autonomous preprogrammed drones had sampled nuclear testing environments in the Cold War. In Vietnam, "special purpose" aircraft flew reconnaissance and battle damage–assessment missions at a fraction of the cost and risk to manned machines.

In wars with Egypt and Syria, Israeli UAVs laden with explosives had killed missile sites, armor, and 150 aircraft.

Incorporated as a subsidiary of Edwin Land's Polaroid Corporation to help Lockheed photograph Cuba from eighty-thousand feet, Aerotech had missed the warning signs of the decline of high-altitude reconnaissance in favor of strategic low-altitude surveillance, and thus entered the UAV market late and halfheartedly. Its inaugural machine, *Rotor*, was a poorly designed dual rotary wing that looked more like a flying birdcage than a sophisticated aircraft. *OVAL*, a failed nine-foot saucer, was captured on film by the tabloid press and ended up as Hollywood movie prop. A Canadian oil firm purchased *Gray Wolf*, Aerotech's third and last UAV, but filed negligence lawsuits after the machine's fuel tank burst during its first assignment on remote pipeline patrol.

Aerotech's reputation—and earnings—had continued to free-fall through the Gulf and Bosnian wars, and the war on terror, while aerospace giants like Boeing and Lockheed had gobbled market share. To avoid bankruptcy, the company had left mainstream design for radical miniaturization, and hired a radical group of thinkers to integrate flight. A second strategy focused exclusively on the military—war fighters had a growing love affair with UAVs, not to mention deeper pockets than their civilian counterparts.

Peter's eyelids felt like they'd been at war. He

stretched. His joints sounded off in a creaky roll call. He dabbed a tissue over a document entitled: "Aerotech/DoD Tiger UAV Project—Lethality System Specifications." The Defense Department logo was a coffee-stained blur. Work had become that: the breakneck demands, scrambling from crisis to crisis dragging Band-Aids or a fire hose. The satisfaction of pure outlaw development was gone; so was the exhilaration of success. Cash was king. Failures, once treated as minor setbacks that strengthened techno bonds, simply weren't tolerated. Financial losses brought layoffs and outsourcing. The VP of personnel quietly admitted in a staff meeting that the company wanted a younger contracted workforce. He was quietly released. Those who stayed learned to dance, picking up additional workload along with shiny empowerment badges that lost all luster when flashed. The pressure to perform created bitter resentment toward contractors. Legacy employees scrambled for positions like children playing musical chairs. Management preached teamwork from its headquarters in San Diego, but everyone knew the rhetoric concealed a short-term profit mentality—one that failed to realize it was people who made bottom lines come true, not some feel-good mission statement.

Raised in West Salem, Wisconsin, on a small dairy farm—a lifestyle fading into the ages, crushed by high costs and low prices, easy prey for the large cooperatives—Peter had first flown at age five. Not in some metal box with wings, but alone, arms outstretched with speed, altitude, and maneuvering achieved only by thought. Fortunately, a superboy leap off the family tractor with a grain sack for a cape produced only a mild arm sprain and a lesson in gravity.

Educated in aviation engineering, Peter had two decades of unmanned aircraft design experience, but credited his success to an easygoing nature and farmboy common sense—sadly, workplace attributes also fading into the ages. At forty-nine, his deep eye creases and haggard appearance weren't due entirely to corporate burnout, but from a rare combination of narcolepsy and sleep terror—conditions diagnosed as a child. He was guilty not of any criminal offense, but of eyesight too poor to qualify for a pilot's certificate, and of the heinous crime of dreaming.

It began on his twelfth birthday with a miniature replica of a World War II Flying Tiger airplane complete with white teeth and a gaping red mouth. Before remote control (and after chores), Peter used tethered nylon to twirl the gasoline-powered toy around in circles in the cornfields. The tiny plane tucked under his arm, he'd climb to the flat sandstone summit of Table Rock and sit for hours watching a stringless machine sail over the countryside, strafe herds of grazing livestock, dive-bomb flotillas of marsh ducks, and torment squadrons of pigeons mustering on the silos of neighboring farms.

Over time, the marriage of childhood flight fantasies and adult work stress turned so oppressive that he couldn't close his eyes for more than a few minutes without dream-piloting all types of flying machines he'd either seen or worked on, soaring into whatever places his mind happened to choose. He would never be a superhero, but he *was* a UAV, able to dream through airspace at will, hover and silently watch, undetectable master of the skies until jolted awake by some freak distress or alarm.

That was his punishment. And it continued unrelentingly, with even daylight naps now interrupted by panic. Better than any doctor's prescription or physical exercise, only visions of contented black-and-white cows from the pastures in western Wisconsin helped provide what he termed "farm sleep." Holsteins were his pardon. And they surrounded his life on clothing, coffee mugs, and family memorabilia—an array of visual drugs with the power to transport him away from the stress of workplace realities, back to the farm and the best times of his youth.

As he prepared for a meeting with his DoD program sponsors in Washington, this was Peter's twentieth consecutive working weekend, and he was tired. He was always tired, but project timetables couldn't care less. Voice and e-mail accounts were hopelessly backlogged. High priorities mingled with low, and all demanded attention like wailing infants.

A message flashed over the Internet from lacroixd@dia.dcd.gov. Defense Intelligence was one federal agency that rarely sent junk mail.

Peter scanned the contents and clicked his mouse. A postscript mentioned grapefruit. His eyes drifted shut to the soft rhythm of the print carriage.

"Hey—wake up!"

Peter's kneecap banged into the desk edge. "Jesus— you scared the hell out of me."

"Good. Sleep at home. When I find the person who sent me this, they're gone." Sue Pritchard unfolded a flyer from a local gentlemen's club. The north woods were famous for some of the sleaziest. The headline announced an upcoming gala review of midget porn stars.

"I swear I never saw that before. And I wasn't sleeping. I was . . . thinking."

"Well, think about the fact that productivity and net income both stink, and you owe me three status reports. Your last one said something about increased motivation if we all went casual. So here I am. Let's see the presentation. Mister, you'd better be ready for Monday."

"If I don't die of a heart attack." Peter stopped short of serving *ma'am* right back. He didn't have the energy to start a war just yet; they'd get into it soon enough.

Ultradefensive about her four-foot, five-inch height and twenty years his junior, his boss had little respect for subordinates who were older or taller. As for fitting in with the troops, there was no respect for casual, either. She was wearing a suit and heels.

She tried to set a package on Peter's desk but

couldn't find room. He shifted a stack of printouts, exposing stains on his paperwork and his pants. She didn't like Peter. She thought him old-school and unprofessional. Their business relationship was contentious at best, and even personal chats carried an undertone of argument. She claimed it was a generational thing. Of course, it had nothing to do with the fact that she was plain mean—a cute but ill-bred terrier that would bare teeth and snap at anyone but its master.

Aerotech's third director of research and development in as many years, Pritchard was spawned by the downsizing frenzy brought on by economic recession and margin-cutting competition for new surveillance technologies. So many New Agers— Peter called them CIRCUS leaders, Clueless In Real CUstomer Service—had shuttled in and out that he'd grown numb to the performances. Empowered to reevaluate and if necessary fire whole workgroups and redirect salaries to fund new projects, she was smart enough to leave the *Tiger* team alone for now. They were too close to producing something that might actually sell.

CIRCUS leaders were always external hires with God-like credentials and satanic people skills. Pritchard came highly touted from Boeing Electronics Information Systems and viewed managers as nothing more than expensive head count. Income good, expenses bad. Mud turtles—less expensive submanagers who made bricks in the mud pits—existed to further that agenda, period. Insulated by the consulting firm du jour, she spent most of her time at corporate perfecting speak-change—the ability to create grandiose plans of little or no substance. The strategies, unveiled to the corporate pharaohs with lavish fanfare and bold themes, accomplished nothing but new ways to pile more and heavier bricks on the turtles.

On tiptoe, Pritchard peered over a glass partition into the adjoining UAV control center at Sam Nasrabadi's head between the hardware. "Where is everyone? I lug your present halfway across the country and he's the only one here? Well, happy birthday anyway. What are we now?"

Peter watched her trying to calculate his age. She regularly sent him e-mail on retirement planning. His eyes spied the cash receipt taped to the gift box. It was from a doughnut shop outside Green Bay.

"Forty-nine, and you're a little late; the rest left hours ago. They've got a date in the forest tomorrow night, remember? I won't be around, so Sam's making last-minute performance checks." Peter did a double take at the fifteen-by-fifteen-foot projection screen mounted on the control center's front wall. His eyes grew wide when he saw Pritchard's body on the screen filmed in real time from the *Tiger* UAV hovering above the flagpole outside his office window. Fixed crosshairs zoomed in on the center of her buttocks.

"God, these back roads are a pain in the ass, but I wanted to bring the good news in person." She handed Peter a folder. "Your friend in there agreed to work six months into maintenance. Should put us in good shape if we ever get that far. Oren signed off last night. We bent over backward."

Peter tried to maintain his composure and thumbed through the contract. "I'll be damned. I was sure he'd take Canadair's offer to build their intelligence-gathering rocket. Sam's the best in the industry and worth every nickel. What'd we have to give him, a seat on the board?"

Pritchard strolled to the window. "The signing bonus alone would probably upset every other subcontractor on the payroll. You'd think this was the NFL. Please keep it confidential. Where's the machine?"

"What? Great . . . fine . . . we're on schedule. It's in the air right now." Peter fumbled with his telephone keypad, trying to remember the flight control desk extension.

The overhead screen showed that Sam had moved the *Tiger* into a gated test area and was flying tight figure eight turns around a series of vertical posts.

"Is he just playing or is that really necessary?" Pritchard tapped on the control center glass. Eyes fixed on his video monitor, Sam heard it but didn't acknowledge.

Peter released his finger from the intercom and pointed outside. "Know what that is? The Nicolet. If you expect us to fly through it, we might have to negotiate some small obstructions. I think they're called branches."

"Don't you dare try and lay that on me. Playing hide-and-seek with reindeer in the woods was your idea. I went along because you sold the board on stealth."

"And I stand by it. It means a lot if *Tiger* can approach such skittish targets. Sam's running a pool. Twenty dollars a square. Calculations show we should be able to get within twelve feet. Defense wants quiet. That's what sells. And they're not reindeer."

Pritchard sensed a power victory anytime she got Peter to raise his voice. She squinted to read the phrase on his sweatshirt. " 'Dairy farmers make better lovers.' Really? And why is that? Some country secret?"

"It's butter," Peter answered coolly. "I need a new laptop. Mine is literally falling apart and there's not enough memory to access Defense's networks."

"Butter?" She rolled her eyes. "That's sick. Pornographic flyers and sexual innuendo about body lubricants border on harassment. Personnel has a code of conduct that I think would support my interpretation."

Peter gently pulled the fabric taught across his chest, straightening the text. "*Butter* lovers—with a *U*."

The power victory vanished along with her interpretation.

"There's no money for laptops, and frankly I'm tired of what you think will happen with this machine. Enough of the calculations, okay? Test it, get

Defense to sign off, and show me profit. Simple. And I don't approve of your people wagering on company time—especially Sam. We both know he's under enough suspicion—"

Peter slammed a desk drawer. "I'm not going to be threatened with that. I've known Sam for eight years, and if he's a so-called sleeper, I'm JFK come back from the dead. I stand by his personal and business reputation one hundred percent. I know his family; we've vacationed together. Sam has never, ever espoused any political or religious views on anyone or anything. I know his mind. He's a passive, intelligent, and very American guy. We're damn lucky. There's a hundred other companies who'd buy him away tomorrow. Do me a favor? Drop it, or at least start allaying management's fears. We need support, not distraction."

The printer stopped. The room went silent. Peter offered the output as a peace gesture. It was always a good idea to let CIRCUS leaders feel as though they had the final win. Besides, a subordinate–boss conflict was always a losing effort—especially if the boss had zero emotion and the battle wasn't technical.

Pritchard glanced through the document stone-faced, well aware of the project's latest cost overruns. "What's the chance of finding an executive overview in all this clutter? With a *U*. Defense won't release a penny until the lethality's approved. Advanced Flight Systems has a rollout next month that's bound to raise eyebrows. You need to keep

things brief—one hour, max. We can't afford
LaCroix running off on another tangent. I hear he's
being forced out at the end of the year, so agree
with him, even if he's wrong. Don't blatantly lie, of
course. I just don't want anyone else sticking their
nose in. Without that funding none of us gets paid."

Peter despised corporate politics. So much for his
empowerment badge. Who was she to judge La-
Croix, having met the man twice? What was she so
worried about? he wondered. "Trust me. DIA'll do
cartwheels for a machine with eyes like Annie Oak-
ley."

Trying to decipher what she thought was some
cryptic reference to designer sunglasses, Pritchard
inspected Peter's collection of black-and-white farm
photographs hanging on the wall behind his desk.
One showed Peter with five siblings, Huckleberry
Finn–ragged staring into the sun, posing with a
family pet. None had shoes.

"You do know Monday is a formal presentation?
I'd rather we didn't make any fashion statements.
I'm just trying to protect your image. When's your
flight?"

"Thanks." Peter dug for his ticket. "Late . . . I
should get to DC around eleven."

"If you sleep on the plane you might get enough
rest for a change. And you are *not* to agree to even
one tiny engineering change proposal. I will not allow requirements creep. If you need decision help,
ask for a nature break and call in." She drew a nail

file across her thumb. "What kind of dog is that in that picture? Great Dane?"

"Huh?" Peter turned.

"What happened to its ears?"

Peter bit down on his lower lip, hoping the pain would head off the impulse to burst into laughter. So young. So clueless. With a *U*.

"We never did figure out exactly what breed it was. It came out of the barn one spring. I think it's called a calf."

Pritchard brushed off her skirt. "We're having fun today aren't we? But then I forgot—you're one of those farmer wanna-bes. I suppose you let that ugly thing sleep in the house. Probably had its own bed. I saw a cow relieve itself once at a county fair and its trainer made some disgusting comment about beer. Yvonne's teleconference on workplace diversity kicked off yesterday and I heard Carl Richter refused to dial in. Please see that he participates." She nodded three times and reached in her purse for her personal data assistant. "I've been invited to speak at the Civilian UAV Workshop in Paris on the fifteenth, so I'll need some ideas before you leave. One more thing—I'm concerned about timetables, so skip the DC sight-seeing. We absolutely can't afford any more problems. And speaking of that, how about a confidence check on your team? I'm due back tomorrow so I won't have time to baby-sit. Can they handle it? Scale of one to ten. Be honest."

That was pure technical avoidance. *Do your own*

damn research, Peter wanted to scream, but thought better of it. "What assurance can I give? Tomorrow night four talented technicians—some folks might question that—will conduct a surveillance test of Aerotech's newest unmanned flying machine. There aren't a lot of military targets to choose from around here, so we do the best we can. Spy on a moving train, spy on some stationary animals. Low-speed and isolated. No one can guarantee off-site security. It's a dangerous but necessary part of the game. They'll be fine."

"Okay, you just gave me an eight. I can live with an eight. But I can't live without status reports. Oren and I are doing brunch when I get back and he wants an update. Just the highlights. We pull Monday off and it'll be a nice feather for everyone."

Oren Hackl was Pritchard's personal mentor. She couldn't resist name-dropping—a subtle reminder of her other corporate position as liaison to the pharaoh of engineering.

The terrier trotted off into the main corridor.

Peter lifted the barnyard picture from its hook. They had named that bull calf Magic. He chuckled. He was certain no other human in rural America ever referred to a cow peeing as "relieving itself." Months of twelve-hour workdays and not one word of thanks—for himself or his mud turtles. Six figures to brownnose the board, rewrite status reports, and ignore those who really made a difference. Yvonne's entire workgroup got new laptops. *Go, team, go.*

Peter paged through Sam's personnel file attached to the employment contract. It was the first time he'd seen all the investigations. Multiple interviews with INS, DoD, FBI, and Homeland Security. It had reached the point of ridiculousness, and was almost routine. Sadly, Sam raised every red flag in the book—and then some.

Asamal "Sam" Nasrabadi was Azeris-Arabian by birth, which put him at religious odds with the radical fundamentalists in his native Iran. Fled to America during the Shah-versus-Khomeini turmoil. Family killed in civil rioting. U.S. citizen. Computer science major, University of Chicago. Expert light-aircraft pilot. Trained at Meigs Field. Founded the Flyboys, an elite aviator's club that flew annual exhibitions at the Experimental Aircraft Association Fly-In in Oshkosh.

Sam referred to flying as his first calling in life. A prankster who sometimes carried humor too far, he gently reminded team members that all joking stopped when he was flying the *Tiger* UAV from *his* chair at *his* flight control station. Sam lived on-site in an efficiency unit, while his wife, a data entry clerk, maintained their condominium near Chicago. He commuted whenever possible but preferred shorter jaunts to the Native American blackjack tables. When he played, he fingered a gold-winged money clip etched with the initials **AOTF**—Ace of the Flyboys. It helped him defeat his most hated enemy—the dealer's up card—while gambling at Green Bay's Oneida Casino, his second calling in life.

Chapter Four

Northern Wisconsin
Village of Argonne

The butcher turned a key and locked his grocery store's front door for the evening. He pulled a frayed string on the neon sign and bent under the counter for the radio. It was the end of another slow day. He lit an unfiltered cigarette and stared at the faces of Lincoln and Washington, good tenants occupying the compartments in the cash register. He licked his thumb and counted, then paused at the low rumble beneath the floorboards. Bad tenants were acting up again. The energy-guzzling compressors that cooled thick wooden lockers in the basement continued to eat into the already bleak profits. The grip on his meat-cutting monopoly had nearly slipped away altogether after the interstate bypass rerouted traffic to the new supermarket on the opposite side of town. Sympathetic customers continued to visit, but rarely bought anything other than a token loaf of bread or some other staple. He'd been forced to secretly add venison to his ground beef and famous old-world sausage. The community was outraged after someone shot and killed a blind old buck a local 4-H club had befriended. It wouldn't have survived the winter.

The butcher walked outside to his Ford pickup truck and noted the items under a canvas tarp: chain saw, rifle, knives, clear wrap, and a five-gallon plastic container of gasoline in case he got into a lengthy chase. He'd been salting forest trails for weeks. Arrest and conviction would destroy his family name and pocketbook—the state penalty was $3,000 for each violation, but he'd take the chance. The Department of Natural Resources wardens were more interested in enforcing laws for opening day of the fishing season—much too busy to worry about a few missing tenderloins.

The night air in the Nicolet was a crisp thirty-six degrees. A steady wind had grown strong enough to mask the low hum of the *Tiger*'s fan blades, which had been spinning for nearly an hour fifty feet above an active pair of Burlington-Northern railroad tracks. Although a menagerie of animals had crossed the area, only an opossum stopped to forage below the UAV, preferring the warmth and shelter of the wooden ties.

*   *   *

Twenty miles to the east, Aerotech employee Carl Wilhelm Richter sat at his workstation stretching a rubber band tight enough around his head to make a mentholated inhaler stay up each nostril. The rose fever season plugged his sinuses like Boulder Dam did the Colorado. A thick red mustache completed the perfect walrus face. In charge of *Tiger*'s audio/ visual systems, Carl was the company patriarch of high-altitude photoreconnaissance and also of sarcasm, the brunt of which was directed at know-it-all consultants and "Noisers"—Illinois residents who despised the Green Bay Packers, crowded area casinos, and mocked Wisconsin highway laws. Raised on Milwaukee's segregated south side, where his father operated a firearms dealership, Carl had shifted his support for the NRA and related hunting activities over time—along with his appetite—to the indoor sport of eating. He was technically obese on anyone's fitness scale. Much to the relief of Aerotech management, Carl's racial bias against anything that wasn't white and male, overt in earlier and less sensitive times, had also shifted to a militialike, albeit legal, bias against the U.S. government. It had something to do with an overzealous prosecutor and accusations against his father, who had served in Hitler's Third Reich. Only fifteen at the time, Carl watched his father's health deteriorate until he went into a nursing home still defending against the two-year witch-hunt.

Seated in front of Carl but on a lower tier in the control center, Sam Nasrabadi applied light forward and backward pressure to a *T*-shaped military joystick. He watched *Tiger*'s nose dip and rise from his video monitor. Obviously bored, he slid his thumb clockwise across twenty-four buttons on four pad matrices on the joystick. He clicked on "scope surround." A chartreuse grid appeared on his monitor and another simultaneously on the room's overhead projection screen. A second click produced a movable box. A third brought crystal-clear focus and locked telescoping crosshairs onto the opossum's heat image directly below on the railroad tracks. He knew the vibration insulators surrounding the ultra-wideband antenna-transceiver could handle impacts up to twenty-eight Gs, so there was minimal danger from a fall at this height. Hovering and low-speed flight were as easy as a child's video game, although higher-speed and maneuvering tactics required formal airman-style training. If the UAV literally lost its mind, a separately encased memory origination module—MOM—with encrypted final instructions would help it "limp-float" back to its last control center launch point unassisted—a procedure dubbed "home-to-Mama." MOM knew to save the precise amount of battery charge for the return trip—a nice feature in territories absent a wall outlet or friendly Radio Shack. For targeting, the machine could isolate and track heat patterns moving one meter per second inside a quarter-mile radius from hover or dashing flight. Stationary targets were best. Tonight's was late.

There was a vomitlike stink in the control center,

thanks to Carl's fondness for potent cheese sandwiches. Muffling a two-second belch, he unwrapped a powdered doughnut and forced a huge bite to one cheek. "So how much did we gamble away to the Indians last night? Five hundred . . . a grand? Mrs. Nasrabadi know about your expensive little habit?"

Sam adjusted his grip on the joystick and jotted a note, ignoring his tormentor.

Carl pressed. "Hey everybody, look. Osama's targeting rats. Big game hunter. What do they hunt in I-ran—camels? Ever eat one?"

"I try to watch my weight," Sam finally said. "Perhaps you'd interrupt your hourly feeding to explain why we're waiting for a rusty train with a National Guard Armory, Fort McCoy, and the extremely low frequency assets in the area. This is work for a child."

Carl tilted his head and swallowed slowly, producing a mild pop in both ears. "You've been here, what, twenty years? It's called *play*, Osama. Child's *play*."

It was twenty-three years. Sam wanted to raise his middle finger and puff his cheeks like a bullfrog, but controlled the impulse. The last time he joked about Carl's appearance and eating habits, a nasty and very public argument ensued, mediated by Peter in a closed-door session. He typed out a brief message on his keyboard instead.

Caroline Bell Jennings—she preferred CJ—cracked the sliding doors on the exterior flight balcony. Observing a pair of owls hunting the edge of the forest, she took one last drag off a cigarette and flicked it to the parking lot, narrowly missing a vehicle below. Pale-skinned, with a Joni Mitchell–like physique, CJ managed the UAV's power transfer system from the batteries to the electric motor. A hopeless nicotine addict with a heavy North Carolinian drawl, she regularly received deliveries of homemade sweets along with cartons of cigarettes concealed in newspaper as if that would somehow square with the company's smoke-free policy. Carl hoarded the bakery. Occasionally, outdated business attire would appear, a motherly hint that jeans, sweatshirts, and ponytails at work showed poor Southern manners. In a once-famous nepotistic monopoly, CJ's entire family had worked for the old Bell System's Western Electric Company, where, as Daddy's tagalong to the Winston-Salem plant, she picked up the basics of digital technology. But acting on a deep-seated urge to work in aviation, she merged electronic communications with physics, and renounced a preordained career at Lucent Technologies for flexible consulting stints with the navy and now Aerotech. She had broken the news to her father gently, suggesting that telephony was too ground-based, and that even Alexander Graham Bell himself was fascinated by flight. Dogged by the Office of Naval Research, she continued to long for the Carolina coastal dunes, and as a deferred signing bonus for committing to pursue jet noise minimization after she finished at Aerotech, the navy agreed to guarantee—and pay for—her future relocation to Norfolk, just eighty miles from home.

The last member of the *Tiger* team was Ricky Benavides, a young Mexican-American who had gained Peter's attention via a series of technical e-mails on solid air-fuel systems. Boyish faced with street-smart black eyes, Ricky had traded the gang life of southeast San Diego for Cal-Tech engineering studies. Motivated by intense hatred of the barrio, and unmotivated at the prospect of giving his talent and earnings away to some Silicon Valley corporation, Ricky quit college after his junior year and started an Internet business selling radio-controlled model airplanes and helicopters. The Hobby Wing was so successful that he hired family members and opened a storefront warehouse in Chula Vista, five miles from the border. They had recently built and introduced a flying wing with a seventeen-inch wingspan and a weight of fifteen ounces. Remarkably easy to control and fully assembled in less than two hours, the craft was powered by a small fan and launched with a gentle push. At just $99 per kit, a national market of teenage males bored with remote control monster trucks and eager to act out *Star Wars* flying fantasies bought out the initial inventory in only two weeks. Ricky was reluctant to accept Aerotech's offer, but the position was temporary, and the chance to work for the great Peter Wescott, with his reputation and knowledge of supplier contacts in the unmanned industry, was worth interrupting a growing cash flow for a short six months.

Sam gave a sharp whistle.

Carl hurriedly sucked the sugar off his fingers and focused the *Tiger*'s forward camera lens on three faint lights twinkling in the distance. Thanks to the UAV's circle vision, a picture-in-picture window on the screen's lower right-hand corner showed empty track ahead. His video monitor displayed a bright green outline of the dusky scenery, thanks to the E-O/IR—electro-optical infrared—wide-angle sensors that detected radiation in the visible spectral bands, providing one hundred times greater vision than TV or forward-looking infrared. Both were essential elements in establishing positive target identification required by U.S. rules of engagement.

Sam released his grip on the joystick, allowing the UAV to briefly hover unassisted. He pressed his face into a moistened towel, leaving a sculpted four-inch stalagmite of black hair on his head. He wondered why he was the only one who showed any sense of urgency. The rest seemed more interested in food, cigarette breaks, and private business affairs. If it were a resentment conspiracy to his being placed in charge while Peter was in Washington, barking orders would only make it worse. He didn't dislike any of his coworkers personally, but simply struggled with their carefree work ethic.

"What's the status on the battery charge?" Sam spoke into his monitor, but loudly enough to be heard across the room.

Ricky quickly minimized the Hobby Wing's Web site on one monitor and double-clicked the UAV's on-line system icon on another. Initialization was too slow.

"Fuel?" Sam asked, raising his voice.

"All right, I'm on it," Ricky responded. "Don't you think we need to be higher?"

"The debate on that is over, so don't even go there. Take your position. We've got three minutes," Sam ordered, his eyes alert to see that the youthful technician did his job as instructed.

"You heard Osama," Carl's voice replied evenly. Sam swiveled his chair.

"That's three times. I'm going to tell you once. Don't call me that."

"What's the big deal? It's a fair question."

Sam exhaled a long breath. "*People*—why are you fighting me on height? We don't have time to argue geometry. Whoever's running that train would have to have either a periscope or Doppler radar. So let's all agree that at the present height the *Tiger*'s invisible."

Carl pondered that. "Aye, Admiral Osama. Invisible we shall be. Cloaking device activated. Shall I engage the warp drive?"

"Funny you should mention that. There is the possibility that the engineer is stuffing his face, like someone else I know, causing his extremities to be almost as warped as yours."

"How do you say 'jackass' in I-ranian?" Carl retorted.

"It's Farsi—jackass."

"Quit!" CJ barked to both men, but she was glaring at Carl. "I can't believe we continually have to listen to your bickering. This isn't grade school. Sam, fix your hair. You look like a conehead. Ricky, is there any fuel at all?"

"It's fully charged, but I still think the machine's too low. All somebody in the caboose has to do is look out the back door."

CJ shook her head. "There is no caboose. Nobody pays employees to sit around all day and play games. Railroads did away with them years ago."

Ricky got the not-so-veiled message. "I was just thinking out loud. I'm not a train expert. I didn't figure to cause a war. It won't happen again. Promise." He hung his head like a bad puppy. It worked. CJ liked him. He was close to his mother, too. The woman's years of cleaning homes for the middle-class had taken their toll. The multiple sclerosis was in remission but she was bedridden from muscle loss. He did volunteer work and donated a percentage of his business profit to the MS Society.

Tonight's mission had three objectives: hover above the cars of a moving freight train; overtake the engine to simulate attachment of a delayed explosive; and approach and record thermal images of white-tailed deer. Carl first suggested using the animals as targets because of sheer numbers, and the fact they were one of nature's wariest creatures. He faithfully joined six hundred thousand hunters in the Wisconsin woods each fall, where annual kills reached a quarter of a million. The threat posed by chronic wasting disease finally convinced him to give it up. As for the animal rights activists, opening day began with hunter dummies strapped to vehicles that paraded through Madison. All in all, these were rather odd assignments for UAV surveillance, but rookie flying machines couldn't be too particular, especially those forced to prove themselves in the middle of a national forest. The nearest hostile country was on the other side of the planet, unless one considered Illinois—major-league baseball had started with the Cubs playing the Brewers. Carl had memorabilia pinned to his workstation and was nearly euphoric at finally being rid of the hated White Sox now that Milwaukee was back in the National League.

At a distance, the seven-million-pound freight train made no sound and had a deceptive, lumbering sway, appearing to cover the last quarter mile of track in slow motion.

As the first of 120 cars passed underneath, Sam lowered the UAV and rotated forward to pace the train. He was in no particular hurry. Burlington-Northern ran through some of the most deserted parts of the Nicolet, giving them all night to play with this hulking python headed to Duluth-Superior for a refill of raw coal.

No one knew about the behemoth construction crane lashed to five flatbeds.

One boom section, pointing forward like a giant lance, extended sixteen feet above the car tops and was gaining on the UAV at a net velocity of fifty mph.

Ricky recognized the steel juggernaut's outline with just four seconds to impact. "Collision—*break* left!"

Sam nearly twisted the joystick off its base.

The drone's left wing dropped sharply as twelve tons crushed by one foot from the underbelly. Fighting for control, he managed to veer the UAV away at an angle, narrowly avoiding the crane's midsection on the next two flatbeds.

The cocked video picture showed the ground zooming closer.

"Power, power! Up, up! I can't hold it," Sam shouted.

Absorbed in the blurred image on the projection screen, CJ had lost all concentration and carelessly reduced fan blade speed, precisely the opposite of what was needed.

The *Tiger* plummeted downward toward the No. 3 granite stones on the graded embankment, skipping over the jagged edges like a plastic Frisbee.

Pummeled by digital voice warning messages synched with a cacophony of bleating alarms for low altitude and power loss, the four team members sat helpless at their workstations. Somehow the machine had maintained an upright position; its forward video lens focused on the end car.

Two orange-red reflectors gently winked good-bye.

Chapter Five

Sam scurried to each workstation like a supervising sand crab.

CJ and Carl both raised their thumbs, indicating controlled status. Ricky stared zombielike into his monitor at the thought of damage to the UAV's delicate battery frame. Sam read the conditions himself.

"Damn board," CJ said disgustedly. "Peter tried to tell them this was too dangerous, but they wouldn't listen. The wicked witch convinced them how easily we could blow up a supply line."

"Khoda have mercy on them for their stupid World War Two tactics. No one uses trains anymore." Sam bent next to Ricky's ear. "We don't have all night. Shake it off."

Carl increased the *Tiger*'s circle vision for a wide-angle look at the surroundings. Four feet away, the opossum lay curled in a ball, mouth agape, eyes closed, apparently concerned that the strange object from the sky was an owl, albeit a clumsy one.

"Doesn't *anything* work in this place?" CJ swore to herself and scuffed the mouse roughly across the pad, trying to free the sticking ball. The pointer responded. "Increasing to fifteen K."

At the flight workstation, Sam pulled back on the joystick.

Rising out of a dust plume, the *Tiger* floated up and over the moonlit rails toward the forest interior.

The opossum ambled off in the opposite direction.

"I hope that train derails into hell." Sam cursed at Carl's reflection in his monitor. "With you on it. Your cargo research was shitty—if you did any at all. May Khoda have mercy on us, too, because Pritchard won't."

Strong thermal images faded off the overhead screen as quickly as they had appeared.

"Why don't you fly a little faster?" Carl fired back, deflecting the rebuke.

Frustrated that he had allowed anger to interfere with flying, with typically sloppy results, Sam slowed the *Tiger* into a circular descent and moved into a hover position above and behind a rare opening in the forest.

Six white-tailed deer, heads lowered, were browsing in a grassy clearing surrounded by mature Scotch pine. There was a seventh heat image a short distance away concealed in a thick outcrop of scrub oak. Probably the dominant buck, aloof and unconcerned about his harem until the fall rutting.

Carl clicked on each image, recording a signature of digitized degrees and heat patterns that provided a very low error rate to target identification. Since no two "fingerprints" were the same, *Tiger* could key on a subject in virtually any weather or light condition. If the signature was stored on a previous mission, high confidence of reacquisition was only a mouse click away. It always helped to know if you were eliminating the right target.

The UAV continued to descend, pausing fourteen feet above ground level, thirty feet behind the largest doe.

"Pushing twenty-two at ten thousand." CJ announced the decibel level and fan rotation speed. "Lowering. Twelve, eleven, ten . . ."

The doe's head snapped up, freezing the group. Her left ear twitched backward in some primitive reflex, her brain linked with unseen danger.

"You know we are here," Sam observed. He drew two circles on a notepad, representing the number eight, reference to feet. "Initiate simulation . . . prepare to disengage cub."

He stopped all downward motion and eased the *Tiger* toward the clearing's perimeter, tucking it neatly under a shroud of low-hanging pine branches.

There was an eerie lull. The motionless deer seemed to form a digital wildlife mural.

The beam of a million-candlepower spotlight

burst from the forest, illuminating the clearing like a brilliant sun. The deer stared into the light; their eyes glowed white like fireflies stuck in the on position.

Two seconds later, a Winchester .30-06 shell smashed through the doe's neck, severing her spine. She buckled forward.

Before the echo faded, another shot cracked, fatally injuring a second animal.

Confused, the remaining deer frantically dodged back and forth.

A third shot rang out, then a fourth, spattering tree bark into the *Tiger*'s video lens.

Ricky tapped out a password on his keyboard. *Cub Disengaged* was the confirmation.

"What's happening? I've got live separation here." Sam's voice was tense. He twisted the joystick fully to the right, then to the left.

Ignoring the commands, the tiny cub drone floated forward into the clearing.

Sam reached across his workstation and activated a second joystick, stopping the cub's motion and setting it on stationary hover. Deftly working two controls, he raised both machines vertically, pressing the *Tiger* host airframe up through the soft branches, breaking limbs that were either small or dead.

"Someone shot at us!" Ricky shouted from across the room.

"You fool—it's not us." Sam turned to Carl. "Please tell me we're still tracking."

Carl's eyes were locked on his monitor. "Right below . . . I've got good heat."

The butcher lifted his ski mask and cocked his ear, trying to confirm that the rustling of branches and wood-snapping sounds were nothing more than turkeys startled from their roosts. When he heard the soft but unmistakable humming of some type of motor, he quickly ducked into cover, pawing his hands over the ground for spent shell casings. Motors meant people. Wardens.

Both UAVs slowed to a preprogrammed hover at three hundred feet above ground level.

Carl panned the *Tiger*'s video lens across the area, zooming in on a human figure digging through what appeared to be a backpack.

"I can't believe it," Ricky spoke at the image. "He knew. He was waiting for us. I heard about corporate sabotage in school. It's big business and it happens."

Carl put a finger to his lips at the youth's conjecture. "He's only a poacher—and we got caught in the middle. Probably a Noiser. They love venison. Be a pleasure to turn him in."

Sam pinched the bridge of his nose and lifted a telephone handset. "That's perfect. Here. Call State Patrol headquarters and give your statement. Excuse me, Officer? This is Aerotech. Our secret flying machine was just cruising through the forest when its imaging sensors detected a maniac with a rifle."

Carl's eyes narrowed. "I don't know about anyone else, but there's been enough mission failure to go around. I vote we end it."

Sam was still shaking his head at the idiocy. "That's the first intelligent thing you've said tonight. Put our friend on the screen once more so I can see his face. Mr. Benavides, if it's not too inconvenient, would you mind preparing for recovery? Thanks. I appreciate your help. Give me some time for direction and distance." Sam's neck pulse was visible.

With the cub safely locked into the host airframe, the *Tiger* sped over the forest canopy. It reached the control center flight balcony in eleven minutes.

At the last DIA acceptance meeting, Peter had committed to full operating capability in nine months. They had less than six left, which meant mid-fall. It wouldn't sit well if word got out to the other intelligence agencies that the unveiling of Aerotech's breathtaking UAV was delayed by a stampede of frightened deer. *Bambi tramples* Tiger *in tense forest confrontation.* Some world-class surveillance weapon.

Wearing a grounding bracelet to protect the electronics against static discharge, Ricky carefully gripped the hovering UAV's wings and walked it inside. He squeezed needle-nosed pliers and gently peeled a piece of sap from a wingtip. He was thankful there were no punctures.

"The cub looks okay, considering," Ricky said sheepishly. No one commented. "Guess I screwed up, huh? I can't believe I did that."

Seething, Sam rose from his console. "I can. Because you're an amateur who doesn't think. And if you can't make a decision under pressure, I will. Exactly how long do you think it'll take before you understand the difference between real and simulated? Wait—don't answer. Tell me something. Where were you when the rest of us practiced the most basic of tactical operations? Obviously paying more attention to toy orders. There's no way that guy would've detected our position. Never. A few moments to evaluate, and we find a dark escape path per normal procedures. That's how things should have gone. Instead you initiate a live separation and ram the cub down his throat exposing both machines. He saw us plain and simple. He's probably on a phone right now to cable news. By morning the forest will be overrun by tabloid reporters looking for UFOs. Now how do you suggest we contain it?"

Ricky tried to speak.

"Be quiet; I'm not finished. Now think physical damage. Acceleration into something this thick"— Sam held two fingers together—"would set the project back a year, minimum. You're absolutely right . . . you did screw up. I'm suspending you. Get out."

Carl stood.

"Back off . . . I know what I'm doing." Sam pointed to the door. "I mean it. Go."

Ricky turned to his coworker. "Can he do that?"

CJ lowered her head and exhaled a long breath.

Ricky pursed his lips and calmly pulled at the Velcro on his wrist.

Sam followed him to the doorway. A small phone directory sailed into the corridor in a long arc. "Did you know your mother raised an imbecile pig that knows nothing? You can come back when you start taking this job seriously . . . do you hear me? Come back here! Ricky—please . . . I'm sorry."

Tripping over an electrical cord, but maintaining momentum, Carl charged around his workstation like an enraged hippopotamus. "Who made you VP of personnel?"

"Your face is purple. Sit down before you have a heart attack."

CJ saw Carl clench his fists and squeezed herself into a neutral position between the men. "Okay, this is getting way out of hand. Let's pick it up in the morning. We're in enough trouble. We don't need violence."

Sam started pacing, repeatedly opening and closing his mouth. "I can't believe Peter hired that amateur. He has no flight sense whatsoever."

"That amateur is twenty-six years old and runs his own UAV business," Carl reminded him. "He's been working with remotes for years. Give him a break. He made a bad decision. We all do. Deal with it."

"Shut everything down," Sam ordered. "I'll try to bring him back. Peter'll have enough to explain. He doesn't need any more personnel issues."

The control center door slammed shut just as all

video monitor screen savers timed in, filling the room with panoramic scenery of surf lapping Salt Cay Island in the Bahamas.

CJ stared at her coworker. He *was* purple. "That was fun. What's an imbecile pig?"

Carl shrugged and wiped a thick film of perspiration from his face.

The fax machine behind his desk began printing a document with a single line of text: *For Unlawful Carnal Knowledge*.

"What the hell is this?"

CJ stared at it a few seconds and chuckled. "It's definitely for you. Better brush up on your old English history. Bailiffs used to write that in the court record when people got caught, um, messing around. They got tired of writing out the words and simply used initials."

Page two printed: *You*.

Carl reached for his wallet. He placed a twenty-dollar bill on top of the fax and crushed it and the papers into a paper golf ball. He pitched it at Sam's workspace. "There . . . you're a witness. One day things might get a little ugly around here. See you in the morning—maybe . . . maybe not. I might be sick. I'll call."

CJ lit a cigarette before methodically turning off the room's electronics.

At Sam's desk, she unraveled the crumpled ball and examined the money briefly. It was an older twenty with a smaller portrait of Andrew Jackson on one side and a broad sweeping view of the White House south lawn on the other; newer currency showed only the northern facade. She slid the bill underneath a crystal paperweight and turned away.

Something caught her eye.

She peered back through the thick glass at a tiny but now magnified sketch of the *Tiger* UAV hovering over the South Portico.

Nicolet National Forest

When the pull cord on his chain saw broke, the butcher angrily spewed out his own succession of four-letter words. Normally he'd fire a lantern and cut the deer where they lay, but the possibility of someone else in the area convinced him to settle for a rapid field dressing.

After dragging two carcasses back to the truck, he propped himself onto the tailgate and lit a cigarette.

The *Tiger* located the butcher's thermal image in ten minutes and thirty seconds.

From a distance of twenty yards, crosshairs locked a target point on a red plastic container. A sharp snap sent a pencil-thick stream of gasoline flowing onto the truck bed.

The butcher turned.

A second ceron round neatly pierced his blood-stained hand.

Burning tobacco ash tumbled into the vapors.

Ignition . . . explosion.

Exit.

The targeting mission had lasted twenty-six minutes and fifty seconds.

Clean.

Chapter Six

Hornets. Angry hornets. Buzzing.

The air above Washington was thick with fog . . . and hornets. Sucking into the fan blades.

A distant airport came into view. Towering monuments and empty train cars lined the approach.

Two giant cows stood upright. Tails slapped the surface of the Potomac. Hooves motioned clearance to land.

Ringing. A klaxon of warning alarms, but from where? Fuel gauge? Altimeter?

Clogged.

No power.

Gut-twisting vertigo.

Falling headfirst toward the runway.

Shocked erect in bed like Dracula rising, Peter blindly pawed the nightstand for the snooze button. He finally found the telephone.

"Wescott? Where the *hell* were you last night? I called three times." Pritchard's voice was irate.

"Huh? I . . . What time is it? . . . Jesus, let me think . . . my fight had flog. . . . We couldn't . . ." Peter's vision started to clear and he spotted something alive and black on the hotel room's carpet. It was buzzing. He scooped up his pager and shut it off.

"They blew it big-time, mister. Your whole train idea was a damned fiasco."

Peter grimaced. "Fiasco?"

"That's what I'd call your machine actually bouncing on the ground, for Christ's sake. Thermal detection wasn't much better. One of your people even walked off the job. I don't have all the details, but it was complete fiasco. I'm just ill. . . . Hello? Did you hear me?"

Peter flung a pillow against the wall, disturbing a glass-framed painting. Odd that it wasn't secured, he thought, but then most guests in this place probably weren't prone to taking souvenirs. He could barely bring himself to ask about structural damage.

"A few bumps and scratches," Pritchard said disgustedly. "That's the only good news. Not a single conclusion and no one documented a thing. We could have hired a team of third graders to run a better test. Don't you talk to your little darlings?" She waited for an answer but there was none. "I want three things: a detailed report on what happened; who was responsible; and someone's butt— by Friday. I'm late . . . we'll have to talk later. Not one word to LaCroix. We tell him everything's on schedule. That's our position until we figure out what went wrong, understand? Call me!" *Click*.

"Damn," Peter swore, and fell back to the mattress.

He scrolled through the messages on his pager. Sam's number. *Welcome to Washington*. Just what he needed: paperwork and another deadline. He hated it when Pritchard called him *mister*. He rubbed his eyes, promising himself not to think about that or the word *fiasco*. The only thing that mattered today was his presentation.

He got up and split the drapes in the suite's living room, exposing a view that cost $750 a night, in case DIA preferred doing business in arguably the finest hotel in the city. The obelisk poking through haze over the right shoulder of the White House two blocks to the south looked sort of Egyptian. He tried to spot the aluminum-coned tip. A nice height from which to dive-bomb Mall squatters on a hot summer day, just like the family herd.

After staring in disbelief at the price of Jamaican Blue specialty coffee in the room service menu, he glanced back into the bedroom at the picture frame now dangling crookedly above the black walnut headboard. He moved closer, peering beyond the crack in the glass.

Holsteins grazing in a flowery meadow. There was a bluff with a tablelike flat peak silhouetted against the sky in the background. And a farm. It was *his*.

Playing chicken with the Potomac at Washington National Airport was the world's worst aviation experience, especially in low visibility. Fog at Brown County Airport in Green Bay had delayed departure for nearly three hours. When approach control finally allowed the landing at National, the passengers experienced a ride equaling that of any thrill park. It was that harrowing. After multiple deplaning delays, all he could think of was horizontal rest. He had never noticed the cows.

The painting's size seemed small for the room until Peter remembered Hay-Adams's motto of power with civility. He studied the artist's signature. A genealogy buff, he knew there was an identical name deep in his family tree—a hardy immigrant who brought the first Holsteins from the Canton of Graubunden, Switzerland, to LaCrosse County in 1833. Margaret Reudi, his maternal great-great-great grandmother.

Struggling with an overfilled garment bag and media headlines describing petty theft, Peter waited for what seemed like an eternity to check out.

The registration clerk behind the counter was conferring with another hotel employee. Something was wrong. They suspected. But how? Hidden cameras? Two-way mirrors?

Peter studied their faces warily. Those things were illegal.

"I apologize for the delay, sir," the concierge finally said. "Our communication system isn't very cooperative this morning. Anything else we can do for you?"

"Who could I see about making a purchase?" Peter asked.

"Certainly"—heel click—"how may I help?"

There was a red-and-gold emblem on the little man's tuxedo sleeve boasting membership in Les Cles d'or. Some elite customer service club, Peter guessed. He scrawled a signature on the authorization slip. "I'm not sure how to explain this but I grew up with cows; they help me sleep"—the concierge smiled briefly—"and I think I'm related to the artist who paint—"

"Yes, we do have several interesting pieces. But I'm afraid none are for sale."

Certain it was a prelude to an ill-mannered bidding game, Peter tactfully exposed cash from his pocket. The cheesy smile vanished.

"I'm terribly sorry, but the owners . . . We have explicit ord—"

"You don't understand. There's a small painting in room eleven hundred. Of cows. That farm has been in my family since the early eighteen—"

"Sir, I know the one. May I suggest something private? There are reputable galleries in the area that would be more than happy to—"

"Never mind. A taxi will be fine."

Washington's fickle sky was misting. Peter caught a brief glimpse of the White House. Two crowds huddled under umbrellas outside the perimeter fence: one, anti-something protestors. The other, routine visitors waiting for the daily tours. He'd stood in that very line. As a vacationing nine-year-old, he'd endured the sweltering heat and humidity just to see all those important things in the buildings. They had to be important because guards were everywhere—entrances, exits, side doors, ramps, and especially the monuments. His favorite was the robotic soldier who strutted back and forth at that cemetery.

Stuck in the nation's second-worst morning rush hour, after New York City, Peter's ride crawled east on Pennsylvania Avenue, connecting to South Capitol before crossing the Frederick Douglass Memorial Bridge into Anacostia, Washington's highest crime area. He marveled at how a city with such intimidating scenery could transition from national glory to third-world slums just three blocks from the rotunda.

"How long have you been battling this"—Peter squinted at the driver's ID—"Sanjeev?"

"Ten years in the District," the man replied in a rolling-tongued Hindi accent. "Two in Calcutta."

"What's your favorite—?"

The cabby interrupted him. "The Mall at night. Spotlights surround Washington's Monument. Tickets are free at Madison and Fifteenth. But there are checkpoints. Unfortunately, these are security-conscious times."

How did he know? Peter wondered, stung at being such a predictable tourist. What if he were really asking about restaurants? He wasn't.

A delivery truck was unloading in the parking lane ahead. The taxi accelerated, swerving to avoid it.

Peter groped for a seat belt. "So what does your country think about the war on terror?"

Sanjeev eyed Peter in the mirror. He didn't look like a government employee. "The biggest problem in India isn't terrorism; it's television. Cable television. Everyone can get it now and thinks that is how life is supposed to be. No one gives a damn about anything anymore—even family. Young people are brainwashed by media that attacks the very foundation of religious culture. The freedoms we enjoy in America have gone far beyond original intent. The government cannot stop it because it's already out of control. They protest to the president, but he doesn't control culture. Take the Muslims. America is viewed as moralistically evil. It is something they fear will ultimately spread and infect their homelands. You cannot have a country where so-called personal freedoms attempt to legitimately coexist with a religion that despises sexual deviation, antireligion, sorcery, pornography, and even outrageous music. The list goes on and on. The Muslims are simply acting against it first. It's not really about government."

Peter shook his head. Fascinating. Immigrant cabdrivers always seemed to have uncanny insight into the tempo of world politics. Perhaps the man's views were exaggerated, but it was unnerving to think that it all came down to culture.

Sanjeev brought the vehicle to a stop, honoring flashing school bus lights.

Peter smiled at the innocent faces. Sadly, his wife couldn't have children. They'd considered adoption, but Peter was torn by corporate America's unwritten expectation of a dedicated work life. And if that accounted for the traditional 110 percent, then what would be left to give? Was it possible that the demands of business profit might be a leading cause for family breakdowns? *Nah*. He still would've been a great parent. If he could handle consultant supertechs, he could handle children. Besides, they often behaved the same.

"You have kids?" Peter asked.

Sanjeev clicked the windshield wipers and raised four fingers.

"Good for you. I'm not into television much, but I've heard it's pretty raunchy. I guess advertising dollars keep that kind of trash alive. Kids grow up. They'll eventually figure it—"

The taxi started forward but braked suddenly. Two young boys, presumably late for school, darted across the street for the bus.

Traffic moved on.

The seven-story DIAC—Defense Intelligence Analysis Center—building stood three miles south of the U.S. Capitol on the grounds of Bolling Air Force Base along the eastern shore of the Potomac. Adjacent to the Anacostia Naval Station, the Defense Department's unassuming intelligence headquarters were placed outside the Pentagon to gain more workspace and the privacy offered by an obscure yet restricted military site.

Sanjeev dropped his passenger at the main gate, where a base security escort was waiting.

After a short ride down Laboratory Road, Peter passed through two security stations, each requiring visual ID and metal checks, and boarded an express elevator to the sixth floor. The doors opened into a brightly lit but windowless room fashionably decorated—for a government building—in tones of light gray to charcoal, carrying on the color scheme of the center's concrete and glass exterior. Neatly framing one end of a large oval table, three sequential easel charts showed a trajectory curve of the *Tiger*'s lethality system. DIA had done its homework. Almost an hour early, Peter helped himself to the continental breakfast on the table and drifted back in time through a series of photographs on the wall of the chronology of American-made UAVs.

Peter had completed the *Tiger*'s design at Johns-Hopkins University's Aeronautics Division in Laurel, Maryland, while working on the EXDRONE for the Marine Corps. Impassioned with aerial surveillance, Peter and LaCroix became professional friends and held late-night brainstorms on functionality, deployment periods, and how to someday acquire enough talent and capital to make the *Tiger* a world-class flying machine. It took less than a year before the marines had had their fill of army leadership, sending the project into jeopardy. Truthfully, more time and energy had been devoted to

Peter's UAV after hours than on EXDRONE's daytime development; thus milestones slipped farther behind on an already beleaguered schedule. With cancellation imminent, LaCroix sold the *Tiger* concept to DIA's Directorate for Analysis and Production, D1. But openly calling for the elimination of manned surveillance embroiled him in conflict with manufacturers and pilots alike who believed UAVs would eventually threaten their employment. He finally gained DoD attention with irrefutable evidence that U.S. forces had never fought using unmanned flying technology, and that Britain, Italy, Japan, South Africa, and even Greece had active, well-funded programs. In an organization that strongly resisted change, LaCroix tried to consolidate army, navy, air force, and marine UAV functions into a single DIA department under his control, but failed due to the political infighting. His vision of diverse military organizations working as one with all their logistical and cultural complexities was admirable but naive, and trying to reach common ground on airborne intelligence tactics, theater boundaries, or even priorities was an ongoing nightmare. Once it had taken six months to agree on how to *proceed* to define a common landing and recovery system. The army and marines were interested only in who or what was over the next hill; the navy needed the ability to land on moving ships; and the air force falsely claimed the only use they had for UAVs was the lowly task of airfield damage assessment. When Congress tried to force military cooperation by eliminating individual branch funding, LaCroix spent two years coddling executive, acquisition, intelligence, appropriation, status, and whining oversight committees layered in bureaucracy and foot dragging. After the air force announced it was creating its own reconnaissance squadron at Nellis AFB in Nevada, he tried an end run for centralized control of U-2R, Naval Tactical Intelligence, and all unmanned technology. If he couldn't beat them, he'd take over the functions. The undersecretary of defense acquisition and technology denied the global plan, but gave LaCroix and D1 a green light to build *Tiger*. It was enough of a mandate to forge an ACTD—advanced concept technology development—fly-before-buy process that ignored DoD's formal acquisition guidelines. No more closed bids, mandatory cheapest price, open debates, or awarding contracts via an archaic crony network. If his neck and his pet project were on the line, La Croix wanted the best UAV possible and didn't give a private or public damn what company could produce it. After LaCroix left, Peter considered one of the U.S. military's own unmanned programs, but discovered they *all* had a history of canceling projects late in development. Contemplating field openings in Israel, but not ready to shift allegiance, he joined Lockheed Missile and Space Company in Austin, Texas, managing the development of the army's *Aquilla* UAV, a Soviet radar jammer with an onboard microprocessor. The eighteen-hour workdays under General Blalock carried constant pressure from an unnamed intelligence agency to add sniper capability to the design. The project was disastrously over budget and riddled with software glitches; a fiscal shakeup at Defense finally killed *Aquilla*, sending Peter into yet another job search—one that mysteriously ended just twenty-four hours later after Aerotech offered him the team leadership of a project that focused on UAV miniaturization and silence, two bellwether features of his *Tiger*. When he learned development and testing would take place in his home state of Wisconsin, it was Miller time. LaCroix patiently waited for Peter's flying prototype before admitting he had arranged the career path.

"Hiya, Peter! Nice to see you in person again," Harold Floring sang out, referring to the flood of prior videoconferences. In charge of procurement and testing, Floring followed LaCroix from project to project due in part to personal friendship. But if the need arose, he also had the rare financial savvy to circumvent most of the 5000-series directives created by Defense's acquisition board. Floring was a stocky, fit man in his early fifties with an affinity for white short-sleeved shirts. It wasn't the cropped flat top that dated him, but the bifocals balanced on the end of his nose. A scent of strongly spiced aftershave wafted through the air with his entrance.

"How's the ulcer?" Peter asked.

"Not bad, but I still have to watch the menu." Floring squeezed Peter's hand firmly and lowered his voice. "A friendly warning. The old man's grapefruit is sour as hell, but don't let on. Bring up fishing."

Peter smiled suspiciously and removed his laptop from his travel bag.

LaCroix entered the room and went straight for the coffee. Peter noticed a cherry-red glow on his face and a receding hairline. The man owned a vacation home in Florida and was toying with a real estate business after government service. It was common knowledge that he had been reprimanded for using military resources to acquire old but still classified reconnaissance photographs of Cuba—which happened to include the Keys.

"Looking trim, Colonel," Peter said. They shook hands.

"Cholesterol's down thirty points, thanks to Lipitor and vitamin C. Have some of my grapefruit. I sent a case to Wisconsin the other day."

"Thanks." Peter wrinkled his nose and obligingly placed several small pieces on his plate. Although the fruit was rich in calcium, a recent AMA study had suggested they were the leading cause of kidney stones. "You get all that sun fishing?"

"You would have to mention that subject." LaCroix groaned and unbuttoned his stiff shirt collar. "Wake me up in an hour."

"You're looking at the king of Lake Erie." Floring beamed. "I finally netted a prespawn female. She was forty-one inches, seventeen pounds. Should be an official record by the end of the month. If I die tomorrow it'll be with a smile on my face."

"You caught a *seventeen-pound* walleye?" Peter loved to fish. The fact that it had been over two years since he'd wet a line left him with a twinge of jealousy. He extended his hands sideways to air-measure the length. "That's just shy of Wisconsin's."

"You two and your Great Lakes. I chartered a head boat out of Marblehead once near Port Clinton and must've drowned a thousand minnows. We got soaked. The weather was so bad even the ferries shut down. To hell with that Ohio birdbath and its hurricane winds."

Peter was amused at LaCroix's continued bad luck in fresh water. "You realize that birdbath has seventy million fish?"

"You want real action? Try night fishing for black-tip sharks. Even the ones under five feet can snap eighty-pound line."

"Sharks in the dark?" Peter asked incredulously, remembering one off Martha's Vineyard with an appetite for boats and a man named Quint.

LaCroix laughed. "Barracudas start feeding at sunset two miles off Port Canaveral. We spread cut bait to build up a frenzy, then change to squid. Black-tips go nuts for it. And if the swells get high enough, hammerheads usually nose around for a handout."

Peter felt his stomach. He got motion sickness closing his eyes on an escalator. "A seventeen-pound walleye . . . damn! I'd retire my rod and reel."

"Now that the obligatory fish stories have been told, let's get down to business," LaCroix directed. "All we want is reasonable assurance that this UAV's weapon system works, and our procurement lawyers'll mail the contract—all five pages. To be honest, I need help with your figures."

Peter passed out two sets of specifications. He approached the easels and extended a metal pointer. "You'll recall that the lethality is two-pronged: a projectile targeting system—PTS—and a detachable cub. The *Tiger*'s body structure serves as a host carrier, much like a seven forty-seven does with the space shuttle. Both UAVs are hand-launchable. The cub is a featherlight drone that sits inside the host. It can be released independently and has a hinged compartment capable of carrying up to six ounces of—"

"Peter," LaCroix interrupted, "in the interest of time, we're comfortable with the cub and its lethality."

"Sorry." Peter rearranged his notes. "PTS has the capability to detect and confidently identify targets, and to ensure that those targets are engaged without collateral damage. Targets can be partially obscured and even in hidden environments. The system is semiautomatic, internal ejecting, and can hold and fire ten high-velocity center-fire twenty-two caliber rounds between the top surface area, here"—he touched the center chart—"and here. There are three capabilities. Number one is movement. The upper housing can swivel in any direction, so there are no blind spots above or below. The engaged barrel can extend horizontally from any position. With respect to tracking, the ultra-wideband radar transmits pulses that are shorter in spatial length than the target, but larger in signal frequency. Thus, the receiver provides high-resolution imaging. We use a narrow sixteen-degree radar beam and direct-path sensor returns."

"Tell me about noise," LaCroix demanded, stirring his coffee.

Floring started a small tape recorder.

Peter's mind went blank as he connected a data cable from the room's television monitor to his laptop. He couldn't believe he had stumbled already, and he paged through a folder. He noticed how much the room's fabric-covered paneling deadened sound. He swore he could hear his watch ticking.

He booted the *Tiger*'s flight operation program. The laptop's screen flickered on, then off. Peter tapped it several times with his finger. "I'll cover the discharge numbers in a moment, but let me get back to you on the startup decibels. Number two: power. Muzzle velocity is three thousand feet per second." Peter remembered to pause. "I'd also like to add that our range tests have shown minimal trajectory loss. Gentlemen, at two hundred yards, this weapon has zero drop."

"That's physically impossible and you know it," LaCroix scoffed, stabbing a slice of melon. "In the remote possibility of breaking from defensive mission priorities, we'd need at least a fifteen-inch barrel and triple powder loads. How'd you manage it?"

"C'mon, Colonel. Undetected entry and assassination are the *only* reasons for building this kind of weapon into a surveillance aircraft. That being the case, we figured the round must reach and penetrate a human target quickly while maintaining near silence. And we achieved that by replacing a traditional fifty-grain lead bullet with a ceramic-boron composite that weighs eighty percent less. Believe it or not, it's as hard as titanium. There were some problems with overspin until we lengthened the shell casing. We named it ceron."

LaCroix shook his head. "Why couldn't our people ever think of that?"

"Wasn't in the manual," Floring muttered. "And recoil?"

Peter wondered if he felt nauseous from thinking about ocean swells, or from talking so casually about killing. He found the screen menu he was looking for and clicked an icon. A video started with one of the *Tiger* team members standing in Aerotech's test yard literally heaving the machine into the sky like a weighted paper airplane. "A BB gun from Wal-Mart has more recoil. Still, we had to absorb enough to stabilize flight and hovering balance. *Tiger*'s propulsion design is identical to that of larger fan motors. Batteries spin blades that force air through a single airway. Essentially, we added a quarter-inch-diameter hollow ring, shown on page two, to distribute the weapon's discharge. When PTS fires, ejection gases are measured, and that precise amount of balancing pressure is siphoned from the primary airflow into the exhaust. Because the gas is too slow to counter any recoil, it simply replaces the primary air and keeps the entire system in balance. It's all a matter of manipulating deficient and surplus air—"

"Okay, that's fine. I'm sure our people will have a field day with it, but what about the noise?" Floring persisted.

Peter paused the video. "We lined the inside of the barrel with a silica fiber netting tapered from front to back. It's really nothing more than a high-grade silencer. When fired, the sound measured eight decibels." He knew the number fell squarely within parameters.

Floring peered over his bifocals. "If we're all on the same team, why can't we get any performance data?"

Peter shifted. "Let me apologize for that. As a matter of fact, we ran two tests last night on maneuverability and stealth."

"Stealth? What target?"

"Multiples, actually. I'll make sure you get a full assessment." Peter neatly avoided the subject and jotted a note.

"The last capability?" LaCroix reminded.

"Right . . . number three: accuracy. We fired from a mix of different ranges and achieved these results." Peter produced a detailed computer drawing of target positions and distances. "The internal gyros maintain enough midair balance for this kind of lethality, but at two and a half pounds, I wouldn't recommend any more weapons; it's not a Tomcat."

LaCroix smiled at the F-14A artwork poster framed over Peter's shoulder. "Why so touchy about this little bird? You familiar with Rainbow?"

"Somewhat, but never worked on it," Peter admitted.

"Tacit Rainbow was a cheap suicide drone that could hover anywhere from five to fifty thousand feet and wait for enemy radar emissions. It could follow a signal track home and blow out the transmitter," Floring explained.

"Too bad the air force stopped funding it," LaCroix added bitterly. "Claimed it detracted from manned operations. When we showed black-and-white figures comparing the cost of one Rainbow UAV for one Shrike missile, the savings would've grounded half of their first-strike Weasel squadrons."

"Hmmm . . . I see your point."

"And we see yours. Just one weapon, for now."

"Fair enough; let's move on. For comparative purposes, if you matched the UAV's accuracy against that of a trained sharpshooter, it'd be a long day for the human. At two hundred yards, *Tiger* consistently hit a five-inch circle." Peter bowed his head theatrically as if apologizing for the achievement.

Floring picked up the bait and ran with it. "I've seen guides in Wyoming shoot varmints at twice that distance like they were plinking cans off a fence

Joel Narlock

at twenty feet. The twenty-two caliber is just naturally accurate. I was expecting a little more from a machine as sophisticated as this."

Peter took up the slack. "*Tiger*'s firing module is complex and simple rolled into one. The wideband technology calculates distance to a solid object, and pinpoints that position on the earth the same way GPS does, only far more accurately—three inches, to be exact. GPS has waypoints; we call ours target points. Once one is defined and locked, the PTS barrel will follow that point until it reaches the end of a firing sequence or range. Locate, acquire, target, and escape. Limited functions, nothing fancy. See for yourselves . . . this'll take a few moments to load. Even under unusual operating conditions like . . ." Peter paused in midsentence to inspect the fruit. His confidence level was flirting with cocky— a line he vowed not to cross no matter how smoothly things went. He bit into a huge sweet strawberry, blaming his smug facial expression on that. ". . . flying parallel to the target at one hundred miles per hour."

The hook set deep.

Chapter Seven

"Our circle vision program should make you feel as though you're inside the machine itself," Peter continued. "Very similar to watching a film in one of those round movie theaters. Hopefully, you'll enjoy the sensation. We'll demonstrate the lethality at a targeting range coming up on the right. First we need distance."

The *Tiger*'s omniview opened to bright sunshine and a picturesque view of the Nicolet forest from three sides. From a height of thirty feet above ground level, the UAV's video zoomed onto an armed and threatening mannequin positioned in front of a large earthen mound. A black kerchief covered the mannequin's face.

A pair of crosshairs rolled smoothly across the screen and intersected on the target's head. In the right-hand corner of the monitor, an arrow appeared and clicked "Lock" on the control menu. The screen responded with a sharp rectangular bull's-eye sight and a distance display. Next the arrow moved to load sequence, a series of geopositional coordinates, and a three, indicating number of rounds.

Peter paused the program and highlighted the target. "Once we've determined a relative position on the earth—the target point—PTS will maintain those coordinates and direct fire into it. This can happen from any direction, angle, weather, or light condition as long as it's fixed. Tracking and hitting an evasive target is a little too sophisticated. For this shot, we need a few minutes to get into position."

The UAV began moving away from the test range the required seven thousand yards.

At the calculated distance—nearly four miles into the forest—the UAV accelerated until the speed indicator read *100 mph*.

A screen display box showed descending digital distance to target starting at four hundred yards. A high-pitched tone sounded and another descending counter appeared on the monitor—*00:14, 00:13, 00:12, 00:11*—indicating there was a seven-second window of available targeting time on the approach and an equal amount on the exit.

The arrow pointer clicked on "Fire."

Three rounds in three seconds.

The UAV's passing speed made it difficult to determine exactly what happened. After circling back from the south, without losing sight of the target range, the *Tiger* lowered to ground level. There was a tight triangular grouping of quarter-inch holes in the center of the mannequin's forehead.

Floring leaned sideways. "I wish HUMINT were here. They won't believe this."

"I'm not sure I do," LaCroix whispered back, still trying to comprehend what had just happened.

Peter closed the program. "The lethality works well even while inverted, but we'll forgo the showboating. I doubt we'd ever use that position so long as we have Top Guns."

"Impressive," LaCroix admitted. "What if I steal *Tiger* and turn it against you?"

"Be my guest. We digitally encrypt the audio, and scramble the video just like landline cable. Real hard to fly if you can't see."

Floring propped his glasses onto his forehead and peered at LaCroix. "How's it feel to have a hook in your mouth?"

"About as sore as one of those sharks."

Peter continued. "There's not much more to detail except for minor programming changes to accommodate *Tiger*'s new weight, but those should work out. The software program was written and integrated by our senior flight technician, Sam Nasrabadi. As of last week, we own the code. We're on schedule for the Den sometime in early fall."

Aerotech's UAV was required to complete one undetected test flight in D1's Bear Den, a 150-acre proving ground located on the southern edge of the Bolling base. A special-op sister to Huachuca managed by a civilian security firm, the Den had perimeter sensors and radar that acted as a final exam for preproduction aerial or ground-based vehicles.

"*Tiger* good enough?" LaCroix referred to the Den's long-standing record of never allowing either a prototype machine or even a human operative to breach the complex undetected on a first attempt.

Peter shrugged impishly. "My team's confident. In fact, they were thinking about a wager. Any other questions or comments?"

LaCroix motioned to stop the recorder. "Before we pony up funds for that, what would you say to providing *Tiger* with some greater, shall we say, challenges than sneaking past security guards and barbed wire?" He rose from the table before Peter could answer. "I'm sorry to blindside you, but I've got no choice. The *Tiger*'s testing schedule has just been accelerated and enhanced. We want your team in DC now, not fall. And unless Aerotech can agree, some purse strings might tighten up indefinitely, if you catch my drift."

Peter sat down, trying to assess the impact of what was being proposed—transferring people, material, software, and essentially duplicating mission control operations in Washington seven months early. "Who decided this and exactly what kind of enhancements are we talking about?"

"Does is matter?" LaCroix countered. "Suffice it to say we want reality."

"Reality? I thought the Bear Den was supposed to—"

"For Christ's sake, we all know the Den has its place and certainly don't want to abandon it. But we've got other surveillance objectives in mind that'll put this project on a faster track." LaCroix poured himself a fresh cup. "Peter, in case you haven't noticed, the terror defense mind-set in this town has turned out to be more serious than any of us expected. There are rumors that whole intelligence organizations could be restructured into Homeland Security, or even eliminated. And Defense is next on the block. Produce or give way. We've got to perform like private industry to survive. Low cost, quality, and timely results."

Distracted with what he thought was an implication about government head count being placed on Aerotech's payroll, Peter completely missed the comment on other objectives. "If you expect Pritchard to take on extra bodies, forget it."

"Our people won't touch *Tiger* until it's ready," LaCroix said firmly. "Just give us enough feedback to evaluate the progress. You'll use our control center with base clearances to come and go."

Peter massaged his temples. "I suppose Bolling has on-site housing?" Floring was nodding repeatedly.

"You'll even get one of the new SUVs our motor pool just leased. Suburbans."

LaCroix snapped his fingers. "Thanks for reminding me about the mobile issue."

"Mobility's not a problem," Peter responded prematurely. "My people are okay with relocating provided there's light at the end—"

"An MCS. We want that tested, too."

"You have a mobile control station rigged for *Tiger* already?"

LaCroix sat down and reached under the table for his briefcase. "Not exactly. We gutted a cargo van from another project that got a little too big for its own good. The thing needs work, but I'll have it ready by the time you move in. Say, two weeks?"

Two weeks! Peter tried not to show reaction and calmly checked the date on his watch while wondering about the nature break his boss had mentioned. On one hand, it might make sense to ask for more time to evaluate all the logistics. On the other, it would take Aerotech senior management weeks just to weigh the pros and cons. They'd fumble around a new organization chart, hire some babble-speak consultants, run it past the attorneys, and then bring in the accountants. *This is what I get paid for*, he thought. *Empowerment or bust.*

"Agreed," Peter blurted.

"Any other questions from our distinguished walleye killer?" LaCroix asked.

Floring shook his head.

"Excellent—that settles it. Peter, you'd better call what's-her-name so she can run to Hackl and collect her brownies. *Tiger*'s classified on this end as of now, which means background checks by Defense Security Service. The usual forms and interviews. Will you call Gavin Murphy and kick-start that?"

Floring was writing furiously. "Time frame?"

"Yesterday or ASAP, whichever comes first."

Floring tucked a raisin bagel into a napkin and gathered his materials. He gave Peter's shoulder blade two sharp whacks. "Congratulations. Tell your team they do nice work. You all right? You look tired."

LaCroix slid a folder across the table. It bumped Peter's chest and snapped him out of a mild daze. "Peek at that for a while. You'll get a kick out of it. I'll be right back. Take your time. I heard you like baseball."

The title said, "Tiger STAT1—Stealth Aerial Test One: Camden Yards."

Both men watched Peter break the seal before closing the door.

Peter perused the document briefly and chuckled as he tucked it back into its folder. It was obviously someone's idea of a UAV gag. Still, he was glad to see that an agency as stuffy as DIA could embrace even a small sense of humor.

He let out a lengthy yawn. His eyes slowly drifted shut—a reward for a presentation well done.

LaCroix reentered the room. "I didn't expect you'd be bored to sleep. What's your honest assessment?"

Peter cleared his throat and volleyed the folder across the table. "Interesting. A little peculiar, but still interesting. Would you consider giving us a little more time? Two weeks just destroys our operational test plan. We'll need at least that long to handle the physical equipment moves."

"I asked you for an assessment," LaCroix quietly repeated. "But before you jump to any conclusions, please know that we take public testing very seriously. In today's environment, the slightest action out of the ordinary tends to raise security levels—especially Homeland military action. I want your project team to prove it has total mastery of this flying machine and its capabilities."

"Assessment of what?" Peter asked innocently. "What are you talking about?"

"You probably think it's peculiar because it has nothing to do with military surveillance, and you're right. We're running a different edge here. Military comes later." LaCroix put his hand on the folder and slowly escorted it around the table, placing it squarely in front of Peter. "I think the best way to view it is from a point of a stealthy simulation. I can assure you that the mission is serious in the sense that detection could jeopardize the *Tiger*'s worthiness in U.S. intelligence. My staff has put a lot of time and effort into this plan, not to mention acquiring some very choice seats—right behind home plate."

"You can't be serious?" Peter asked incredulously. "A baseball game?"

LaCroix unfolded a contour map of the city of Baltimore. "Have you ever been to Oriole Park?"

Peter's mouth was hanging open. "A stealthy simulation flight over a major-league baseball game?"

"We want the UAV out in the open," LaCroix said matter-of-factly. "High enough not to be seen, but in front of the civilian public. A baseball game attracts thousands of spectators. Using that theater as a test format can be an invaluable component of UAV surveillance. While the crowd is busy looking one way, you simulate a modest tactical maneuver and exit in the opposite direction. We want to see how well your team can bring it off."

Peter figured he was being played as the straight man in some bloopers film for a DoD Christmas party. "But what about . . . the media? What if we're spotted?"

LaCroix shrugged. "Darkness will help minimize that potential. Keep it simple and safe. We're not asking that you harm anyone."

Peter started to laugh. "Is this serious? Because if it is, I've changed my mind. I don't think it's peculiar at all. It's off-the-moon dumb, and you're crazy. Since when did the Defense Department—our own government—start conducting surveillance tests on the American public? Tell me you do this all the time?"

"After nine-eleven, more than you could ever imagine. Without anyone getting hurt or finding out about it, for the most part. D-one will provide rapid and responsive all-source intelligence to the world's most capable armed forces. In our view, it's essential to ensuring military information domi-nance in the twenty-first century. A matter of national defense. You and I both know the war is coming here, on our soil. And when it does, we'll need every tool and weapon available. It's simply serving the security of the country."

After a long silence, Peter realized it was no joke, and strange as it was, he started to rationalize that the UAV's battery capacity could hold it in a loiter or hover position overnight if necessary. "I must be as crazy as you for even considering this. Jesus, I like baseball. You say it's been done before?"

LaCroix hesitated. "In the early eighties we played a rather comical game of hide-and-seek above the Goodyear blimp during Monday Night Football. It wasn't very dramatic and no one suspected a thing. But I'm afraid we want a little more than surveillance this time."

Peter raised one eyebrow and cocked his head. "Don't stall me, Colonel. What do you mean?"

"We want you to target something in the stadium's interior."

Peter stared at LaCroix for nearly ten seconds. "I need to go."

"Peter, sit down."

"No—*you* need to see a doctor, because this is certifiable. It's complete paranoia. You people have been reading too many Tom Clancy novels. I will *never* allow my *Tiger* UAV to be used in the commission of a crime. Furthermore, I will never even consider using the lethality in an area where there is a high risk of injury to innocent people. I will not allow it to happen. You want to float through Baltimore and shoot up the place—rent a hot-air balloon with a rifle; you're not using mine."

"Will you please listen? You don't understand. You're viewing this as a personal matt—"

"You're damned right I am. No—I've got a better idea. Let's make the home plate umpire dance at the All-Star Game. Yeah, that's it. We'll target his foot and watch him hop all the way to first base. In a couple of months we'll blow away the game-winning home run at the World Series. Why not go all out with your stealthy simulation? Do you know what'll happen when this reaches twelve very old, rich codgers on Aerotech's board? Their hearts will explode from the shock of all the lawsuits. The San Diego hospitals won't be able to handle all the strokes. This is dumb, Dan."

Peter burned his tongue on fresh coffee and LaCroix waited for him to settle down. "You're funny, you know that? What happened to the bright engineer I knew at Hopkins who used to crave the radical? The one with all those wonderfully creative ideas, especially after good wine? Listen for one minute, okay? No one gets hurt or breaks any laws. We're talking simulation here. Fly in, acquire a target, *simulate* the lethality, and get out. DIA's got complete authority to legally test intelligence-gathering surveillance devices on the American public. Hear that? Complete authority. Granted, we're pushing a bit, but that's my problem. This is the right time, the right place, and the right machine. I'm not going to give it away."

Peter ran his fingers through his hair. "What authority?"

"The USA Patriot Act gives DIA the exclusive right to test UAVs on the private sector, if—and this is key—if it's in the interest of homeland defense. We have determined that the action fits the criteria. Now, what else would you like to know?"

Peter was flustered—too many baseballs flying around his head. "Patriot Act? When did they do that?"

"Senate Armed Services wrote a section that allows for covert testing of unmanned surveillance machines on the American public. We've used it a number of times after nine-eleven; it's real."

"Real doesn't make it right, and you still haven't answered me. Why would you chance the exposure?" Peter turned to the contour map. "You've done this before?"

LaCroix sensed he was winning and placed his hand on Peter's shoulder. "The authority rivals CIA's on a domestic basis. If it'll make you feel better, I'll get you a copy of the legislation, but it might take a while; it's highly classified. And the answer to your first question is that it's such a perfect public venue. Think about it. If the machine can accurately sight and lock a target in front of a few witnesses—"

"A few witnesses! You call a stadium filled with people a few witnesses? There could be ten, perhaps twenty thousand."

"We're talking surveillance here, not terrorism,"

LaCroix reminded him. "And for your information, the Orioles sell out their games. The attendance will be over forty."

Peter started laughing at the ceiling. "I can't believe you think this is no big deal. You sound like Johnnie Cochran telling the jury O.J. hit himself in the nose with a golf club and that's why there's blood all over his driveway. Anybody with a pulse knows it's totally obscene, but no one has the balls to say so."

"Mind if we stick to baseballs here?" LaCroix countered.

Both men cracked up at the deadpan remark.

Peter paced back and forth, stopping to shake his head at the line of professional ethics. What would Aerotech's reaction be? Was there even a line? He let out a long sigh. "I can't believe I'm agreeing to this. Give me some time to think things through."

"Good, but don't take too long. There's a twinight doubleheader the last Sunday of next month. I want it done then. Oh, and one more thing. If anyone on your team has so much as a dirty handkerchief in their past, tell them to get it out on the table. The agents in DSS are very thorough about background checks. It'd be a shame to have a security problem hold up your funding."

Peter wondered how private companies managed with such drab department names like personnel or human resources. Only Defense would call theirs a damned directorate.

He gathered his materials, feeling like a realtor who had just sold his first luxury mansion—to buyers who swore they had the cash and wanted to move in tomorrow.

Chapter Eight

Nicolet National Forest

John Eljay Turner stepped out of his log cabin and surveyed the blanket of fresh snow. He bellowed into the crisp morning air, "Black folks don't like winter."

He leaned his twelve-gauge shotgun firmly into a notch in the porch rail and stared at it suspiciously while he zipped his jacket. "Don't . . . even . . . think about it."

Finished with her morning jog and still under arraignment, his four-year-old Brittany spaniel, Tress, obediently froze, certain the unfamiliar but stern command was meant for her. Bred for game birds, she had uncharacteristically given chase to a sassy chipmunk the day before and stumbled into the weapon.

Turner's eyes rolled down the barrel to the dab of epoxy on the red-beaded sight. The dog waited for the verdict. Shooting distance would be the judge.

He spied a weathered piece of plywood next to the shed and propped it against a tree stump. He loaded one shell and pumped the action. The crack of the three-inch magnum gave a long echo as the lead sprayed into the board evenly, but did little damage.

Convinced the line was good, he reached deep into his pocket for a special high-brass Remington load with just fifteen thirty-two-caliber pellets—double-aught buckshot. He braced himself before squeezing the trigger. The impact tore a two-foot hole. The barrel was smoking as he ejected the shell.

All was well. Not guilty.

He slung a backpack over his shoulder and started out, the dog dutifully sweeping a narrow path in front, her stubby tail motoring back and forth at the freedom.

Turner's legs ached after only a mile, but he pressed forward like a modern-day prophet, driven by inner voice and spirit through the wilderness, seeking holy ground. A sanctuary. His own fortress of solitude.

He reached the entrance and stared up at the majesty.

John's cathedral.

He was no saint, but after all these years, the

name still fit. Rome should be so lucky.

Seeded in 1931 by the Civilian Conservation Corps, the double row of tall white pine broke the northern wind so efficiently it reminded him of a silent church. He removed his hat and walked inside. A lone deer reluctantly fled its warm pocket of fallen evergreen, so he decided to lay claim to the bed. There wasn't a peep from his birds. Thermos coffee had never tasted so good.

"Black folks don't like winter, girl," he quoted his grandfather again, but this time softly to the dog.

Turner knew he was different; so did his friends and family. Different for owning property in northern Wisconsin in such close proximity to towns with less than stellar racial reputations. But in a county with twelve people per square mile, he never had any problems. His closest neighbors—eight miles away—were friendly enough and kept an eye on his property. They knew he lived near Washington, DC, and sometimes did work around government buildings. Something with the grounds or landscaping. They referred to him simply as "that colored fellow."

The man in charge of the Secret Service Uniformed Division at the White House complex cherished the anonymity.

Every year Turner returned to the upper Midwest, spending part of his precious vacation with his family in Chicago, and the rest on a jihadlike ruffed-grouse hunt in the middle of nowhere off Fire Tower Road. It made Washington seem like another world. Sometimes he missed human conversation, but the feeling quickly passed when he remembered urban civilization. Normally fastidious about his appearance, he secretly relished his current homeless-style clothing. Best of all, he kept his worst nemesis at bay. Of all the great things about his career and high-profile position, he hated most that confining piece of clothing whose only purpose was strangling blood from throats—a necktie. He especially despised being held prisoner by someone else's idea of style. He was thankful the only fashion decisions in the Nicolet were those of warmth and camouflage. One was particularly relevant today. He stuck out like a tourist against the snowy background.

Turner's father had retired from law enforcement. Restless and filled with youthful make-a-difference energy, Turner had figured his own destiny pointed to police science at the University of Minnesota, where he received a commitment-to-hire notice from the Secret Service late in his senior year. During his probationary period, he enrolled in a graduate program in criminology. Surprisingly, his first field office assignments were far from adventurous and involved mostly white-collar crimes like credit card fraud, ATM theft, bad checks, phone fraud, and even counterfeiting.

After four years as a special agent in Minneapolis, he relocated to Washington and was promoted to assistant to the resident agent in charge of the U.S. Capitol. He quickly concluded that the congressional interior, anterooms, maintenance passages, and ventilation ducts were vulnerable to terror attack when 9/11 still meant an emergency phone number. When the assistant director wouldn't even consider recommendations to overhaul building and airspace security during State of the Union addresses, Turner called him an asshole to his face. The problems were irreconcilable, so Turner transferred to the vice president's PPD, Personal Protection Detail. The deputy director thought Turner's ideas should have been implemented, but couldn't see overriding his longtime crony; it was easier to transfer the young troublemaker. After serving sixteen years in managerial positions in both protective and investigative assignments, Turner returned to the Uniformed Division after a fifth promotion.

With Tress curled comfortably beside him, Turner felt that the current status of the White House perimeter was light-years away. He stroked her head and neck. He didn't blame the birds. It had been a light year for snowfall, with the seasonal average down by almost two feet. With such easy access to food, there wasn't much need to move.

The wind picked up in longer intervals, indicating winter was still alive and well. Spring had passed, according to the calendar, but dates meant nothing to the Nicolet.

The sharp flutter of a muffled wingbeat brought Tress to her feet.

Turner scanned the ground for quiet access into

a thick circle of pines off to his left. Unlike the Brit, he had to rise slowly to let the blood start flowing. The dog was already making her way to the sound on the exact path he would have taken. She was a natural hunter and waited patiently for him to catch up before easing into a frozen point between two evergreens.

Turner reached the clearing and cocked his ear. He knew the bird was in there; he could feel it. His mind laid out the strategy.

Just one more and you can go home, John. One shot. Don't screw it up. Anticipate the flight path. That's the secret to hunting these things. Anticipate. Find the escape route and beat the bird to it. He had learned to respect these flying bolts of lightning. Anything that could accelerate from zero to sixty mph in three seconds deserved it.

He clicked the safety and readied himself for the explosion that was sure to come.

What seemed like an eternity of silence ended with the bird's preflight warning: the distinctive three *eek*s.

Like some feathered propeller, a blur of reddish-brown energy darted around the pines with heart-stopping speed. In one fluid motion, Turner raised his shotgun and locked the bead on the target. His mechanics were good, but there was a problem. The bird was on the wrong path! His smooth barrel lift and follow-through collided with a spruce branch, resulting in a faceful of powdery snow. No grouse breast tonight.

Tress plunged into the brush that held the bird's luscious scent only moments before, just for the smell of it. She emerged with her head cocked in unmistakable canine confusion. He knew what she was thinking: *What happened, dummy? I wanted to fetch something.*

At the cabin, Turner unlaced his boots, bittersweet about canned supper. He hated to dress those damn birds anyway. All the feathers and mess for one lousy meal? Yeah, that was it. He'd settle for beef stew and a side dish of sour grapes.

DIA Center
Directorate for Administration

DA Support Services handled security and suitability interviews for all military and contracted employees working on sensitive Defense projects in the National Reconnaissance Office, Central Imagery, NSA, DIA, and all four military service intelligence organizations, claiming to bring to the military what the DoJ did on a domestic front. In truth, the civilian FBI simply wasn't as trusted.

Harold Floring regularly worked with Support Services and knew the normal wait time for completing one criminal background investigation for one individual in the preterror era was thirty days. The postterror workload would probably put his clearance request at the end of a long line—if the store were open at all.

Amazingly, a human voice answered the phone after only one ring.

"Gavin? We're all in trouble if senior directors are working weekends."

"Thanks for reminding me," Murphy replied. "I only have to cut the bottom fifteen percent . . . you?"

"We were lucky. The angel of ventilizing passed us by this time—at least until the next budget crunch. They figured LaCroix already took a pay cut last year."

"Ventilizing?"

"Consultant-speak for combining fresh air with down- and rightsizing," Floring explained. "It still translates into blowing old farts like you and me out the door."

"Speak for yourself," Murphy scoffed at the remark but knew the claim was partially true.

"What's the chance of opening new clearance work ASAP?" Floring asked. "I've got a short fuse on a project that just got funded."

Murphy let out an audible sigh. Everything had a short fuse. "In-house?"

"Contractors. You free for dinner, say . . . seven-ish?" Floring heard papers shuffling.

"I can do that," Murphy confirmed. "Seafood?"

"How about that new place by the markets? I forget the name. Something about a ship."

"The Mast . . . but don't park south. Gangs had a bit of a shoot-out last night."

TARGET ACQUIRED

Nicolet Forest

Turner sopped up the last bit of stew gravy with a crust of bread while watching a PBS videotape on super predators. Tress had assumed her usual begging position on a braided rug between the stove and kitchen table. She let her eyes follow every table movement, hoping for a tidbit. A pride of lions had surrounded a Cape buffalo. Stuck chest-high in a mud hole, it bellowed a death call. Turner stabbed the last forkful of meat just as a lioness mounted the hapless bull from the rear. He tossed the morsel into the air. The Brit's mouth snapped it down instantly.

Turner took his share of criticism for these sabbaticals, mostly from single friends and colleagues who preferred to stalk female prey around some Caribbean island. The DC rumor mill said he had some weird drive to punish himself at this time of year, but it was simpler than that: he desperately needed the annual recharge. Virtually no city entertainment appealed to him anymore, other than selected sporting events. He routinely visited inner-city schools to tout law-enforcement careers, but gradually shifted his message to that of hope. Once, a principal interrupted a speech to proudly proclaim that *only* 110 students had been suspended that morning—a school record. Addicted to failure, the black culture was disintegrating before his eyes. Students literally cornered him in the hallways, begging for help against neighborhood horrors that had become routine. He tried in vain to rally local and even national media, but concluded that the shocking cases of Hollywood celebrity shoplifters apparently took precedence. People simply didn't care.

He started a fire and settled into his sofa with a stack of unfinished *National Geographic*s. He couldn't stop thinking about her. Lt. Sheri Walker taught calculus at the Naval Academy and spent every plebe-free moment commuting to Washington. It had been two years since a freak but fatal blood clot had taken his wife. Sheri was the only woman he'd met since who ordered him to stop dwelling on the past. She made him feel young again. No one else had the guts, and thus fed his sympathy addiction.

As he listened to the dried birch crackle away his last night in the north, his drift into sleep was prolonged only by a desperate battle to forget, for just one more day, the grind of the Capital Beltway and one of the most stressful jobs on earth.

Potomac Shoreline
Wooden Mast Restaurant

The Mast was a smoke-free establishment, so Floring waited outside the entrance to draw a few more puffs off his cigarette. A wobbly customer accidentally brushed against a fire-red sports car in the parking lot and triggered a piercing alarm. Murphy pulled next to it just after it stopped.

"Gavin, don't touch that car." Floring flicked his

butt in a long arc that landed neatly underneath the vehicle. Murphy exaggerated his stride away from it.

They walked inside to a reserved table overlooking the Potomac. The water was calm and offered crystal reflections of the opposite shoreline. A waiter outlined the dinner specials and jotted a drink order.

Floring noticed weather imagery on the bar's television screen and squinted to read the forecast. "Did you know the NSA has enough satellite power to track every single motorized vehicle in the U.S.? They could effectively wipe out auto theft."

"Along with a few amendments," Murphy quipped, his constitutional law diploma curling at the suggestion. A self-proclaimed slayer of intelligence injustice, Murphy viewed his agents as first-line defenders against internal anarchy and now terror. His swept-back silver hair resembled George Washington's. He had purposely fitted a walking cane with a polished silver handle and tip to enhance the stately effect. "NSA's got more than its share of knucklehead power, too. You actually have to keep up with them?"

"No, thank God. My head spins enough at all the changes. And not just software and numbers. Hardware technology's gone to the edge, too. Maybe more so."

"So what's all this furor in Analysis, and how can the SS help?" Murphy asked. Both men knew he meant Support Services.

"The investigators can't delve into project details," Floring said firmly. He knew this was a double-edged sword. D1 needed thorough background checks, but not at the expense of technical leaks.

"Who gets the results?"

"Everything comes back to me. I'll feed LaCroix." Floring paused while Murphy produced a pen and notepad. "We're exploring a new technology here, and I need assurance that four contractors have absolutely spotless records. Their work could send us into the next generation of covert surveillance. If this thing goes to potential, sabotage would be unthinkable. Can you skip any formalities to save time?"

Murphy winced at the suggestion. He wanted to be as accommodating as possible to internal customers, but when his agents skipped procedures and things went wrong, the ramifications were often visible and embarrassing.

"Depends on the level. You said it's already rated?"

Floring raised a finger as a waiter approached. They ordered.

"If it's that urgent we might bypass education and start with family. We can usually get some element of comfort if there's a stable home unit. Of course, that assumes no flags on their DFEs."

The Declaration for Federal Employment was the U.S. government's official questionnaire for sensitive positions. A twenty-five-page paper inquisition, it sought data on friends, family, relatives, job history, financial status, tax returns, court orders, even traffic tickets—parking included if over $300. It also examined legal and illegal drug usage. The rule on that was honesty. Best to admit bad judgment up-front and minimize it.

Floring was already craving nicotine and fondled a breadstick. "What about psychologicals?"

"Who has resources for that?" Murphy laughed. "We can barely keep up with our own evaluations. What exactly is this technology?"

"It's aerial surveillance–related. Aerotech developed the thing and gave us our first look a year ago. It's still a prototype, but from what we've seen there'll be lots of interest. Peter Wescott's the project manager. There's no reason to suspect anything, because we solicited them first. One's Iranian, if that matters. He's been here quite a while."

Murphy shrugged. "Probably means we can't get at the family and have to look for evidence of latent loyalty, like frequent trips to neighboring countries or patterned communications. Fairly routine. Remember, we stopped doing business with Iran after the demise of the shah. If the subject has friends or relatives back there and has sent them so much as a postcard, it won't sit well."

"I'm sure Wescott would've brought that up," Floring surmised. "The fellow's already been through several interviews with Justice."

"He may not know. You'd be surprised how close

you can get to someone without seeing another side."

"Didn't Iran recall all its citizens to join the military under penalty of death?"

"Sounds familiar, but that's a question for State. If he's a U.S. citizen, Iran's the last place he'd want to visit." Murphy clicked his pen. "What's his name? I'll start the preliminaries."

Floring spelled it. "He's their flight control specialist. Peter speaks highly of him. By the way, you can bypass Wescott."

"This prototype have seats?" Murphy asked.

The *Spirit of Washington* dinner ship glided down the Potomac for its evening cruise. Floring smiled into his drink at the tactful pumping. He owed a better description. "No passengers or pilot. It's a UAV."

Murphy repeated the acronym. "Unmanned. . . . something."

"Aerial vehicle. This one's ultra high-tech. Code-named *Tiger*. Very small and whisper quiet. Takes interesting pictures in interesting places."

Their entrées arrived.

"LaCroix's still building UAVs? I thought his consolidation program petered out."

"Two years ago," Floring said. "It almost killed him."

"Military cooperation at its finest." Murphy grinned.

"It was bad. Just imagine the navy and air force trying to agree on flight tactics. LaCroix had teams, designs, bids, functionality, and pet projects coming out his ears. It got to the point where departments did their own thing anyway. He figured there was no value in false control."

"So why is D-one still involved?" Murphy wondered.

"Because we challenged our top contractors to design a machine that we'd keep for ourselves. The best of the best for covert intelligence. If the services want in, they pay our price. And from what we've seen, Aerotech is way out front. They'll be in the Den in a few weeks."

Murphy squeezed a lemon over his plate and neatly accounted for every sautéed shrimp. "I think we've got a file on Wescott. He was with Lockheed. Be easy to update."

"No, he's fine. He and LaCroix are old pals. Jesus, you talk about people like they were some real estate title policy."

This observation was very true, Murphy thought. "Aerotech's on the West Coast."

"Corporate headquarters. Their test facility is in Wisconsin near the thriving metropolis of Eagle River, the world capital of snowmobiling."

"Good for them." Murphy was from Georgia and hated winter. He casually jotted *stealthy undetectable aerial surveillance* on his notepad. "Your Bear Den's got quite a reputation; so does that gentleman who runs it. I believe his name is Miller. I hear his bank account rivals his ego."

Swirling the last of his drink, Floring was distracted by an attractive woman sitting at the bar. He took a deep breath and remembered his wife of twenty-nine years. "I hired Dutch Miller. His company is SSI—Surveillance Systems, Inc. We lease them the space. He's retired military. Championed unmanned deployment for years. He tried to convince the entire U.S. Army how dangerous UAVs were to ground forces. He riled some general in Missile Command. Finally turned in his papers. Miller's no gentleman."

"That's him," Murphy confirmed. "We considered sending some of our own investigators through SSI for the operations experience, but the cost was outrageous."

"He's not cheap, but then the best never are," Floring said. "Damn, look at that!"

Murphy turned to the window. Black smoke was billowing out of a cabin cruiser in the center of the Potomac. "Could be nasty if the tanks go. I think they're in the floor."

Restaurant personnel scrambled for help. The vessel's owner was a wealthy eccentric who attempted suicide before.

Metro Police Harbor Patrol reached the area just as the cruiser exploded. The bow and stern sections launched apart in opposite directions like pieces of a wooden toy. Debris reached the restaurant pier fifty yards away.

Floring picked up the dinner tab and carried a drink onto the river patio. His cell phone chirped.

"How'd it go . . . he get nosy?" LaCroix's voice asked.

"Not bad," Floring answered. "I had to explain what a UAV was, but nothing more. He's assigning two agents on Monday. He didn't appear too interested."

LaCroix laughed. "Murphy's no dummy. He knows exactly what that means. His people cleared the *Predator* team at General Atomics. Well, let's hope he puts this on a fast track so it's nice and legal. I suppose we ought to brief Mr. Miller that his impenetrable facility is about to get a workout. I'm afraid the Bear Den's perfect record might have come to an end. Technology doesn't give a damn about tradition."

Chapter Nine

Oakton, Virginia

Turner's leg muscles were burning, but he raised the treadmill's angle another notch in his bedroom in the upscale suburb west of Washington. The machine purposely faced the windows so he could watch the buffet line of songbirds at his feeders, and turn his back to the snakes writhing on the tie rack in his closet.

He glanced at the dog on the floor. Sprawled on her back and deep in dreamland, she pawed her own doggy treadmill in the air with her hind legs, chasing a bird in some crop of grass. Time in the forest flew by faster than that damn grouse, he thought. One by one, as if by some evil voodoo, work projects he had buried away in temporary memory graves started rising like freakish ghouls, their faces contorted in proportion to their priority: protection . . . budgets . . . head counts . . . performance evaluations . . . special projects . . . new hires. Turner's day-shift supervisor, Eugene Michels, was on extended disability after knee replacement surgery. The second shift position had been vacant since the incumbent had lost his fight with esophageal cancer.

When Turner finished on the treadmill and set out for the White House, the most dreaded ghoul rose last: traffic. Turner wasn't in the flow on I-66 for three minutes before someone cut him off and flipped him the finger. He just let it go; his mind was in the cathedral.

It took an hour to reach White House reserved parking between the old executive office building and the west wing.

The gate officer bent through the window. "Morning, sir; welcome back. I hear we're getting a new face today. I just wanted to tell you that Paul Bristol and I worked together in the Atlanta field office. He's a good man."

"That's nice to hear. I'm sorry it took so long," Turner said. An affirmation from one of the troops was always a good sign that he'd made the right choice. "Looks like the place is still standing."

"Yes, sir. Mr. Evans has been in early every day. He cracks a mean whip. He wants to know if you're ready for your walk."

"Huh?" Turner frowned. "A walk where? What the hell's he talking about?"

"Not sure, sir. Just relaying the message."

"Thanks, Henry. Appreciate the feedback."

Turner pulled into his assigned space and walked briskly up the steps. He turned to look back at the city. A deep breath confirmed that his cabin was indeed a thousand miles away. His Remington 870, standard training shotgun for the UD—Uniformed Division—was now a briefcase. The honking in the air wasn't geese.

A former DC Metro police officer known for his crisp uniform and spit-polished shoes, third shift supervisory officer Joe Grant had the somewhat embarrassing honor of being the oldest employee out of twelve hundred in the UD. He'd been working double tours to help ease the coverage deficiency and would faithfully sit outside Turner's office every morning with a status report of the previous shift's activity.

"Welcome back, stranger." Grant grinned. "Am I glad to see you. I figured you couldn't stay away."

"That's an understatement," Turner replied. "What's it mean when you can't stop thinking about work even when you're on vacation?"

"It means you're dedicated."

"Or just plain stupid." Turner noticed the fatigue in Grant's face. He leaned over his secretary's desk and ran a finger down the appointment log. "How are you holding up?"

"A little tired, but I'm okay. Not as much fire as I used to have. Geno's up and walking around. His knee's still swollen pretty bad. He's bored silly. Can't wait to get back in here."

"Jack holding a meeting this morning?"

"Yes, sir, he wants you to go for walk . . . with a pair of gloves and a shovel."

"Sounds like O.J." Turner chuckled. He loosened his necktie before the office lights flickered on. "Well, I suppose you're gonna give me an earful of—"

There was a large metal bowl on his desk. It was filled with dried dog food.

Grant raised his hands in mock innocence. "I had nothing to do with that."

"That SOB." Turner cracked up and set it on the floor.

"This'll only take a few minutes," Grant promised. "I know how you like to ease back into things. Besides, I'm meeting someone special."

"A date?"

"Just my daughter." Grant beamed and opened his notebook. "Let's see . . . all in all it's been fairly quiet. The gangs gave the E Street fence a new paint job. One hotshot sprayed his sign on a column last Friday night for some initiation."

"His sign?" Turner remarked.

"The latest thing. Everybody's got their own personal symbol so they know who did what. He set off I-5 before Raider cornered him on the fringe near seventeenth. Roughed him up a little bit, though."

Turner grimaced. "That dog'll eat one of the press corps reporters someday and we'll all have hell to pay."

Raider was a Belgian Malinois imported for the service from a breeder in the Netherlands. The dog's dingolike brown body and black face had been achieved in the early twentieth century by crossing German shepherds with hounds. An excellent bomb sniffer with short hair and extremely fast reflexes, the dog was considered too vicious by some, but could tolerate DC's voracious heat and humidity better than most attack dogs. At 110 pounds Raider was bordering on madness, per his own handlers. A red Doberman had bitten the dog's ears as a pup. Payback came when the full-size Malinois had scaled a nine-foot kennel fence and tore the Dobe's ears off before handlers intervened. Diet and medication helped, but there was still talk of injection. Even the trainers were at risk.

Grant made a note to muzzle the animal. "Anyway, we got the kid without a lot of commotion, but damned if he wasn't carrying a three-eighty just like mine. That Beretta's worth six hundred bucks. Then he tells me he's got a Desert Eagle. When kids start owning fifty-caliber handguns, it's time to bring in the marines. What's with DC?"

Turner stared out at the west wing and shook his head. "This isn't the only town with guns and spray paint. Once they start formal training, I'm transferring north."

"We had a drive-by at E-eight last night at oh-one-hundred but couldn't make out much. Caught some of it on tape and turned it over to Metro. I figure they should handle the gang wars." Grant flipped pages. "Here's a good one. The day after you left, a pilot flew a helicopter into the zone to let some Saudi bigwigs take pictures. He tried to warn them no one was allowed in the air around here, but they swore they'd fix any problems. Said they had friends in FAA who'd close their eyes. Can you imagine that? Jack's people pulled the whole party at Dulles. Last I heard they're still locked up."

Turner knew that the pilot's certificate would be gone for five years, minimum. Code of federal regulations part 91, FAA rules for restricted and prohibited airspace. "Hate to hear that, but dammit, we've got to send a message. The air traffic around here is still scary. Don't think I'll ever get used to it."

"Now the bad news," Grant said. "The president's here until mid-September. A few travel days later this month, but nothing extended."

"That even makes me more nervous. I wish they'd get out of here in summer. Humidity brings out the crazies."

"I need to hit the trail." Grant tried to muffle a yawn and started for the door. "The rest is in e-mail."

"Hold on." Turner opened his desk drawer for an envelope. He intended to take full advantage of the government's new performance-recognition program. Success depended on rewards that were meaningful and immediate. Ten crisp hundred-dollar bills were meaningful. "Breakfast is on me. I want you to know that I appreciate all the extra time and effort you've given over the past weeks. It hasn't been easy. In about fifteen minutes we'll have another body on board. You tell Nicole I said hello."

Barb Dwyer, Turner's personal secretary, walked in with a pot of coffee and a bulging folder. "We missed your smiling face. Have a nice time?"

"Next year I'm taking eight weeks."

"But you don't get that much vacation."

"I'll ask the president to arrange it . . . he owes me a favor or two."

"How're Mom and Dad?"

"Fine, but they need to migrate out of Chicago. It's too fast-paced," Turner confided. His parents were approaching eighty and continued to battle the winters.

"You know your father . . . he'd be lost without a snow shovel." She slid three documents out of the folder. "I'm upgrading my PC's RAM and need those signed right away."

"Your what? Where'd you learn that?"

"I finally finished my class," she said proudly. "Now don't get mad, but Jack said the Doberman he hired to fill in for you worked just fine and you owe him lunch."

"The dog or Jack?" Turner grinned.

"I'll let you get caught up. Coffee's strong." She smiled and pirouetted out the door.

Turner nudged the dish on the floor. He still believed his White House complex record was a compliment to the professionalism and skill of his officers—not to the notion that the job was overrated. The UD simply focused more on the external grounds than directly on human protectees, at least up to 9/11. After that, Turner's officers had seen their status and respect levels skyrocket. Anyone interested in breaching the physical grounds probably had more on their mind than picking flowers from the Rose Garden. The PPD got all the past glory for protecting the president and first family mainly because of the higher visibility, but so what? They knew routes and routines, thanks to AMPS. The Agent Management and Protection Support System was a live database that assigned and tracked all current and future movement of the service's valid protectees. With a million lines of code, AMPS had several security modules to limit and control access levels. Unbelievably, a budget reduction task force under the previous presidential administration had made the moronic recommendation to transfer IT programming support to a sweatshop of foreign coders just to save the labor costs. He remembered the turf battles in personal protection and had a right to criticize. Glorified bodyguards with sunglasses who thought they were bad. He loved to rap those nervous prima donnas. It always made the first day back a little easier.

Turner started signing his name in unintelligible scrawls on documents that were nothing more than triplicate proof of a paper bureaucracy. But he couldn't complain: top management pay grade, a team of quality personnel, and respect from all levels in the service. His ninety-five officers safeguarded the personal residence of the president of the United States. He hated his team's other reputation, but to a certain extent, the canine label fit.

He glanced at the plaque coworkers on the Capitol detail had given him when he transferred to the vice president:

> The Capitol has guard dogs; the VP has Turner.
> The only difference is, dogs clean up after themselves.

The sound of someone whistling filled the outer office.

"Heeeere, boy . . ."

An arm stretched into Turner's doorway dangling a thick leather leash.

Jack Evans was the special agent in charge of the Presidential Protection Division. Known for his tailored suits and flamboyant neckties—Turner was convinced it was purely to spite him—Evans had selected today a tie that sported a tennis theme. "About time you showed up for work around here. Cereal have enough crunch?"

"Nice tie," Turner remarked. "You pick that out all by yourself?"

Evans hiked up a trouser leg and sat on the desk corner. "Pure silk. Guess I have a natural talent. How're things in the arctic?"

"Come with me next year."

Evans smirked. "John, I want you to get professional help. Normal people fly south, where it's nice and warm. What's so special about northern Wisconsin except cold, wind, and snow? There's nothing up there. No people, shows, opera—nothing. Lunch says you don't even have cellular access."

"Peace, quiet, no crime, and no neckties," Turner said evenly. "I'm lucky to have electricity."

Evans shook his head. "When are you going to end that crazy vendetta? You might want to buy a nice suit and impress that Annapolis lady. Take her dancing. Navy officers like to dance. Mark your calendar and we'll go shopping. It'll be my treat. My wife says I've got a stylish eye for that sort of thing."

"Paul Bristol's here," Barb gently interrupted. She collected the folder and peered inside Evans's suit coat. "What a nice tie. I'm glad Rose took my advice and picked the one with the rackets. They're so cute."

Turner laughed out loud. "What were you saying about your eyes? You going to hang around or just collect the Purina?"

Evans's demeanor instantly turned serious. He glanced at his watch and took a seat on Turner's sofa. "I've got ten minutes, tops. We need to take a walk in the park."

Turner sank deep into his soft leather chair. He closed his eyes and tapped the leash against his cheek. "Damn . . . I hate walks in the park."

Paul Bristol was thirty-one years old and, in keeping with the dual missions of the Service, had completed investigative time in the Cleveland field office. Both men rose to greet the new supervisor as he entered the room.

"Welcome aboard, Paul. Where do you see yourself in two years?"

Bristol had never met Evans but knew him by reputation as the man being groomed for director of protective operations. "Well . . . you'll have moved up to the DPO, so I thought I might backfill the vacancy."

"With your performance record, I don't doubt that one bit," Evans remarked. "I hope you have better luck working with these belligerent uniforms. I'm sure you've heard rumors about all those rifts."

Bristol smiled politely at the compliment. "I don't pay much attention to rumors."

For years, an invisible yet distinct undercurrent of resentment had arisen between UD officers and PPD agents based on who wore suits versus uniforms and who had lead protection authority at any given time in the White House complex. It had gotten so bad that the director of the Secret Service had to issue a memorandum of clarification stating that UD authority took precedent whenever protectees were off-premises. He ended the memo stating he wouldn't tolerate any rifts. The term had become a comic mantra.

"The first thing I want you to do is observe," Turner suggested. "Learn the layout and the officers' routines before recommending any changes or improvements. There's a rhythm to the complex that takes on a life of its own. Are you up to speed on alerts?"

"Yes, sir," Bristol confirmed. "I'm current with my refresher training and have had plenty of routine intrusions at the Treasury facility. But I've never had any experience with Platinum."

"No one has," Evans spoke up. "Nine-eleven would've been the first. Let's hope it stays that way."

After each of the Lebanon, Oklahoma City, and Pentagon attacks, the Secret Service had continued to reinforce protected structures and perimeters with concrete barricades, pop-up road bars, heavy metal fencing, and a two-block shutdown of Pennsylvania Avenue. All protective agents and officers assigned to the White House complex were trained to use and recognize a series of operational alert levels that announced physical incursion type and severity. Level Gold, a call for overwhelming military force, had occurred once during the civil rights movement in August 1967, and again during violent student protests to renewed bombing in Vietnam in May 1972; Silver identified ground-based intruders who had already managed to gain unlawful access onto the premises; and Platinum was a blood-pressure-raising level that signaled an approaching airborne threat. All three carried protectee assassination urgency.

Turner handed Bristol a thick package of documents. "The physical layout is really childlike in simplicity. Circular and pie-sliced, the internal sectors are designated I-one through I-eight and range from the perimeter fencing inward to mirror similarly numbered external sectors, shifted slightly for coverage overlap. After nine-eleven, we extended E-sectors out an additional quarter mile in all directions. As a White House UD supervisor, you have full authority to assign patrols anywhere in the sectors. Your officers know their jobs and regularly post outside the perimeter—tourists, vehicle squatters, et cetera. Some pass through the area as part of the regular crowd."

"What's my available head count and are any reductions planned?" Bristol asked.

"Thirty-eight and possibly. There's always someone looking to cut expenses, but I'll worry about that." Turner reached in his pocket. "SCC access keys and cards. Spend time in there. You can cover a lot of ground through the cameras."

Manned twenty-four/seven by a staff of thirty-six, the White House SCC—Security Control Center—located in the old executive office building, observed all eighteen acres via visual-, motion-, and vibration-sensitive alarms placed throughout the complex. To supplement the ground patrols and minimize shoulder-to-shoulder armed guards, a network of Series 6000 Intrusion Detection Units—IDUs—were synchronized with optical light sensors and video cameras to monitor aboveground movements. Active at various times and locations, depending on complex activities and schedules, they were positioned along key fence lines and tree penetration points that could serve as blind spots or hidden runways. By the time a would-be trespasser reached what appeared to be a safe, concealed position, alarms would have already been triggered. A secondary grid of underground pressure plate sensors protected areas where IDUs were not practical. If a brick were thrown onto a pressurized area, its combined weight and impact would produce enough vibration to set off a silent internal alarm. Twenty pounds was usually enough, although settings varied depending on the size of the first family's pet.

Bristol shifted slightly in his chair. "I wonder if we could set up a training schedule to review the background of the Cessna flyovers. I studied quite a lot of the postevent critique data, but I still have questions."

"Not at all," Turner replied, impressed that his supervisor was already showing more interest in aerial than ground-based incursions. "Even though they carry life-and-death severity, Gold and Silver threat levels do not require safe resolution within a hard time frame. Platinum is a different story. Military aircraft patrolling our beloved capital, ready at a moment's notice to engage airborne threats, are half-useless. There simply is no time. And with all that hoopla about the Emergency Response Team and its infamous Stinger countermeasures, the . . . Jack's policy is to not use shoulder-fired weaponry on Washington air traffic. There simply is no need."

"Who started the theory?" Bristol asked.

"It's no theory, son; it's a fact," Evans corrected. "In the spring of 1992, with oversight from the White House chief of staff, we hired a small aircraft to penetrate the Washington no-fly zone during a staged vulnerability test. At the first PEC, security experts from FAA and CIA's Office of Technical Collection determined that high-energy explosives either dropped on or flown into the complex would have caused massive damage to the facility and everyone in it. Detection and prevention results were even worse. Based on those conclusions, and a little shouting from your boss, the secretary of the treasury approved funding to install, test, and deploy a White House air-defense system, including full radar tracking. Remember, a potentially hostile aircraft approaching DC is tracked on radar surveillance at least twenty miles out of Washington. Whenever *any* aircraft fails to follow strict approach procedures—seated passengers, area passwords— the SCC gets notified first over secure fiber. This sets a general minimum time mark of forty seconds before the earliest possible airborne impact. Pilot maydays or claims of misjudged coordinates are unverifiable and unstoppable—especially those departing northbound from Reagan National—given the time frame and risk to the nation."

"There are countermeasures in the complex not used in other protected facilities. Don't worry if you're a little overwhelmed at first. But hear me. Forty seconds," Turner repeated. "It's a number you'll never forget after you've been here awhile. Barely enough time for the president to grab his bathrobe and slippers. On the brighter side, no terrorist aircraft, we call them long threats, carrying explosives or excuses can alter course one degree without the SCC and on-premise PPD agents doing what they do best."

Bristol nodded. That meant whisking the protectees away to ride out the assault—real or accidental.

Evans stood. "I've got to go, gentlemen. Congratulations on your promotion, Paul. Welcome to the team."

Bristol politely rose halfway from his chair, and then sat back down. He was visually more relaxed now that he and his boss were alone. "Overwhelmed is an understatement. We never really had to concern ourselves much with aerial threats at Treasury. The building itself is a fortress. What's the main difference between a long and short threat?"

"Distance," Turner answered. He could go on and on about the subject that had earned him respect through the ranks of two presidents. He was the first person in the service to recognize the danger potential. "White House aerial radar coverage spans a hundred-and-twenty-degree arc out to the Jefferson Memorial. There is no need for a northerly sweep because the average building height will force low air traffic into National's radar. Short threats literally appear out of nowhere. The only defense is a combination airborne/ground-based Hunter-Target-Acquisition radar and Rapid Aerial

Defense System modules to detect aircraft that have either eluded traditional return signals or originated inside the forty-second boundary. RADS features two batteries of Talon antiaircraft rockets that serve as a last line of defense against low-flying planes with kamikaze intentions. They're hidden from ground level in two separate closets on the east and west sections of the White House roof. RADS is designed to lock the positional signature and target any airborne intruder approaching the complex from the Jefferson Memorial, Mall, Ellipse, or the south lawn. The three-foot weapons have never engaged an aircraft in the zone, although every penetration is tracked. When a Cessna crashed on the south lawn near the president's bedroom window in 1994, critics called the incident red-faced proof that our air defenses were all bluff and the zone had no early-warning capabilities. They were half-right. To divert public attention away from RADS operations we allow errant commercial pilots and suicidal drunks in Cessnas to stay airborne as long as protectees are deemed safe from CDP. You familiar with the term?"

Bristol nodded. "Certain deadly peril."

"Very good," Turner complimented. "Barring gross incompetence by our countermeasure officers, any craft intending to penetrate Washington's prohibited airspace undetected must either be small and agile enough to avoid radar altogether or stealthy enough to blend into the cluttered background. Birds notwithstanding, very few things that fly meet the criteria."

Bristol's eyes were starting to glaze over from information overload. "My education's in business administration, not engineering. Do you think I can add value to the UD?"

"I do or I wouldn't have approved your transfer. And don't worry, you'll get plenty of training starting with Target Tracking in Sensor Systems, or TTSS. The details are in your folder. It's a four-day course at the threat assessment center specifically designed for White House UD personnel who operate tactical defense systems. It provides overviews and hands-on training on target tracking, radar, sensors, and countermeasures. In case you don't know, I don't promote anybody who can't make the next two levels. Like it or not, people are watching you. But that doesn't cut any weight with me. Adding value isn't enough. I need you to learn this complex's nuances and procedures thoroughly and fast. My other supervisors are damn fine officers who could damn well retire tomorrow. That's a void I'd rather not have to deal with right now." Turner noticed the time. "I've bent your ear enough. We'll go over ground-based threats and off-site radar later."

A 9/11 terrorism task force concluded that the White House perimeter was indefensible, specifically due to public access and proximity. Multiple assailants could storm and/or fire short-range weapons into the complex in seconds, leaving occupants no time to react or take defensive measures. Even with protectees out of public view, overwhelming structure attacks were still possible but recognized as hit-and-miss potentials. Security forces simply could not defend a structure the size of the White House from every person or faction intent on damaging the building or its occupants. Accepting that vulnerability, the PPD constantly maneuvered protectees away from openings.

The Secret Service AAOP—Aerial Assault on Principal—simulation record for escorting the president out of harm's way from a daydreaming or lunatic pilot anywhere on the White House grounds was thirty-two seconds flat.

The procedure was somewhat misnamed.

Carrying the president like a sack of potatoes into the nearest bombproof safe room was a better way to describe it.

White House South Lawn

Presidential baseball.

It was something White House Security dreaded: very casual and very exposed, the commander-in-chief on one team, his eleven-year-old son on the other.

Aaron was an only child and had captured the hearts of the American public with his long eyelashes and active imagination. An honor-roll student in the sixth grade, he loved to bring schoolmates into the complex to play *anything* that would ease the boredom and formality of what his parents called proper behavior. He owned a variety of video games—except those with heads and limbs flying off in combat—but baseball cards were his real passion. He and his friends would spread out their collections in the Rose Garden and trade for hours. He knew the delivery schedule of the latest price-guide magazine, and memorized player statistics in his room late at night. Ultramischievous when the opportunity arose, he had once found a secret hiding place in the hedgerow next to his father's Oval Office and disappeared there for over an hour, sending the PPD and his mother into raw panic. Turner had spotted an autographed 1957 Henry Aaron baseball card worth $6,000 facedown near the shrubbery entrance. Luckily, neither of the Aarons suffered any harm. After he'd received a stern scolding, the conversation shifted into an hour-long story about the man who had hit 755 home runs. By then, the boy knew he was named after the slugger.

It wasn't the Olympics or Super Bowl, and therefore didn't rate national special security event status, but south lawn frolics featuring Secret Service protectees still invoked a directive, code-named Walk in the Park, that cleared I and E sectors four and five from the south portico to the Washington Monument.

UD officers and PPD agents were assigned positions, some doubling as outfielders, with additional ERT and countersniper units posted to visually monitor movements in the Ellipse and center Mall. Even from a distance of three thousand feet, DC park police confirmed that the monument itself was secured from long-range rifles, handheld launchers, or even a crazed hang-glider. Although traffic was allowed to continue on Constitution Avenue, no one could stop a vehicle between Fifteenth and Seventeenth streets. Pedestrians on E Street along the south fence had the best seats. This event was especially troubling because it was scheduled on a Saturday, which meant the backup RADS crew was on duty.

Turner watched Aaron tightening his shoelaces on the grass near the portico drive. It brought back fond memories of his days coaching in Minnesota, T-ball, Little League, and Junior Adult League. Once he took a group of six-year-olds to a major-league game in Minneapolis, paid a security guard to get inside the stadium early for autographs at the dugout, and wound up in a shouting match with a player who refused to even acknowledge the kids. The incident soured him on haughty professionals who forgot how they got to be superstars.

"Excuse me, is that Mr. Hank Aaron? Listen up. Keep your hands back, eye on the ball, and shift your weight when you swing. That's how you get power. Show me."

Determined, the boy lifted his bat and proceeded to bounce and wrap it behind his body like so many of his pro idols.

Turner shook his head. "You'll never get it around on a fastball."

"Oh, yes, I will."

"Bet?"

"Bet. Get up . . . get up . . . get outta heeeeere . . . gone—for Aaron." The boy's eyes sparkled with pride as he picked up his glove and trotted off.

A large crowd had gathered along the south perimeter to catch a seventy-five-yard show of the president pitching to his future Hall of Famer.

After an hour of playing time, father and son walked to the E Street fence to greet fans. One wanted an autograph on Aaron's home-run ball, and stuck it through the bars only to have it reexamined by attending PPD.

Turner was standing on the south portico overlooking the event when he heard the electrifying call.

"Platinum . . . I repeat, we have short-threat platinum . . . E-four . . . south southeast, dropping fast. We have an inbound," a youthful voice crackled over the communicators.

Evans was out of position. Turner was already sprinting down the steps, screaming into his radio, eyes on his watch. "All sectors! Mark is thirty-five . . . move them east!"

Mentally counting down the deadline, eight PPD agents lifted the confused president off his feet and raced in unison like some multilegged giant ant at a right angle away from the projected flight path and into the eastern shrubbery line. Another agent carried the boy.

Executive staff and advisers scattered in all directions. On the run, agents frantically deployed protective vests and whisked their cargo along the footpath to the east wing. The crowd at the south-lawn fence flattened like a squad of boot camp recruits when told to take cover from the overhead attacker.

"Inbound is slowing . . . speed is choppy . . . we can't track—"

"Whaddya mean, choppy? Where is the god-damned thing?" Turner interrupted harshly. There was no response. He tried to shield his eyes from the bright southern sun. "Dammit—what the hell is going on? Shut them down."

"We've got it, John," Evans's voice answered.

Turner reached the portico driveway in time to see the threat approaching. He turned to the roof. On the lawn, a dozen of his officers braced as a black wire-framed airplane kite floated to the grass on the very spot where the president had stood just moments before.

Outside the fence on the sidewalk, a tiny Korean girl gingerly crawled over her parents and tugged at the irresistible colored string draped across the iron bars.

Six E-section officers with weapons drawn materialized from the crowd. They were dressed as homeless people.

"Clear the metals," Turner ordered. "What the hell happened, Jack?"

"This is Officer Watts, sir. Mr. Evans is with the president. Our forward cameras glitched out. That's the first time it's ever happened to all three. No one lowered the sensitivity, sir, and once we locked, we had no choice but to—"

"Cut the chatter and get your butt back to normal in there . . . out."

"Yes, sir. SCC out."

"I hate walks in the park," Turner muttered as his officers dispersed the rest of the crowd and brought the kite in for routine examination.

Chapter Ten

Nicolet Forest
Aerotech Flight Control Center

Sam set the *Tiger* on stationary hover forty feet above the forest floor in Rocky Land, a heavily wooded ravine overshadowed by the height of the hillsides and a foreboding canopy of dead trees. The area was inaccessible to hikers or other trespassers, and a small creek dribbling through the center made the only sound. The approaching dawn provided just enough natural light to eliminate the need for infrared.

Dating herself, CJ had affectionately named the area in deference to the famous flying squirrel of a bygone cartoon era, due to the fact that the jerky motions of the little creatures tended to fool the UAV's targeting sensors.

Through the forward omniview lens, Sam noticed movement in one of the trees and pressed the zoom toggle. He placed the joystick in front of CJ. "You're right-handed . . . good. There are four control pads on top of the controller. Radar, omniview lens–type selector, sensors, and target matrix-type selector. Each pad is further divided by function so that there are twenty-four controls within four square inches. You should be able to reach all of them with your thumb. Let's see what we have."

A single, regal sunray had managed to find its way through the treetops and bathed a fat eastern gray squirrel grooming itself on the branch of a jack pine. Unaccustomed to being chosen messiah of the forest, the animal froze.

CJ applied steady pressure to the radar pad button labeled BFC, for beam focus control, which eventually drew out a circle engulfing the animal's body on the target matrix. Next she touched the track/lock button and used her mouse to drag two movable crosshairs together.

Sam's eyes moved back and forth as he compared data from the wideband target matrix to the video. "Easy does it . . . okay . . . you've got good reflection."

"I think the mechanics are even smoother than the cub controller," CJ observed. "Is there any order to the alignment?"

"I do vertical first, then horizontal, but there's no rule. Whatever is comfortable."

The squirrel moved slightly to the left, its target

outline following shortly thereafter in some slow-motion game of shadow catchup. CJ turned the system's autotracking feature off and repositioned the scope lines manually with relative ease.

"Good . . . very good," Sam observed. "You can almost feel the radar pulses reflecting back to the receiver, eh? Stationary targets are easy."

"Feel the radar?" CJ mocked. "I think I get the drift. This is getting a little morbid."

"This is no time for sentiment. Take the shot," Sam said firmly.

CJ flexed her hand several times before grasping the joystick. A screen grid on the monitor recorded a single burst of light hitting the branch two inches below the rodent's feet.

The little animal calmly began stroking its furry tail, unaware it was ever a target, albeit a simulated one.

Sam shook his head. "Range was perfect . . . positioning good . . . load initiation was set correctly. That was some of the smoothest aligning I've seen. Right up to the part where you were supposed to set a target point. This isn't *Star Wars*. You do have some responsibility for accuracy."

Carl burst through the doorway. "I give up. Where is it? We've been waiting for half an hour. Peter's sound asleep in the conference room."

CJ glanced at her watch. "Are we finished?"

"For now," Sam answered, and reset the target matrix. "That kid . . . Ricky wants me to show him how to initiate a solo flight from one workstation.

It's a little delicate because you have to carry the machine while it's running and operate a wireless mouse at the same time. We'll start later this afternoon. You're welcome to sit in."

Carl was opening and closing desk drawers in rapid succession. He paused over CJ's shoulder at the video monitor. "You missed him. You probably squeezed too hard. It's a plastic joystick, not a Smith & Wesson."

"Calm down; there's no need to tear the place apart. It's in my car. The world won't end if you don't eat." Sam winked at CJ. "We'll get the bakery if you bring the machine in."

Carl raised one eyebrow. "I don't want to sit here all day. Where is it?"

"Rocky . . . less than a mile out."

Irritated, but willing to accept the proposition for his stomach's sake, Carl slipped into the flight chair. "Fine . . . just go . . . I'm starving. And don't forget the napkins."

Before closing the PTS program, Carl touched the omniview zoom for a wider look at the forest. He pressed his thumb on the "Target point" button on the selector matrix pad. The squirrel had retired to its tree trunk nest through a three-inch hole. Carl gently wrapped his hand around the joystick and squeezed off a rapid succession of light bursts that neatly framed it.

"I don't care about penalties . . . they can kiss my ass," Ricky screamed into his cell phone in the corner of the conference room. He quickly covered his mouth in embarrassment. "I've got to go . . . *adios*."

Peter's eyes opened and he gathered himself.

Ricky took a seat and folded his arms like a brooding child.

Peter saw a flash of himself in the youth. A generation apart, they had chosen similar paths in life, pursuing a love of remote flying machines. One was a novice, fearless and in the game for career success and money; the other was a veteran with more wins than losses, but needing ever more intense successes to even stay interested. "Pritchard and I discussed your memo on the cub accident. You okay?"

"Depends. Am I still employed?"

"I'll share the feedback in a minute. Where is everyone?"

"CJ and Sam were cross training."

Peter glanced at his watch. "How's the business?"

"Great . . . everything's great. My goal is to be a millionaire before I'm thirty. Our new twin-turbine jet model took in twenty-eight thousand dollars in three days." Ricky filled a water glass. "Now all we have to do is give half to the government. California's talking about Internet sales taxes again. There's so much more to running a business than simply selling product. Who can understand all these rules?"

"Taxes . . . now that's an ugly word," Peter observed. "Save yourself the aggravation and hire an accountant."

"Don't have to. My father does our bookwork. He doesn't understand much about remotes but he's good with numbers. I don't know what I'd do without him. He's been staying up nights because the IRS says we owe more than he figured. They can get really nasty and it bothers him. I swear I'm going to buy him a new car. He's had to drive junk all his life. Then I'll get him a PC. He's still into pencils."

The remaining team members filed into the room.

Sam set a circular pastry ring on the table. Carl tore open the wrapping and slid two slices onto his plate.

CJ dutifully filled Peter's coffee mug. "No offense, but you look like hell. Another bad night?"

"Nah, I'm fine . . . let's get started. Speaking of nights, I've seen the video of the deer exercise and thought it went well; so does our boss. You encountered and handled something that's a fact of life in the surveillance world and will happen again under live circumstances. We need to get *Tiger* back in the air. It's the nature of the business. But I think some of us need to remember we cannot work together and succeed without making and tolerating mistakes. Nobody on this team is perfect."

Sam cleared his throat. "This is for everybody. I'm sorry for my conduct the other evening. I had no right to go off like that. I apologize to you personally, Ricky, and to your mother. I meant no disrespect. You are a valuable part of this team. I guess the pressure over the past months got the better of me."

"What exactly did Pritchard say?" CJ asked, touched by the speech.

"She trusts you and your judgment and supports your successes and failures." Peter chose to hide the fact that he and Pritchard had had a ferocious argument on the inevitability of human mistakes—fundamental concepts she couldn't understand. She wanted Ricky terminated for negligence.

"There's been a slight schedule change," Peter announced. "We all knew up front that Defense would run external testing out of their Bear Den facility in Washington. Those time frames have moved up considerably. I know it's short notice but I had no choice."

"How considerably?" Carl asked.

"We start packing tomorrow. Plan on at least eight weeks. LaCroix has already handpicked some surveillance targets, and I agreed as long as none of their people get in the way. We'll complete the assignments, evaluate performance, answer a few questions, and head home. If everything checks out, we'll leave the machine behind."

"What kind of targets?" Ricky wondered.

Peter hesitated. "I don't know specifics, but it looks like we'll be staying at Bolling AFB. We might get our feet wet with the military. There's a good possibility that *Tiger* might do something off-base as well."

Sam had a confused look. "You mean military airspace . . . with traffic?"

"Bolling's home to the Eleventh Air Wing, but

it's mostly a ceremonial center. I don't believe their runway is even active anymore. I'm still trying to confirm the details. LaCroix wasn't sure he even wanted to pursue it," Peter lied.

Tiger's onboard flight computer chip took instructions from Aerotech's 120-billion-operations-per-second digital processor. A sophisticated data-fusion module coordinated all technology instructions into a single stream. The transfer to the DIA's facility was virtually seamless because both companies had agreed to bridge gateways and system infrastructures months earlier. Both also conformed to the International Organization for Standardization and Open System Interconnection and had compatible hardware, data links, network, transport, presentation, and session interfaces. All that remained was migration of the application software.

TRACON ZAU Airspace—Eastbound
(Somewhere over Michigan)
32,000 Feet Above Ground Level
C-130 Military Transport

National Mall. Parade. A crowd standing, waving.
  Twist the propeller tight. One more turn.
  Puff of gas smoke.
  Rising . . . floating . . . the Washington Monument.
  Cheering. Flags. The Fourth of July.
  They loved Tiger.
  Climbing . . . circling . . . champion of the Mall.

Capitol . . . Liberty. Jefferson . . . dome. Pentagon . . . tracking me? Lincoln . . . reflections. White House . . . danger!

Concierge and cabdrivers with guns.

Bullets . . . piercing.

One . . . two . . . three.

Searing pain.

Four . . . five . . . six.

Ricky tapped Peter's shoulder again three times.

Peter jerked awake violently as the dream bullets quietly vanished.

"You wanted to see me?"

"Huh?" Peter's eyes focused and he patted the empty seat. "Have you ever been interviewed for government security clearance?"

Ricky paused to think. "I interned one summer with McDonnell-Douglas and had to sign a confidentiality agreement, but—"

"It's not the same. DSS will screen you and your family. It can be a very intimidating session for everyone. This may be nothing, but I overheard you the other day talking to someone on the phone about penalties. I generally don't get involved with personal affairs, but if you have legal problems, I need to know."

"It's nothing." Ricky lowered his eyes. "Nothing but—"

"IRS again?"

"Partly. The letters have gotten worse. All for a stinking two hundred and eighteen dollars. Then we get this"—he removed a tattered envelope from his pants pocket and slid out the contents—"from the undersecretary for Information Analysis and Infrastructure Protection. Some new department in Homeland Security. They're ordering us to send them the names and addresses of anyone who bought remote-control flying machines over the past three years. *Ordering*. A tiny business like ours. That's bull. How can they do that? I don't want to give anyone my customer list."

Peter put on his glasses and scanned the document. "It's probably not a bad idea. Do you do any background checks?"

"Checks for what?"

Peter frowned suspiciously. "Think about it. Someone could walk into your store or go onto your Web site, buy a remote-control machine, and . . . you know . . . use it for something not entirely legal, even terror. There's all kinds of people in the world wanting to figure out new ways to hurt others. I've worked with these administrative bureaucracies before and some are really a pain, but do me a favor"—Peter folded the letter—"draw up a brief outline of screening procedures just in case the issue comes up. It could save both of us some grief."

Ricky returned to his seat.

Peter opened a map of the Washington-Virginia area and began jotting down a list of suitable surveillance targets. Alexandria was opposite Bolling on the Virginia side of the Potomac, with several smaller towns farther west. He didn't know what to make of a comment LaCroix had made about a mall. Peter tried to visualize the *Tiger* drifting over some shopping center at night. It had better be night, he thought. And what about this baseball business? People surely played that in Virginia in some quiet park with cover or even woods nearby. Why couldn't they do something with that?

Peter gazed out of the aircraft's window at a commercial jetliner traveling westbound far below, a tiny winged machine streaking through the sky toward some unknown destiny. Not unlike his, he thought. Never one to pass up an opportunity, he tucked his head comfortably into a pillow, thankful for the relaxation. Some temporary slowdown of the whirlwind they'd been riding on. Maybe, just maybe, the whole project might work out. A night flight over a major-league baseball game. Dumb.

His eyes opened and he grabbed for his notes and the map. *Damn!*

LaCroix didn't say a mall; he said *the* Mall.

Andrews Air Force Base squadron security met the team and accompanied the UAV on the short hop to the DIA Center. Like most military facilities, Bolling had comfortable accommodations, provided tenants didn't mind the constant flow of air traffic from National Airport across the Potomac. Everyone opted for on-site housing. One look at Washington's motorized traffic made that decision easy.

Located on the seventh floor of the DIA Center, flight control was twice as large as Aerotech's, with plenty of think space in an adjoining conference room.

The UAV was test-ready in just eight hours, but Peter stubbornly refused to allow any talk of flight until every paragraph of documentation was completed. The groaning was enough to impress Hollywood.

Aerotech's senior management insisted that Peter's team maintain strict and ethical business standards should any surveillance test involving the general public appear to cross the line either of reasonableness for the UAV's technology or of Aerotech's good business name—no matter what the contract called for. As for DIA's surveillance targets, Peter was already concerned that the FAA had been excluded from any briefing list, even though it was certain that the UAV would be flying in the surrounding airspace—most of which was already heavily congested. The topic was simply ignored as a priority, and whenever Peter tried to revive it, LaCroix deflected the subject with jargon about intelligence privilege. The issue finally died without resolution.

Peter strolled into the flight-control center and placed his coffee mug next to the *Tiger*'s maintenance platform. He ran his hand slowly over the machine's frame, an evil-looking triangular wedge that looked like a mother F-117 Stealth Fighter had squatted on a runway and birthed a fully-formed lethal infant—after fourteen months of labor.

Sam finished making a fresh pot in the room's kitchen alcove and peeked at his boss standing trancelike in the aisle. "I know it's your life's work, but if you stroke that UAV any more it'll start to purr. Won't be easy to say good-bye to such a beautiful machine."

"She is beautiful, isn't she?" Peter smiled. "Beautiful and quiet. LaCroix had better take care of her. That reminds me . . . he wants an updated schedule. The man's persistent like a bulldog. You miss a completion date and he's got hold of your leg and won't let go. Speaking of bulldogs, I never did talk to you about that targeting stunt you pulled on Pritchard in my office. Don't do it again, understand? Especially here. You'll get us both charged on a security violation."

"Shhh . . . I wasn't targeting anybody," Sam whispered. "It was just video. The line-of-sight selector uses the same matrix. I'm not *that* stupid."

"You wanted to show me something?" Peter asked, noticing that Sam used both hands to set the coffeepot back on its warmer. "Why are you whispering?"

"I hate to be the one to tell you, but there's bad news. It's really got me stumped. See if you notice the shudder at station hold—the ability to circle above a target." Sam leaned into his workstation and clicked his mouse.

The UAV's motor started spinning with a low hum. Emitting as much sound as a bathroom exhaust fan, the noise faded to an almost imperceptible level.

Sam used one finger to prod the joystick. Effortlessly, the UAV lifted into the air. The frame immediately started to vibrate.

"That's not good," Peter observed, the concern obvious on his face.

"It gets worse," Sam said theatrically. "I've always said this machine has a mind of its own. I found a loop in the PTS program. If it ever faulted out, it could simply start shooting at random. We may have to fold our hands and beg again."

Peter's mood sank to the floor at the thought of asking Pritchard for more time and money—not with looming deadlines. He stepped forward for a closer look. He never noticed the tiniest curve of a smile on his star technician's face. It was too late.

A section of the UAV's canopy rose upward, exposing a black gun barrel on a tiny turret. The assembly turned slowly, stopping at a mark in the center of one of Peter's Holsteins. There was a muffled *click*.

"Sam—something's wrong!" Peter snatched the coffee mug out of the line of fire, sloshing the last of its contents down his shirt.

A tiny flag popped out of the muzzle: *Happy Belated Forty-ninth*.

There was a gift certificate taped to the UAV's underbelly.

"Surprise!" The *Tiger* team burst out of a maintenance closet, cake in hand, singing.

"Sorry about that," Sam said sheepishly. "My idea. CJ said it went too far, but I didn't listen. You're pissed."

"I'll live." Peter smiled. Blushing, he blew out the candles and dabbed his shirt. "I knew you people were up to something—I just knew it. I'm giving Pritchard my two-weeks' notice. My wife would quit her job in a minute. Maybe we could finally start that farm. I love working with animals in the morning. It makes your soul rich."

Sam lowered the machine. "We love you, Peter. Don't leave. Who else around here would put up with such a crazy—You serious? Is there money in that? Cows or goats?"

"Llamas."

Peter returned to his office and pressed his foot inside a wastebasket that wouldn't be emptied for three days. DIA cost-cutting.

He thumbed through a leading unmanned vehicles magazine, pausing at the dark-humored vendor advertisements.

Your One-Stop, Affordable UAV Solution
UAVs—Day or Night Solutions in an Uncertain World

He hated the fact that everybody was building UAVs, courting the military with solutions. He loved the fact that when they said *solution*, it meant reconnaissance. In his first DoD abstract document, he had used that term to describe *Tiger*'s lethality. Even with the military need growing, no other manufacturer's reconnaissance UAV could double as a covert sniper.

Peter wiped a smudge off his wife's picture. They were desperately trying to coordinate a phone call.

His speakerphone chirped.

"Look, I'm really sorry about the shirt, but I've got a great idea. Pritchard doesn't trust us, right? Especially you, because she thinks you want her job. So keep the enemy close and invite her to Washington. All our lives get easier. Dinner in Georgetown . . . a quiet hotel . . . something wet and wild?" Sam's lips made a kissing sound.

"That's all I need." Peter laughed. "Besides, I've had enough wet today. Were you the one who sent her that flyer about the midgets?"

"Huh?"

"Forget it. You had to be there."

"So is she coming out here or not?" Sam asked.

"Not her style. Somebody might find out how dumb . . . technically challenged she is."

"Good. I'm sure you know there's no wobble. The machine's running great. You interested in a trip to Atlantic City? We'll be back in ten hours. Feel lucky?"

Peter thought that over, then eyed his desk. "I can't. This place is a mess. You go ahead. Your stakes are too high for me anyway. Listen, try to be a little more patient if anything comes up with Carl that . . . well . . . you know . . . He's a little on edge."

"Are you trying to tell me not to be a jerk even if Carl's a jerk?"

"Something like that . . . thanks. Wait—what happened to your hand?"

"I took my favorite toy out for a ride last night along the George Washington Memorial Parkway. It's like the Grand Prix. I think I twisted something lifting it onto the center stand."

Peter winced. He didn't approve of Sam bringing his motorcycle to DC. "Do me a favor and sell that damn thing. Even you can't operate a joystick from a cast."

Initially christened *Hummer* by Aerotech's board, Peter quietly renamed the UAV after his boyhood Flying Tiger, explaining their selection was taken by the early warning E-2C Hawkeye and a certain squat transport vehicle. He didn't have to mention the reference to oral sex. Titles aside, it was a fair bet *Tiger* would replace every close-, short-, and medium-range UAV in the industry. General Dynamics, Dornier, Lockheed, and British Aerospace Systems, already suspicious of DoD's preferential treatment toward Aerotech, were preparing rival proposals. LaCroix made sure Peter's machine stayed the front-runner throughout the selection process via a lethality specification.

The National Military Joint Intelligence Center at DIA considered an average UAV to cost $500,000—less for expendable drones. When Defense saw *Tiger*'s price tag, Peter tried to soften the sticker shock by comparing the value of one bomb-laden UAV destroying one Silkworm missile site, versus one Silkworm killing one U.S. warship. Development cost of the baseline system had already reached a staggering $30 million—Aerotech desperately needed income. Final numbers came in at $1.6 million each, or $200,000 per pound. Cheap to keep, considering what the army shelled out for Lockheed's failed Aquilla UAV before its plug was pulled. DIA also planned to bring the other thirteen U.S. intelligence agencies into the sales line when the time was right. Rumor said everyone wanted the lethality—a nice terrorist surveillance toy for any agency with its own intelligence collection sector.

Working with peacetime military was always good business. In war, a company fortunate enough to land a multiyear contract with the U.S. Defense Department was comparable to a lone vampire bat stumbling into a herd of fat Holsteins.

Aerotech was betting that *Tiger*'s propulsion, flight control, and targeting subsystems would lead the industry for four years before the technology went obsolete. With maintenance and follow-up contractor support, the company's financial vampires figured to suck an annual margin of 50 percent after everybody got theirs.

By midnight, Peter's desk was as clear as his e-mail folder.

He typed one more message:

To: Aerotech Engineering & Devel
(pritchard.sue)
From: Aerotech Engineering & Devel
(wescott.peter)
Subject: Status and Paris Speech Topics

No specifics on testing. CIA potential customer. DIA grumbling about price. Let's discuss ranges and minimum margins. We may need to discount?! Paris—UAVs as competitive/global as PCs. Three hundred manufacturers worldwide. Homeland Security potential is overwhelming. Fastest-growing security technology. NBC (nuclear, biological, and chemical) weapons detection, traffic control, search and rescue, drug interdiction, monitoring of U.S. infrastructures.

The Future

Attack UAV (AUAV)
A low-flying, solar-fueled military machine that loiters over a foreign target region indefinitely. Carries dormant but lethal precision payloads until directed to strike.

Reconnaissance UAV (RUAV)
An uninhabited UAV that flies independently or works in conjunction with other airborne systems. Loiters subsonically at high altitudes and monitors wide areas via all forms of signal and electronic intelligence. Scans entire regions.

Tackler UAV (TUAV)
A highly maneuverable, fast drone used specifically by Highway Patrol departments. Magnetic and expendable, this UAV is attached to a vehicle's wheel. At slowdown, it is remotely deto-

nated, producing an impact small enough to disable further mobility. Eliminates all high-speed vehicular chases.

Blinder UAV (BUAV)

Same countermeasure concept as Tackler, but attaches to an escaping vehicle's roofline above the windshield and slowly secretes a black tarlike film. Driver visibility is ultimately reduced to zero.

Urban Sentry UAV (US-UAV)

An inexpensive remote drone capable of high-resolution video tracking of urban environments. This UAV would be deployed over city streets in high-crime urban areas to gather visual evidence of criminal action—particularly public drug dealing. Uses infrared night vision and video-radio links to communicate data to ground units.

Hive UAV (HUAV)

A large-capacity vehicle used to recover smaller machines returning from duty. A floating moth-erstation large enough to accommodate human repair crews. Solar fueled for long-loiter time frames.

Lethal UAV (LUAV)

Similar to the Urban Sentry, this UAV is authorized to use on-demand lethal force against criminal activity. The unit is video equipped for evidentiary support, and the lethality is effective from short- or long-range. Includes nonlethal payloads for riot control.

Stun your audience. Predict a UAV presence in every major city in five years.

Call me if you'd like to discuss.

Peter

P.S. I had a great slide presentation to complement your Paris speech, but my laptop locked up and won't let me send it. Sorry!

PW

His screen flickered on and off twice before finally imploding to black.

Peter left the office smiling anyway.

Brownnosing in Europe meant she'd be out of his hair.

Chapter Eleven

DIA Center

To: Aerotech Engineering & Devel
(wescott.peter)
From: Fox River Realty (wescott.elizabeth)
Subject: Poetry in Mooo-tion

Though novels have been penned in force in
honor of the dog and horse,
The cow defeats them handily.
With character and loyalty, in winter snow and
windy breeze,
She squeezes out our milk and cheese.
Test results have surely shown,
All children love a frosty cone.
When up to heaven God doth lift,
The cow—she soars but leaves her gifts.

Purses, gloves, and bright red shoes,
Burgers, steaks, and sticky glues.
Her very bones to birds as seed, yea, even gob-
blers come to feed.
The brief and suitcase left behind,
Contain the plans of humankind, and, last, the
belt wrapped round and round,
Keeps all our pants from falling down.

Found this in an old magazine. Thought you'd
enjoy it.

The family reunion's a go. Gordon and Sylvia
said we could come anytime and stay as long as we
want. They could use help with the chores! You up
for farm time? Thought so. Me, too.

See you soon.

Happy anniversary. I love you!

Beth ☺

"Congratulations. How many years?" LaCroix
asked, peering over Peter's shoulder at the e-mail.
He handed Peter a cup of morning coffee.

"Twenty-four." Peter recited the number instantly. "I feel bad not being there. The real estate
market in the upper Fox Valley near Green Bay is
depressed. She works more hours than I do."

"She's a good woman. I've always liked her,"
LaCroix offered, feeling somewhat responsible for
the separation. "You were raised on a farm?"

Peter fought to keep his mouth closed through a
yawn. "We both were. Hers was sold. My brother
still lives on ours. He and his wife raise beef cattle

and corn. They spend two-forty-five a bushel to make a dollar-ninety, so it's love for the land more than anything else. He's offered me five acres anytime I want to retire. It's my favorite place to vacation."

"A farm reunion." This drew a mild frown. "Sounds like fun. People need people, or something like that. Yours adjusting to the facility okay?"

"I figure they're used to it by now. They've lived in rented quarters for over two years. Besides, they spend most of the time in the control center anyway. Sometimes I wonder how they stay motivated, though. Even I'm getting a little anxious." Peter meant bored.

"Tell me about the *Tiger*'s downsides. Unless it's made by God, no UAV is without its own unique problems."

"Hmmm . . . downsides," Peter said thoughtfully, noting LaCroix's use of the plural. He leaned back and rubbed his eyes. This was foot-in-mouth political territory, and he needed to be careful. He had been dinged on this skill—or lack thereof—on his last performance review. He wasn't too upset, though; he'd written the evaluation himself, and no one else ever read it. Where was Pritchard when you needed her? "Off the record, the battery structure has cracks, either from faulty materials or chemical composition. Smart money says it's not the materials."

"What's your proof?" LaCroix's eyes narrowed.

"We haven't had time for proof. No one's taken

self-consuming fuel this far. Sure, it's exciting to think of the weight loss that makes other UAV configurations seem like blimps. Wideband power consumption is also a problem for battery life. Nobody knows the distress effect repeated fuel drain has in a machine this size. One day it could simply discharge five miles in the air."

LaCroix was taking notes. These were minor. Based on a thorough review of the *Tiger*'s paper specifications, his technicians were already considering reinforcing the exterior with higher-grade silicon. If there were fuel-related problems, a new vendor would solve that. "Anything else?"

"Radar," Peter conceded. "We've never pursued trying to achieve a stealthy profile because of *Tiger*'s size. Sam did some preliminary research into signal strength and even compiled working calculations based on data from civilian airports. He's got a friend at Raytheon who's installing new solid-state digital units at Heathrow International. It was part of our future test plan. From a targeting perspective, the wideband technology is truly an ideal position locator, but there are definite signal degradations beyond a thousand feet. We haven't had the time to look into that, either."

"Tell me more about your team," LaCroix probed, seemingly uninterested in any further radar deficiencies. "Any of them open to new opportunities?"

Now he wants my staff, Peter thought. It was becoming more evident that rumors were continuing to grow about Aerotech's financial problems. "I think most have standing offers. The navy's licking its chops for CJ and her noise reduction work. Someone named Savage checks up on her at least once a week."

"Capt. Harlin Savage," LaCroix said with a snarl. "Deputy program executive officer over their cruise missile project. He's the navy equivalent of the Antichrist. He and I've had some real battles about resources and allocation priorities. He's hell to work for and a real bastard on interservice teams, especially related to UAVs. He believes ninety percent of approved funding automatically slants toward missiles. Thinks cruise technology is the answer to all wartime dilemmas. Calls UAVs 'useless-ass vehicles.' Probably wants to cut down on missile noise, although I can't imagine why. By the time you hear the damn things, you're dead. What about you? Is there life after *Tiger*?"

"I'll putter around here and there." Peter kept his answer short. "So, in addition to major-league ball games, tell me about the National Mall."

LaCroix smiled thinly. "I believe a night flight into the District of Columbia is as good a place to start as any."

"Why not Virginia?" Peter countered. "A suburban environment gives easier and safer access to cover. There's still enough ground security to keep things interesting."

"You and your safe cover," LaCroix chided. "Over the past month I've talked with my counterparts in NRO, CIA, and Service Intelligence, and they agree that it's foolish to waste any more time in some remote forest with such tremendous opportunities before us."

Peter got the distinct feeling that LaCroix knew about the deer fiasco and was offering a way to save face. "We still need to address territory issues and airports."

"No, we don't," LaCroix replied matter-of-factly. "Think about it. Who's going to see anything at night two hundred feet in the air? No one. Ground observers will never spot an object as small as *Tiger* at that distance. It can't happen. I had lunch with Doug Richards the other day, and he told me that a machine like *Tiger*, if it existed, would only need to stay clear of the major airport approaches. I need *Tiger* now—not in two years. So find a quiet flight path in this quiet town and get your quiet UAV in the air. I'm being pressured, too."

Peter knew by whom—the services. Richards worked for army intelligence. LaCroix delighted in whetting appetites and dangling new technology before it was ready.

When a military project failed due to a rush to production, it was no big deal for two reasons: other than the GSA, itself an overworked, mammoth bureaucracy, there was no government Better Business Bureau—especially on classified projects; and there was no personal financial pain. *Every* military project manager and *every* military contractor referred to it as the "poppy effect." Opium. It was druglike: OPM—other people's money.

Peter rose for a coffee refill and noticed there were Holsteins on the pull-tabs of the dairy creamers. "When can we start?"

LaCroix grinned widely. "Good. By the way, I took the liberty of working out a draft surveillance mission for the Bear Den incursion." He unfolded a scaled map.

Peter craned his neck at the layout. The *Tiger's* flight path was highlighted in yellow and ran straight up the main road to their security offices. "We're preempting the penetration with nerve gas?"

"No, as a matter of fact the Den personnel will be wide-awake and alert as ever. And just to make it more interesting, they'll be expecting you."

"What?" Peter asked, dumbfounded.

"They don't know any of the specifics, but I told them your UAV is coming."

"What on earth for?"

"Just a little misinformation to draw a shark close to shore."

"But it's not misinformation. It's true," Peter argued.

"To a certain extent, yes. *Tiger* can sneak in right under their noses—or should I say under the drive shaft—at the eleven o'clock shift change. Just don't get run over."

Peter studied the plan. "Under a moving vehicle,

huh? Since when did you start getting so creative? What's the vertical clearance?"

"Twenty inches. But the key to the operation is getting to this turn." LaCroix circled the position with a marker. "The guards usually chitchat for a while, so it's also your most vulnerable time."

"I assume the Den's got fair radar range?" Peter asked.

"Twenty kilometers."

Peter tried to visualize that distance. "Jesus, who the hell do they think they are, the Kremlin?"

"The Cessna that landed in Red Square would've been detected ten miles out." LaCroix adjusted the map. "There are fourteen stops along the interior route. At number six, you'll drop off to the right of this F-16, here. Use standard stealth tactics so the cub drone can get to the fuselage. Shouldn't take any more than three minutes. The Den uses optical sensors set ten inches off the ground, so your UAV has got to stay low."

"F-16?" Peter questioned.

"Don't look so shocked," LaCroix said. "The Den has over thirty target assets. Decommissioned, of course. Tanks, personnel carriers, artillery pieces, and even aircraft. I think lightning damaged this one. Fried the electronics. Miller got it for the cost of transportation. I want you to place the cub on the tail section. And about those ground sensors— they don't give a damn about overkill. Whenever something activates, security sees it on video and confirms the intruder. Constantly resetting sensors is what they get paid for. Remember, you can't just fly out for the exit. You'll need to catch the vehicle's return to this fence line. I've got a surprise that'll afford you eight seconds before they close the front gate. By then, *Tiger* should be a low blur."

"Noise?" Peter guessed.

LaCroix smiled and reached in his pocket for four two-inch-long cylinders taped together. "A little present. Nothing fancy, but loud enough to wake up their sound detection."

The M-80 firecracker was so named because each contained one-eightieth of the explosive power of a stick of dynamite. This configuration would yield one-twentieth.

Peter examined the device for conventional fuses but remembered there weren't any. The cub circuitry allowed for hardwiring of "presents" and remote signal detonation using the same electronic-code frequency transmission as that of a garage door opener or other keyless entry systems, only with extended range. Peter knew that Aerotech caved to pressure from DIA to display the UAV's potential for additional lethality. Senior management wasn't satisfied with a small-caliber weapon that could hit a target bull's-eye on the fly at two hundred yards. Now they were actively pursuing explosives, too. It was so stupid. *Tiger* had the ability to do real offensive damage without much rework, but it was still incredible that DIA would even consider using such a sophisticated—and expensive— flying device just to plant a bomb.

"Jesus—I used to play around with these when I was a kid," Peter recalled. "A trained rat will do the same thing."

"If you designed it correctly, the cub is both a disposable and a renewable asset. Furthermore, it's not your call to question payloads," LaCroix reminded him. "In case you haven't noticed, *Tiger*'s for sale. When you're through, it all comes to me, including hard- and software. One more thing . . . SSI personnel are civilians and do not carry military clearances, so if something extraordinary happens and you're detected, they can look but not touch. Think you can pull this off in two days?"

Peter shrugged but knew they could.

"I almost forgot . . . this'll help you get comfortable in the skies around here." LaCroix tossed Peter a visual flight rule TAC—terminal area chart—of the Baltimore-Washington sectors. Produced and issued by the U.S. Department of Commerce National Oceanic and Atmospheric Administration, it showed positioning data needed to navigate around sensitive flying zones and airport control towers. "Think of DC as just another flight in the forest. Let me know when you're ready. By the way, your Baltimore plan looks fine."

Peter waited for the door to close and dialed a Washington number from memory. The operator transferred him. He recognized the voice immediately and could almost see the cheesy smile. "This is Peter Wescott again . . . Please don't hang up. Just between you and me—name your price for the cow painting. No one will ever—" *Click!*

Peter walked into the DIA flight control center and made a mental head count. The Cheshire grin on his face turned into a father's concern over a missing teenager.

"Where's Sam?"

CJ glanced at her watch. "He said something about dodging speed traps."

"Is he practicing motocross on that parkway again?"

"Yep."

"Nope." Sam slid into the room and the conversation.

"How many tickets?" Peter asked.

Sam smiled mischievously and made a zero with his fingers. "The construction slowed everyone down to seventy."

"Okay, people, gather round. You won't believe this but we've just been given authorization to fly over the White House. You are all required to sign a document disavowing any knowledge of tonight's actions." Peter passed out copies of the TAC charts and finally burst into laughter at the stone-faced silence.

"Not funny," CJ sang out.

"Seriously, before we do anything with the Bear Den, LaCroix wants us to take a quiet tour of DC's airspace," Peter said. Carl and Ricky exchanged high-fives. "Nothing complicated, just a short incursion to get used to the area. Something over the low-rent district in the southeastern part of the city.

From what I gathered on these sectionals, we'll need to avoid the towers at Dulles, National, and Andrews."

"Dulles control isn't in the sector, but the other two share radar coverage," Sam said without unfolding his map. "Flight training. It's an area you don't forget."

"Bolling's property runs all the way up to the Anacostia docks." Peter recalled his taxi ride. "Seems like a safe place for air surveillance. People keep to themselves."

"Docks are always safe at night as long as you're a hundred feet off the ground." Sam ran a finger down his chart. "It's the prohibited airspace that worries me."

"How ironic is *this*?" Ricky noted. "My brother and I tried to fly one of our machines into the San Diego Zoo. It was the first we ever built—a little propeller toy that we had to keep in sight. We thought it'd be fun to buzz some animals. We crossed one fence and got so paranoid that we both lost our nerve. That was a long time ago, when nobody cared much about uninvited aircraft. This time they'll care."

"What's the worst that can happen?" Peter wondered. "Jets scramble from Andrews?"

Sam shook his head. "No way. Just a pleasant three-to-five in a federal prison, out in two for good behavior."

"Dammit—you're not funny, either." CJ gave him a nasty look. "Did DIA mention anything about police security on rooftops? I know I read about that somewhere."

"Not really," Peter answered. "LaCroix figured it'd be too dark for anyone to—"

"Dark's not the problem." Sam folded his chart. "The latest upgrade of moving-target radar can detect an object our size through rain or even dust. We'll be okay as long as there's clutter on our side. I'll work on it."

Peter figured he didn't have to know exactly what that meant—as long as his driver did. "Any other problems with the docks? . . . Okay—that's our entrance."

Anacostia Night Surveillance

Sam floated the *Tiger* through a pair of automatic doors on the north face of the DIA Center and headed for the Anacostia Naval Station via a relatively empty stretch of the I-295 freeway only a few blocks away. Fortunately, anyone who happened to be peering up would see nothing more than the outline of a black, oversize bat two hundred feet in the sky.

Peter glanced at the room's overhead monitor and saw human and canine heat signatures at fixed positions in National Capitol Park. "We're not in the air five minutes and already have to take evasive action. Find a dark place to cross, and keep your distance."

"Ready," Sam reported back in a moment.

He lowered the UAV to a height four feet above the Anacostia River, and accelerated toward the opposite shoreline. The half-mile flight to the northern section of the Frederick Douglass Bridge took thirty seconds. Pigeons roosting underneath the structure's concrete support ledge scattered into the air.

Sam pivoted the UAV 180 degrees so the tail abutted but didn't touch the bridge. The omniview gave a clear line of sight to the west, but there was nothing much to look at except a row of abandoned metal and wood structures ravaged by weather and vandals.

"Heads up—multiple heat in the vacant lot to the north," Carl warned. "They're too far away to identify, but definitely moving in this direction."

Four figures, walking single-file, appeared from behind a row of junked vehicles and stopped underneath the bridge, forty feet below. The faces on the men were hardened but surprisingly youthful-looking. Their necks and arms displayed cryptic tattoos. One was some sort of prisoner; his hands and mouth were taped.

The scene reminded Ricky of home, a misused word that meant *safe and warm* to most people. To him it meant *ghetto*. He knew this neighborhood was black; he could distinguish the difference by the art. Mexican graffiti had flowers. His younger sister had been wounded by the errant cross fire of rival hatred that went on forever because of brotherhood rituals and vendettas just like those of the Sicilian

Mafia. They all started with predeath taunts.

"Yo, Ridge? 'Sup, Ridge? Amo keel you, Ridge. Like you did to my man, Tyrone. Tyrone say, 'Keel that Ridge.' You gon' die, Ridge."

The prisoner was of the Ridge Avenue Crew, a local drug gang.

His captors were Simple City Crew. They removed the tape.

"Fuck all you Simp-ass muthafuckas. I bitch-slapped yo' mamas las' night. C'mon, man. Do me. You all be dead. My crew kill yo'mamas."

"That muthafucka talk shit, man. . . . Amo do his head," Simp One responded.

When it was obvious verbal threats made no difference, the Ridge broke down. "Wait, now—ho' back, man. I ain't did Tyrone, man. Pleeeease—don't do me!"

Showing zero sympathy, Simp One held an Uzi submachine gun sideways and placed the barrel on Ridge's forehead.

"Fire," Peter told Sam.

The ceron round slammed into the Uzi's action at 3,100 feet per second.

The shooter dropped to his knees clutching his wrist. "My hand . . . I busted my hand!"

Assuming the Uzi had jammed and misfired, Simp Two drew a .45 automatic from his waistband. "I'll do him. Watch me, man . . . this for Ty-rone."

Another round tore the pistol away along with the tip of his right index finger.

Simp Three produced and cocked yet another

huge handgun—a .44 magnum revolver, judging from the size of the muzzle—and aimed it defensively toward the open lot.

Sam slid his thumb and pressed a target point. There was just enough angle.

The *Tiger*'s ceron round struck its mark inside the revolver's barrel, gnarling the lead of the chambered round and plugging the path. The revolver's hammer fell forward, piercing a primer. With no place to go, the magnum round backed up on itself and exploded in the cylinder, spraying burning powder and lead fragments across the man's chest and neck.

He screamed as they seared into bare skin.

The three Simps scrambled up a drainage bank for the street.

The Ridge froze, moving only his eyes back and forth across the area, trying to spot the unseen guardian angel. He wasn't sure if he was next or free.

His hands still bound, he sprinted toward the river.

Peter stared at the overhead screen. "Jesus. I had no idea we had the ability to . . . I don't even know why I wanted to do that. So much for a quiet town. Make flight level one-fifty and take your time. Let's find out if there's such a thing as an undetectable flight."

Sam eased the *Tiger* out from under the bridge and floated southwest toward Bolling over I-295. The 1.6-mile flight lasted three minutes and occurred without incident or detection from the intersecting radar bands at National or Andrews AFB, but then, no one was even concerned with that.

The first test penetration into a public theater was a guarded success.

Approaching the DIA control center, the *Tiger* hovered motionless above a cat stalking something on the grass below the flight path.

The animal paused, and then continued.

Carl's eyes began to water. He hated cats.

Chapter Twelve

Hanover Park, Illinois

The Sunday-morning flight from Dulles to O'Hare had been average except for the diaper aroma of one sour-faced infant, and the dietlike breakfast.

DSS agent Kathleen Beck now tried to ignore the stares as she licked chocolate shake from her straw in a fast food restaurant off Army Trail Road. She knew she was being targeted. This time it was a couple across the aisle.

"Excuse me, we're really sorry. Are you Demi Moore?"

"No, I'm sorry," Beck replied, embarrassed yet flattered. She was finally starting to believe it. She thought her husband had used that ploy to get on her good side. He told everybody his wife had been a stand-in for the actress in *GI Jane*. Same hairstyle, same sexy physique, same raspy voice. A demure Demi Moore.

Her partner sat down. "How much time?" Agent Jim Lange mumbled around the pen clenched in his mouth. His tray was piled with a burger, fries, and notes. He was trying to eat and prepare for their next PARA—Probability and Risk Assessment—report. After each background investigation, DSS agents were required to give their best judgment on where, how, and with whom the subject could cause the worst damage to the country, the military, or the represented agency, in that order, then calculate the probability of its actually happening. The results were kept for interagency reference.

"Forty-five minutes," Beck answered. "I can't believe you stay so skinny. How many times a week do you eat like this?"

It was true; Lange was addicted. A full-time investigator and part-time student, he consumed fast food more out of convenience and speed than for reasons of quality or taste.

"Give me a break. At least I don't look like anybody. How many times a week do people think you're Demi Moore?"

"Everyone has a twin," Beck stated, finishing her meal.

"Okay, who's mine?" Lange asked. "Be nice."

Beck spotted a bulbous water tower in the distance positioned directly over her partner's head. Only thirty-five, Lange was nearly bald and terribly self-conscious about it. The couple was still staring.

Beck bent down to retrieve a napkin, exposing her holstered handgun. "Denzel Washington with glasses." She smiled. "We'd better go."

Sam Nasrabadi's condominium was tucked in a cul-de-sac of boilerplate units, overpriced with signs of neglect. Sonia Nasrabadi answered the door. Swedish-American with a penguinlike figure and hamster-plump cheeks, she smiled warmly. Her husband spoke a few words in Farsi and she retired to a bedroom.

The agents were exactly one hour late.

"Mr. Nasrabadi?" Beck said.

"Please, come in. You are from the Directorate of Administra—"

"This is Agent Lange and I'm Agent Beck," she interrupted rudely.

"How was the travel? Can I get you something?"

"Thank you, no. I'm afraid we're on a tight schedule. The flight was fine. Your freeways are almost as crowded as ours. There's got to be an easier way."

There is, Sam thought to himself. *Stop harassing citizens.* "I suggested to the FBI that remote video conference would save everyone time and effort. The only other alternative is a motorcycle."

Awkwardly positioning his body to try to conceal several *Tiger* documents he had just noticed on a foyer table, Sam collected their jackets and motioned toward the living room.

Lange stretched out a microphone cord and set the mouthpiece in front of his partner.

Sam sat down in a chair opposite the agents and lit a cigarette. His foot wiggled nervously. He had strong feelings about current events, including distaste for the so-called plight of third-world Muslims, and weighed the benefits of openly supporting the war on terror, but concluded that the DSS might take his views as phony. It would probably make them more suspicious. He decided to keep his political opinions to himself. He didn't need any more bias. He was somewhat relieved that a woman would conduct the interview. It might allow him to control the rhythm and line of questioning.

"All right, Mr. Nasrabadi, let's begin," Beck started. "Are you a terrorist?"

Sam's face tensed and he took several quick puffs, searching for an appropriate response. Not even the FBI session had started like this. "Unfortunately, I devote much of my life to my work. I do regret the burden placed on Sonia—a burden that would be compounded by external relationships with political or religious groups. I don't have the mind-set, discipline, political cause, or energy to blow things up. And like most working American citizens trying to earn a living, I don't have the time."

Textbook answer. The urge to protest was strong, but it was all part of the game. Top-secret clearance investigations were not shielded by the usual constitutional legalities—an old but often-used ploy to force the interviewee into a defensive, even angry position from the outset.

"Provisions of the Hatch Act make it unlawful for

you to engage in certain political activities. Are you engaged at present either directly or indirectly in any political activity or organization?"

"No."

"Are you now or have you ever been a member of any foreign or domestic organization, association, movement, group, or combination of persons which is totalitarian, fascist, communist, or subversive; or which has adopted or shows a policy advocating or approving the commission of force or violence to deny other persons their rights under the constitution of the United—"

"I don't associate with any group or political party," Sam answered.

Beck paused. "Sir, please wait until I finish asking a complete question before responding." Sam nodded apologetically. Beck waited for her partner to finish writing. "Have you ever been a member of the KKK or other antigovernment or race-supremacy organizations?"

Sam's nose wrinkled as if detecting a strong odor. He'd been through four interviews since 9/11. None had ever explored such a ridiculous path.

Beck raised her voice. "Ku Klux Klan. They're a white—"

"Excuse me . . . I need to clarify something. Without bragging, I'm an expert chess player. The game originated in Iran. In fact, I enjoy all sorts of word puzzles and games. And I'm especially fascinated by America's love of initials and acronyms. It makes people think. So let me ask . . . are you that ignorant or specifically trying to insult my intelligence? I know who the KKK are and cannot think of a more idiotic question to ask a naturalized Iranian."

"I'm not interested in what you know or don't know about initials. Just answer it," she said firmly.

"Yes—you've exposed me. The letters are tattooed on my rear end. I'm really the grand wizard of Mississippi and have worn a sheet all these years to hide my identity. Tonight I'm planning to burn a cross and hang a few nig-rows."

Lange's eyes stared down at his notes. He finally cracked up at the put-on twang.

Beck tried not to notice. She took a deep breath. "Mr. Nasrabadi, you do speak English, do you not? And you do understand the question, do you not?"

He shrugged.

"Then don't give me any more of your whining about nationality, because I don't care. Answer the question."

Sam slouched into his chair. "No."

"No, what?"

"No, I have never associated with the KKK."

"Thank you." Beck waited again for her partner to finish writing. "Have you ever participated in any overt or covert attempt to defraud the U.S. Government or obtain intelligence information for another country or power other than the United States?"

Sam shook his head repeatedly. This was nearly as dumb as the airline baggage question. He was dying to answer yes and bolt for the door. "Of course not."

"Ever been a member of, or supported, or had any connections with a foreign intelligence organization or its activities?"

"Never."

"Have you ever associated with, met, or communicated verbally, in writing, or via any other medium with any of the following governments. Iran?"

Both agents looked Sam in the eye. Not a twitch. "No."

"Iraq?"

"No."

"North Korea?"

"No."

"Deposed Soviet Union?"

"No."

"Deposed Eastern bloc, including the countries of East Germa—"

"Forgive me," Sam interrupted. "My answer is no to all of them."

"Have you ever traveled outside the United States?"

Sam rolled his eyes. "Yes, I have. I was born in Iran and am a legal U.S. citizen."

"We understand that, Mr. Nasrabadi. Any other countries?"

"After graduate school I traveled . . . for a year."

"Can you be specific?"

"It was years ago—let me think. . . . England,

Spain, France. I lived alone most of the time." He crushed out the cigarette, stacking the filter atop a neat pyramid of others.

Beck sensed slight evasion. "You left the U.S. without any formal plan or network of friends or relatives in any of those countries? No one to vouch for your whereabouts for an entire year?"

"I needed to clear my mind after a computer science thesis. I still have my passport."

"What did you do for income?" Lange interjected.

"My family was killed opposing the stupidity of Iranian . . ." He paused. "Of the Shah's land-reform policies. I was raised by an older brother until I finished school. By then the whole culture was in chaos, so I left. My uncle arranged a trust for college tuition plus necessary living expenses in Chicago. When I graduated, the fund was mine. It was a good way to guarantee an education."

"Where is your uncle now?"

"I've answered that a hundred times. He's dead. I have no other family in the U.S."

"I'm sorry," Beck said. "We have to verify. Friends?"

Sam paused briefly. "The Flyboys. But they will only expose the fact that I am always late for practice."

Beck recalled that several members of his aerobatics club referred to him as the Ace. "How often do you fly?"

Sam crushed the empty pack of cigarettes. He

knew where this was going. "Aviation engineers make good money, but not that good. I share time in a Cessna. The same Cessna I've flown for fifteen years. The airfield's ninety miles north of here in East Troy, Wisconsin. I haven't been in the air for months. I'm so damned disillusioned by September eleventh, I don't know if I'll ever go up again."

"What do you mean?"

"Whenever I request time slots, someone mysteriously notifies the Milwaukee FBI office, and like clockwork, an entourage of agents is waiting for me at the airfield. This has happened twice, and twice I've simply turned around and headed home. So, I ask you . . . why is that? Three of my friends rent that plane, too, and nobody calls the FBI on them. Not *one* has ever been questioned. Is it perhaps that their skin is lighter than mine? Welcome to the land of equality." Sam stood. "I'm sorry for ranting. It's not your problem. Can I get you anything?"

"That travel record." Beck peered outside and grimaced at the overcast sky. Rain began pelting the windows.

Lange casually approached the foyer table, appearing interested in the inscription on a polished Cessna trophy while making cursory notes about documents underneath it. He examined a winged money clip etched with the initials AOTF.

1st Place
Sam Nasrabadi
Ace of the Flyboys

TARGET ACQUIRED

National Aerobatics Singles
Oshkosh, Wisconsin
Sunday, June 26, 1988

"If only the prize money were of equal stature." Sam's voice startled Lange.

"Ace of the Flyboys?"

"A call sign I created. You know, like Maverick. Somehow I don't look like Tom Cruise, but it's still a rather prestigious title in our organization. Those wings are as close to being a fighter pilot as I'll ever get."

Beck placed the passport in her briefcase. She'd turn it over to DIA Reference Services Support; a group that thrived on assembling time and travel puzzles. They made their CIA counterparts in IR—Information Resources—look like bumbling klutzes.

After a brief reconfirmation of Sam's employment history and social habits, Beck turned to her partner. "You have anything else?"

Lange shook his head and disconnected the microphone. The thick file from prior interviews would fill in missing information.

"That's it then, Mr. Nasrabadi. . . . I think we're finished. I need to find a Chicago Bulls souvenir of Michael Jordan." She lowered her voice. "My son's a big fan, but I'm afraid the Wizards aren't very good. Any suggestions?"

Sam felt as if he'd finished a massive college exam—one he knew he'd passed. The feeling actually grew into a strange, almost giddy benevolence to the agents as he drew out a short map. "Follow Barrington Road north. There's a shop on the right called Chicago Collectibles just before I-90. O'Hare's twenty minutes east."

"Thanks," Beck said, extending her hand. "I'm sorry about your . . . treatment. I wish there were something we could do. I'm sure it's nothing personal. We'll make sure you get your property back."

"No, I apologize. I . . . that's just the way it is. I should know better than to lose my temper. I'm sorry for that Southern thing."

Sam retrieved their jackets.

The DSS agents thanked him again and left.

Sam figured the reprimand for his sloppy documentation habits would not be severe. He raised his arms to the ceiling, grateful for the strength Khoda had given him all these years. The Ace had prevailed.

The unofficial profile concluded that Sam Nasrabadi was a low-to-medium civilian threat—PARA ranking twenty—to U.S. Defense intelligence, and that the most damaging act he could commit was to transport aerial surveillance secrets or even the prototype itself into a foreign country—probably Iran.

Chapter Thirteen

Oakton

Turner leaped over Tress like some Olympic hurdler and raced outside to the backyard patio. He opened the grill cover. Luckily, the filets were charred just right. One more minute. He and Sheri had been reminiscing about school and lost track of time. On their first date he had bragged so much about his cooking skills that she decided to let him prove it.

He sipped a beer and admired the blue-orange rays of the sunset. With the precision of a military color guard, a cardinal announced day's end with a melodic *hweet . . . hweet . . . hweet.* Shift change, Turner mused. Birds didn't need checklists. He did and reached into his pocket. Flour . . . eggs . . . salad . . . steak . . . Clint Eastwood video.

White House
E Street Perimeter Fence

"Dude, hurry up. You chicken?" Chris taunted, obnoxious from the cheap wine. Only sixteen, the boy had a large physique that helped him avoid most convenience store ID checks.

"Hold on." His friend drew one last hit off a thin marijuana cigarette stub. "Don't rush me."

"Chickenshit. Deke's a chicken . . . bwaak . . . bwaak . . . buk . . . buk . . . buk."

"Shut up, you stupid ass." Deke choke-laughed the precious smoke out his nostrils in short snorts. "What are you gonna do if the cops hear us?"

Chris reached deep into his baggy jeans and pulled out a compact .25-caliber pistol.

"Dude! Is that real?"

"Of course it's real. Gimme some of that."

Deke passed the joint and finished rolling his own oversize pants up around his knees so they wouldn't catch the iron fence tips. He waved to their girlfriends across the street, camouflaged by shadows, but got no response. Passing their own reefer back and forth took priority.

"Okay, like, can you make a step?" Deke asked.

Chris bent over and cupped his hands.

Deke stepped into the interlocked fingers and gripped the top fence rail for leverage. Propelled by a surprisingly strong heave, the skinny youth sailed up and over, landing in a smooth forward roll across the White House lawn—directly onto an active pressure plate.

Twelve seconds later, lead K-9 handler Wilson Ivory acknowledged the SCC alert and focused his night-vision field glasses from sixty yards. "This is Ivory. Confirm single stationary silver intrusion at point section I-five. Sending Raider . . . out."

The Malinois was already straining against the leash. Ivory carefully removed the dog's muzzle and spoke the command for restraint, along with a brief prayer. He hoped like hell the animal wouldn't go any further.

Raider raced down the lawn.

Floating high and oblivious to everything but his belt, Deke smiled at the Washington Monument and lowered his pants. Completing his assignment— a daring moon—he bent over, head between his legs, and looked back at the White House just as the black-faced, upside-down attack dog rammed him to the ground. With his eyes clenched, the pain sensation gave way to Raider's hot breath and drool just inches from his face.

From the fence, Chris saw the struggle and believed the animal was somehow eating his friend. He fumbled for the pistol and plinked off several high shots, hoping the noise would scare the beast off. Panicked, he flung the weapon toward heavy brush on Constitution Avenue before scattering into the Mall darkness with the girls.

Oakton

The meal worked. Dessert was Lover's Blend coffee and a homemade éclair torte drizzled with semi-sweet chocolate. Impressed, Sheri savored the last swirl of cream filling and vowed to run an extra mile in the morning. After dinner the couple snuggled together, anticipating a relaxing movie.

Turner pressed the remote and the phone rang. It figured.

His pulse quickened when he recognized Paul Bristol's caller ID.

"John? We've got a south lawn intrusion. One perpetrator doped up, with his pants around his ankles."

Turner let out a cautious laugh.

"An accomplice fired a weapon."

"*What?*" Turner sprang off the couch. "How many? Anyone hit? Jesus Christ, I can't believe people. I'm on my way. . . . The dogs post until morning, understood?"

"Yes, sir. Park police are sweeping the Mall."

Sheri caught up with him in the driveway. "Oh, my God, what happened? The presid—"

"Hell, no—he's not even there," Turner shouted. "Some fool on drugs."

Directorate for Analysis and Production (D1)
Unmanned Technology Detection Complex (Bear Den)

Operating under a renewable property lease, Surveillance Systems, Inc., invited contractors from all over the world to bring their aerial and ground-based unmanned vehicles to the complex for reality testing. Inside, twenty-five acres simulated a generic military "town," complete with empty but realistic prefabricated buildings for headquarters, fuel depot, communications, medical, barracks, and command and control. For a price, SSI would arrange any strategy a contractor chose—human-machine inter-action, tactical target approach, silent intrusion, even games—and report the results to potential buyers.

The defenses were formidable.

A double set of sixteen-foot-high link fencing surrounded the rectangular perimeter. Criss-crossing the prisonlike void between the fences, light line sensors were linked to a remote sentry system—RSS—that used video cameras to spot, identify, and kill—in simulation—any human or machine attempting access. Polyurethane replicas of the Canadian C9A1 light machine gun were mounted on posts along the perimeter and would automatically train on any intrusion point. A live RSS installation would cyclically spray a target area with 5.56mm rounds the same way shipboard 20mm phalanx weapons protected naval vessels against low-flying missiles. The system was highly contro-versial due to its lack of human decision making; critics claimed RSS bordered on barbaric.

For aerial defense, the facility's own version of Hunter-Target-Acquisition radar featured a forty-foot central reflector-antenna whose oscillator could generate three billion cycles a second and output nine thousand watts. The radar's maximum search distance could reach 150 kilometers with only a 20 percent loss of return signal strength. At a standard sweep of twenty-five kilometers, the loss was zero. The system also had unique spatial nulling technology to eliminate countermeasure jamming from inbound aircraft. Once HTA located a target, a coordinated series of motion and video surveillance monitors tracked it, simulating the locking mechanics of F-14 targeting systems. The result was a virtual latticework of wave pulses that blanketed the complex. If an airborne intruder penetrated that shield, there was no shaking it, period. In fact, SSI personnel spent a large part of their shift adjusting the tracking sensitivity to stop locking onto all the metal-banded flocks of geese migrating through the area.

The Den's only ingress was Defense Boulevard, a paved two-lane road flanked by heavy guardrail that connected the property to Bolling.

Peter slowed his Suburban to an idle stop in front of an intercom and access keypad at the entrance. He wasn't entirely sure he'd be welcome. He had several professional run-ins with Miller on the use of remote-piloted helicopters as viable surveillance decoys. After a series of public—and often ugly—national UAV forums trying to build industry support for their divergent opinions, they had agreed to a friendly truce and even planned an ill-fated fishing trip to Lake Vermilion, Ontario. Two days from departure, Peter's father died unexpectedly and he had to cancel.

Dutch Miller's face appeared on a two-way video monitor, his forehead distorted like that of some scowling Wizard of Oz. "What the hell do you want? We don't like cheeseheads here. Especially when they try to sneak in one of my facilities."

"Just remember what Frank Morris and the Anglin brothers did to Alcatraz," Peter replied. "Who are you going to blame when I shut this place down?"

The remark drew a laugh, but Peter swore he saw Miller's ears grow pointy like some first-stage werewolf at the sound of someone mocking his sacred defense capabilities.

"Pull straight ahead . . . I'll meet you in front." Miller's image clicked off. The gate fences drew apart.

Peter saw four surveillance cameras follow the SUV up to the steel-framed Quonset hut that served as the main office. Miller was leaning against a shiny Lexus. Its license plate read, DA BEARS.

David "Dutch" Miller, retired U.S. Army captain, first recognized that precise targeting and localization to reduce civilian casualties had become as important as enemy destruction, especially since modern army artillery could reach beyond all reconnaissance. In his final years in Missile Command, he nagged to top brass that UAVs were impossible to defend against if used against ground forces. The fact that no one paid any serious attention had contributed to his early retirement. When he formed SSI, he set his own knowledge as the very standard he now vowed to stop, and outfitted the Den with seek-and-destroy technologies his old command would kill for. A staunch admirer of Mike Ditka, he christened the complex after the 1985 Chicago football team and their vaunted defense that season.

They walked inside to Miller's office. Time truly spared no man; Peter silently rejoiced at the patches of gray sprouting on what used to be jet-black hair. Miller's square-set jaw seemed just a bit softer, too, as did his belly.

"You look good, Dutch. What's it been, five years?"

Miller reached his arm deep into a desk drawer. "All of that. I heard you moved to Cheeseland. Why'd you leave Lockheed?"

"I'd either be unemployed or dead from exhaustion. Nice facility. Nice car, too. Looks like the private security business doesn't have to worry too much about layoffs."

"Keep it to yourself, but after nine-eleven, our volume has tripled. You wouldn't believe all the companies I've got lined up. They all want their machines tested tomorrow. Unmanned this, unmanned that. Mention surveillance to the government and the money tumbles in without a lot of scrutiny." Miller brought a match to a cigar stub. "Why should Uncle Sam pay employees a hundred and twenty-five thousand a year in salaries and benefits when they can hire mine for less than half that? And we're better trained. I've got people working three sites."

Peter heard the contractor-versus-employee comparison a thousand times at Aerotech. It signaled a death knell for company loyalty. It still didn't seem right. Peter casually noticed a row of technicians monitoring radarscopes in the adjoining room. "What are they looking for?"

"There's a group of Nighthawks due into Andrews through our eastern zone in the next day or so," Dutch said. "We're supposed to try to catch the signatures."

Peter remembered some fascinating research by a group of rogue Lockheed technicians who claimed stealth aircraft could be detected on radar if they flew too closely, thus making the formation itself a defined image. He lifted a small gold-plated F-117 off Miller's desk. The design was remarkably similar to *Tiger*'s.

This made Miller's face wince. "Be careful with my retirement present. One of the wings is already loose."

Peter set it down. "Shadow hunting, huh? There any truth to that?"

"Between you and me, the only thing we'll detect is a *ka-chink*ing sound in my bank. I heard you were coming to DC. You wanna tell me about your little bird?"

"It's nothing you haven't seen before. Just a—"

"Shhh . . ." Miller interrupted. He thrust a finger

through the window blinds and peered across the Potomac. "Think I hear Canada."

Peter smiled. "You actually have time for that?"

"Nada. Not with people like you snooping around places you shouldn't. I hear your machine's a floater." Miller's eyes narrowed. "Who's La-Croix's sponsor—navy? Don't suppose you'll tell me the range?"

Peter hedged. This was obviously part of La-Croix's misinformation, but what and how much? "High-altitude," Peter lied a little. *Tiger* sort of met the requirements.

Miller produced two Styrofoam cups and a pint of brandy. "Know what we've got in here?"

"LaCroix tells me things once in a while, too." Peter smirked.

Miller turned his head sideways and spit something off his tongue. "I told D-one that human eyes, heat, and video could spot UAVs, but only radar-guided hypervelocity rockets could detect and kill 'em. So after all my proposals, they finally coughed up funding for a hunter system. Bought it all the way down to the belly. Just like that big northern pike I caught on Lac Seul. I ever show you the belly on that thing? Fat as a pig. Here's to jackfish and the fat women of Green Bay." Miller downed his drink and wiped his mouth across his khaki shirt-sleeve.

"Canada," Peter said, completing half the toast.

"What's the best compliment you can give a female Packer fan? Nice tooth." Miller let out a raucous laugh. "So you really think you're good enough to sneak a floater in here, huh? One Black Angus steak says we beat your machine. And this year my Bears'll kick Green Bay's ass, too."

Peter extended his hand. "In case you haven't noticed, Ditka doesn't take the field on game day anymore. Last I heard he was wearing a wig on some TV sitcom."

"Don't pick on my guy; he'll be back. You start buying pants with deep pockets."

Outer Banks, North Carolina

The midmorning thunderstorm reached the soundside bridge along old Highway 158 and abruptly stopped.

Two blocks south of the Kitty Hawk fishing pier, the house was small and sun-beaten, with weeds and sand grass for lawn. Heavy anchor chain served as landscaping.

Agent Beck stepped out of the vehicle and inhaled the ambiance of the warm sun mixed with the fresh sea air. "Yeah, I could live here."

"Myrtle Beach has great golf, too," Lange added, confusing his Carolinas. He turned off the ignition and let out a yawn, sluggish after navigating the last eighty miles on a two-lane coastal road.

The DSS agents walked up the short driveway. The home's front inner door opened and there stood a short, wiry man with a deep tan from years of ocean fishing.

"Mornin'. Y'all must be from the Dee-fense Dee-partment?"

"Mr. Jennings? This is Agent Lange and I'm Agent Beck. May we come in?"

The tension spring on the outer screen door needed oil. "We fixed us a little lunch, and y'all are welcome. Call me Earl."

" 'Preciate it," Lange said, trying to accent-bond. Beck rolled her eyes.

Earl spit a stream of brown liquid into the scant dune grass and waved across the road to his chubby neighbor laden with fishing gear. "There goes old lard-ass. Bluefish won't run for a month and he's out there feeding bloodworms to them damn crabs."

The living room furniture was arranged around an old wooden sea chest that doubled as a coffee table. The king mackerel mounted on a plaque above the television seemed to stretch from wall to wall.

Lange stared at the fish's girth. "Bet he took some heavy line."

"Balls on a catfish, son. Y'all don't need no billy-goat rope to fish the ocean." Earl grinned widely, exposing a row of tobacco-stained teeth.

A woman entered the room with a tray of thick sandwiches and iced tea. The smoked ham was lean and cured with a hint of whiskey. "Earl Andrew—did you cuss poor Arch Raymond right in front of company? I'm CJ's mother, Pauline, and y'all just help yourselves now. You've had a long ride."

The interview was brief and routine. CJ had no criminal record, no problems in any school, no affiliations dangerous to the military. Nothing extraordinary until the conversation turned to her younger brother, Jarrod.

Arrested in West Palm Beach for drug trafficking, he never could compete with his sister's academic or career success and married cocaine after she left home. After sentencing the youth to fifteen years, an especially obnoxious federal judge—a laudatory presidential appointee—commented that the boy's troubles were a direct result of a father who valued work more than family. The remark brought Earl to tears in the courtroom. CJ was so upset that she threw her purse and shoes at the bench. The contempt fine was worth every penny.

The agents returned to DC convinced that the combination of international trafficking and CJ's clearance level made her a prime target for blackmail—not to mention the fact that the supplying cartel had Middle Eastern terror ties.

Now that he'd eaten enough ham to grow a curly tail, bouncing profile questions off his partner was the only thing that kept Agent Lange awake.

After four congested hours on northbound I-95, they rationalized CJ into first place on the probability scale at twenty-five.

Chapter Fourteen

Bear Den Penetration

Glistening with moisture from evening fog, even the rocks along Bolling's eastern shoreline were federally posted.

The *Tiger* floated along the Potomac to the southern edge of the base property. Three hundred yards outside the Den's entrance, Sam lowered the UAV to the ground between the wooden posts of a restricted-access sign.

Two SSI employees, panicked at the consequences of reporting late, sped past in a company Blazer.

In a scene that resembled a traffic cop nabbing a speeder, Sam accelerated the *Tiger* out onto the roadway after it, pacing behind like some NASCAR driver tailgating a competitor's rear bumper.

The Blazer slowed to an idle stop in front of the gates.

"Mr. Nelson and Mr. Parks," Miller's voice growled from the speaker. "Nice of you numbnuts to show up."

A few seconds later, the automatic fencing slid open.

"Take us under," Peter said, sounding like a submarine commander.

Sam complied, easing the *Tiger* forward between the vehicle's rear wheels.

Both unmanned aerial and automotive vehicles rolled up to the security office. Miller was waiting outside on the wood decking.

"Exactly when did you expect to start your shift? Six in the morning?"

"It was my fault, sir," Parks admitted. "I over—"

"I don't care about fault," Miller snapped. "And don't call me sir. You're the last of seven teams. This damn weather'll fog our cameras. I smell Wescott all over the place. I wouldn't put it past him to try to jimmy the power somehow and cut through our fence line. He's a sneaky SOB."

"But . . . you said they'd probably be flying in high, sir," Nelson stammered.

"High-altitude, my ass. There's no glamour. And if I know LaCroix, he wants glamour. Besides, some of my friends consult for high machines, and they didn't know squat about any Aerotech project."

Peter cringed from two miles away. Predictability spelled detection.

"You're both punched in area six from building

E to the north perimeter. I want *anything* out of the ordinary reported to me personally and— What the hell is that?" Miller charged down the steps and bent to one knee. The *Tiger* team stiffened. They could hear him breathing. "Get some air in this pancake."

Parks leaned out of the driver's door and nodded at the half-deflated tire.

The Blazer pulled away. Sam raised the UAV tight to the gas tank.

Nelson turned his ear. "What was that?"

"That clunk? I dunno. Bad U-joint. Jesus, you sound like Miller."

"I ever get that bad you slap me silly." The men smiled and bumped fists.

Miller watched them drive out of sight. Starting up the steps, he glanced down at the pavement and saw a dry imprint where the Blazer had parked. It was delta-shaped but thinner, with an odd swept-back pattern like that of a bird with its wings tucked and folded, diving after prey.

Something tugged at him. He'd seen that outline before. Alone in his office, he reached in his drawer for the brandy. He stopped in midsip as his eyes focused on the gold-plated Nighthawk.

The Blazer paused at a checkpoint. Parks rolled down the window and aimed what looked like a Highway Patrol radar gun at a meter stand ten feet away. A thin blue laser arced across the road. A receiver pad acknowledged the scan with a soft but audible blip. He read the back of the gun.

Sam lowered the UAV to the ground.

"Den Mother, this is Parks. Station alarm count confirmation is zero. No activity and no trips on the counter. Cameras reset on two . . . out."

"Roger, Willie. Two reset confirmed . . . out."

The rear wheels of the Blazer rolled clear.

Sam pivoted the *Tiger* sideways off the road and stopped in a dark shadow.

The omniview panned a full circle, stopping at the gaping sharklike intake mouth of Lockheed's F-16 Fighting Falcon. It was exactly where the team expected. They didn't expect it to be surrounded by thin red light lines.

"Great entrance so far, people," Peter commented. "Ricky? Slide over. I want CJ to work the cub tonight. Unlock it, please."

She clicked the commands.

Carl studied the infrared view of the Den's central roadway. It was infested with light sensors, and he wondered how SSI security dealt with the vehicles constantly setting them off. Probably some unique banded signal that recognized and remembered the patrol paths. Or was it possible they tracked each vehicle, thereby eliminating the need for any other alarms? That was it, he reasoned. Once something was detected and tracked there was—

"Hold it," he said, his eyes doubting the information on his monitor.

"Stop the movement," Peter ordered.

"I'm getting a thermal reading. Does this jet work?"

"What? No way. Is it accurate?"

Carl opened a diagnostic icon and scanned the data. "The sensors are working. It's weak, but there's definitely heat in that intake."

Peter stepped to Carl's monitor. "That's crazy. The thing's an empty shell . . . a prop. LaCroix said the first thing they do when a plane like this goes down is pull the engine for parts. You could probably crawl right through to the afterburner. There's certainly no fuel capability. What about battery heat from a security camera?"

Carl scratched his head. "Possible, but why mount it there? I don't see any other— Wait . . . it just dropped by half. We're back to fifty-one degrees."

Peter twirled his finger at Sam and returned to his station. He nearly asked if Carl had somehow doubled the outside temperature, but decided it would be too insulting.

The UAV edged closer to the aircraft.

CJ disengaged the minidrone and moved it forward out of its base. "Where to?"

Peter tried to remember what LaCroix had specified. He thought for a moment. If this were real, where would it do the most damage? "Put it on the tail," he ordered.

The tiny fan blades easily maneuvered the cub around the light lines to the rear of the aircraft. In position, a pop-up box on CJ's monitor asked if she wanted it to remain there permanently.

It took eight seconds for the melted cyanoacrylate to bleed out and solidify.

"There it is again," Carl said anxiously. "Inside

that exhaust opening. It reads a constant one-oh-two, then nothing. If we circled around to the rear—"

"Jesus, we don't have the time to go on a sightseeing tour in here," Peter quipped. "And we certainly can't afford to play roulette with their sensors."

"It appears, then disappears," Carl whispered to himself. "Maybe it is mechanical. Human temperature would read nine-eight-six. Jesus—something lying inside? An animal nest? What kind of animal? Raccoon? Dog? No—something that size would trip sensors. Besides, the opening is too . . . Perhaps something smaller, like a rat or even a—"

The cat leaped from the jet's afterburner and broke through two sets of red lines. The sector was flooded with bright light before its paws hit the ground.

"Abort, abort, abort! Pull that cub in and take us up—fast," Peter yelled.

"It's too late," CJ shouted. "We're already stuck."

"Dammit!" Peter cursed. He turned to Sam. "Go!"

The *Tiger* rose vertically. Locked, four spotlights followed the ascension. At forty feet above ground level, the UAV stumbled into the HTA radar like a fly that just touched a spider's web.

Horns wailed and additional lighting came on in succession around the perimeter fence. The facility was bathed in daylight.

All Peter could think of was failure caused by another animal—a bone-skinny stray cat. If this had been a live incursion into a hostile facility, a barrage of simple, conventional small-arms fire would have easily destroyed his machine. An altogether amateur performance against a well-trained enemy in a well-guarded facility. Performance grade? *F.* This would just worsen the team's already fragile morale. Then there was Pritchard. She would absolutely blow her stack. He'd already made up his mind not to tell her.

Patrol Blazers with their flashing yellow lights were screaming to the area. There was no point in attempting any further evasion; Peter knew the UAV's actions were being recorded. He certainly couldn't shake the HTA lock. Then he remembered the wager.

"Plan B?" CJ asked.

"On my mark," Peter responded. "Before we try to save face, I want everyone to take a good look at what happens in a hard, exposed detection. We're now on film. The enemy . . . Miller knows our maneuverability, size, and weight. He can also make a damn close estimate about our thrust ratio, too. And we've committed the cardinal sin of stealthy access by leaving something physical behind. I suggest this is a good time to start building character. It doesn't get much worse. This is why cubs are disposable. Hold at seventy feet with a big view and sound."

Miller reached the area, furious that his personnel were simply staring up at the silent, hovering intruder instead of securing the area for secondary threats. He walked under the *Tiger* with a bullhorn and raised a triumphant fist.

"Light it," Peter ordered.

CJ clicked on a frequency command box that sent an electronic signal to a receiver in the cub drone.

The four firecrackers exploded simultaneously.

The harmless but overly loud blast sent Miller and his men diving to the ground. The echo resonated across the complex.

The UAV accelerated west to the Potomac for the upriver flight to the DIA Center. The last thing on audio was Miller's voice screaming obscenities and something to Peter about "medium friggin' rare."

Four hours later, the unauthorized flight back to the Bear Den had taken just eighty seconds.

The UAV methodically moved over the ground at one foot above ground level. Skirting the perimeter fence line, the omniview spotted the target on top of the F-16's canopy licking its left paw.

The PTS scope lines drew together at cheek level, but the target point was obstructed.

The UAV exited the area and returned through the open doors of the flight balcony. The targeting mission lasted six minutes, thirty-five seconds.

Not clean.

Milwaukee, Wisconsin

Sensitive to the war crimes accusations against the family, Agent Beck thought it best to keep a low federal profile and conduct the Richter background interview alone.

She rented a car at Mitchell International Airport, and followed local directions to an oddly named road—Kinnickinnic—a moniker given by early Native Americans to the trail that traversed the Lake Michigan shoreline. She'd never been to Milwaukee and carried an admittedly negative bias into the city for no reason other than national media coverage of the likes of Jeffrey Dahmer, a number one U.S. ranking in racial segregation, cryptosporidium in the water supply, and ten-year-olds caught up in brutal gang murders.

She located the address of the wood-frame bungalow and rang the doorbell. From the porch, she could see the world's largest four-faced clock a mile away.

Someone was peering through a curtain in one of the windows.

Beck held her ID up to the glass pane and spoke loudly and at half speed. "Dorothy? I'm from the Department of . . . from Washington. We talked on the phone about your son?" There was silence, then metallic unlatching.

"Come—today I baked for him," the prim old woman said in a thick German accent. "How is my boy?"

Beck immediately prejudged Alzheimer's and followed her past a wide carpeted stairway into a parlorlike dining room. The home reeked of urine, and its owner bore an eerie resemblance to Norman Bates in drag—complete with high-top shoes and hair bun.

"Carl's fine, ma'am. He wanted to be here, but he's very busy. Mmmm . . . smells wonderful." It wasn't cookies.

"Please sit. I be right back," the woman ordered before disappearing into the kitchen.

Beck paged through Carl's background dossier.

The woman reappeared—luckily without a raised butcher's knife—wearing a stained apron.

"Mrs. Richter, I have a few questions about your son. It won't take long."

"Who are you?" The woman's head twitched. "Are you looking for Dorothy?"

Beck took a deep breath and considered canceling the interview on the basis of legal incompetence, but decided to continue with her trademark double-edged question. "Mrs. Richter, I need to ask you about the important work that Carl does. I'm sure he's mentioned it to you?"

The woman's eyes twinkled. "Always such a good boy . . . and very smart, too. He would work with zose cameras into the night. He would not go to bed. One time he showed me the moon and it was so close I could almost touch. He would go with his father on the hunt. They would always bring me meat. When they first would go, Arthur was champion until Carl put the camera onto the gun. They would shoot every week—for many, many years they would shoot. Ach—look at that dust. My Carl won all zose. That war business made Arthur sick. Carl was so mad."

Beck squinted across the dining room at the impressive line of marksmanship trophies in a hutch. She presumed Arthur Richter was the stern-faced man in a nearby portrait, wearing a brown shirt and swastika armband.

After a few more minutes of veiled but polite interrogation, she concluded that there was nothing more to gain by further checks into siblings or friends; Carl had none listed. His skill with weapons wasn't that unusual, based on his family's history in the firearm business. Poring through newspaper clippings Dorothy had saved related to the court filing, Beck discovered that the government's lead prosecutor had been the president's father.

On the flight home, Carl's PARA ranking knocked CJ way out of first place.

General Profile:	**Expert in A/V technologies. Expert sharpshooter.**
Keywords:	**//hostile//anti-government//revenge//scopes {executive//judicial}//DOJ197//2tdc09077//INS-57-105//War Crimes//DIA-96-221//SecurityClearance//**
Threat:	**//assassination//sniper//**
Probability of Action:	**//50//**

TARGET ACQUIRED

DIA Center

Sam stared intently at the four remaining chess pieces on his PC. This was his long-awaited opportunity to play against IDIOT, a rude, anonymous opponent, fanatical about protecting his or her identity. IDIOT had never lost an on-line match. Sam was one move away, not from victory, but simply a draw—something no one else had come close to. It was IDIOT's play. He or she was certain to ease a pawn forward one more space, thus promoting it to a queen—a poison-pill trap Sam had neatly orchestrated to force an elegant and nearly undetectable stalemate.

Sam's eyes shifted from his wristwatch to his monitor, telekinetically trying to will the electrons to form P-B8(Q)—pawn to bishop eight, promotion to queen. When that didn't work, he begged. "Come on—*move*! I don't have all day. Promote your pawn." He knew the match was posted live across the Web with tens, perhaps hundreds of thousands of observers—maybe more. IDIOT's games were that rare.

A new formation appeared.

P-B8(R)—pawn to bishop eight, promotion to *rook. You should have studied Saavedra/Dolan.*

Sam stared at the board a full minute before comprehending the inescapable checkmate. His foot viciously kicked a metal file drawer, denting it. *Who are you?* he typed.

IDIOT.

Please! A Rematch? There was no response; the link was gone.

Sam immediately entered CHESS + SAAVEDRA + DOLAN into the browser search window. The combination drew one hit: A biographical reference.

Robert E. Burger, *The **CHESS** of Bobby Fischer*. **SAAVEDRA** versus **DOLAN**, 1895 . . . Most famous endgame ever published with a single forced line of play. "A reflection of the 'champion paradox,' the 180 (I.Q.) figure is considered unrealistic. Fischer's apparent lack of intellectual attainments, in contrast to the champions of the past, would seem to make a high I.Q. unbelievable. He is considered by many to be an idiot savant."

Peter slid a chair over, trapping Sam at his workstation. "Everything work out with your interview?"

Sam minimized the on-line screen. "Pain in the you-know-what. They're all uncomfortable. I hate it. Makes my stomach twist every time. Not to mention that I feel like a third-class immigrant with a green card. Sonia said our neighbors won't even talk to her anymore. It's so unfair. Sometimes I think it'll never end."

"How long was it?"

"All of fifty-five minutes," Sam said disgustedly. "That's another thing. They send two agents halfway across the country and waste time and tax dollars for less than an hour's work."

Peter shook his head. "It isn't fair. Hopefully it's the last and we can all move on."

"Wait—listen to this; it's really unbelievable. But I need to bring in some other suck—I mean, players." Sam stood and faced his coworkers. "Excuse me. Anyone interested in a word-game wager?"

"In," Ricky said at once.

"We won the last one," Carl reminded him.

Deep in her oscilloscope, CJ nodded in trivia allegiance.

"Good. Same stakes," Sam stated. "Ready? I bet none of you knows what the KKK stands for."

"Ku Klux Klan," CJ answered suspiciously. "Am I missing something?"

"Wait, I screwed up," Sam apologized. "Not just the initials . . . what do the *words* mean? And keep your hands off the Internet."

All eyes turned to CJ, hoping her Southern upbringing would offer some advantage.

She scribbled something on a page, and then crumpled it. "I've wondered that myself. If you think about it, they are kind of weird. I mean . . . what exactly is a Klux?"

"It's either a Greek phrase or a southern chicken call," Peter offered. He ducked from a paper fastball.

"Right track, wrong race," Sam hinted.

"Klan isn't that weird," Carl said. "It means club or group—"

"Not," Sam cut him off. "Your language uses another word."

"*C-L-A-N*," Ricky chimed in.

CJ polled the room and got a vote of collective shrugs. "We give up. It's worth a few dollars."

Sam made an entry on a clipboard on the side of his cubicle. "They are the phonetic sounds made by a rifle when first lifting the bolt—Ku—opening the action to load a round—Klux—and then closing and locking the bolt—Klan."

Carl shook his head. "Stupid word games. Or should I say weird games? Do you have a hard time sleeping at night? Where do you come up with these?"

Sam laughed. "My background interview. I thought it was one of the dumbest questions ever asked by any investigating agency, so I researched the origin. Think about it. An Iranian in the KKK? Your government is not the brightest. Peter was close because the initials themselves were taken in part from the Greek word for *circle* but the early membership related better to word sounds that came from a weapon."

The team members groaned and turned back to their workstations.

Carl whispered to CJ, "See? What did I tell you? That really burns me. Isn't it *his* government, too?"

Dutch Miller appeared in Peter's office. His face had a humbled look and his walk lacked the usual swagger. Something was wrong.

"You okay?" Peter asked.

"I dunno, just feeling some age," Miller said

softly. "I used to think I was one hell of an expert on UAV tactics, but I guess you woke me up, huh? By the way, I wanted to tell you that LaCroix let me see *Tiger*'s specs up close before the penetration. I even knew the timetable. You aware of that?" Peter bristled. The look on his face gave Miller the answer. "I would have never guessed that someone could build something so small yet so sophisticated—and actually make it work. Bottom line is, we spotted you because one lone pussycat happened to live in the area."

"Maybe it wanted to be our mascot?" Peter tried to lighten the moment.

"It's gone. I doubt it'll ever come back after that fireworks stunt. That Blazer entrance was brilliant, and something I never would've picked up. Your Alcatraz story got me thinking. Did you know that after just one successful escape, Robert Kennedy closed that place down in less than a year? Bang— just like that, the world's premier prison is gone."

"Hold on, now," Peter objected. "You're reading too much into—"

"No—here's what I'm reading. My instincts tell me we're in for a flurry of tiny birds like yours that can travel in and out of every place they want— anytime and anywhere. And if I'm right, you can kiss the Bear Den and places like it good-bye. Think it's time to pull the pin."

"Stop right there," Peter said firmly. "You have too much knowledge to quit. Besides, where would you go?"

Miller thought for a moment. "Mazlat need consultants?"

"Nope—they don't," Peter countered. "So forget about making any midlife career moves you might be sorry for in a year. Israel's a whole different animal. They've got enough on their plates. There's no football over there, either."

Miller frowned deeply. "Hmm . . . that's a problem. I'll have to think on that. Anyway, I'm not letting you out of my sight until I get that steak you owe me, you sneaky son of a bitch."

Chapter Fifteen

DIA Center

Peter stopped the video, anxious for comments.

LaCroix calmly walked to the far end of the conference room and made two brief calls, the first a private conversation to an outside number, the second to Bolling's main gate security. Finished, he started for the door.

"Wait a minute," Peter said. "Where are you going?"

"My office." LaCroix brushed past Carl, who was standing in the doorway. "Rewind that and don't leave this room. I'll be right back."

"He's upset with the gang shooting," Carl surmised. "I knew we shouldn't have interfered. Let me edit it."

Peter pondered that for a moment. "No—I've

got a feeling that's exactly the kind of thing they're after."

"Then we need to talk." Carl closed the door. "It's Osama. I can't work with him anymore. I don't know what else to do. My blood pressure rises when he just walks in the room."

"Carl, if you don't stop calling him that, *I'm* going to get pissed," Peter raised his voice. "Whatever problems you have, that is really a terrible association. And yes, I've noticed the tension. Granted, Sam may need work on interpersonal skills, but you've got to see past it."

"It's more arrogance than anything else. The guy can do no wrong. He comes and goes as he pleases, no set hours, and probably makes twice what I do. The way he treats CJ really pisses me off."

In every job Peter had ever held, every group he'd worked with or managed, every team he'd been a part of, there was always someone who begrudged another, personally or professionally. *Always*. The urge to begrudge was as deep and as powerful as that for sex or even survival. Forced harmony by gentle recommendation or not-so-gentle law stopped the urges for a while, but they always reappeared. Like mold in a cellar, his mother would say.

Peter rubbed his eyes and prepared to speak the words all effective managers used in situations like this, soft, soothing expressions of comfort most employees wanted—needed—to hear. It made them feel good. The teamwork speech. It always worked to bolster spirits and start healing. He really wanted to scream, *I'm not your mommy, so stop your damn whining! Learn how to interact with different types of people. If you don't know how, then take a course on team building.* "You've worked together for what . . . three years? C'mon, Sam deserves more than that. He's a damn good technician. Secondly, CJ's a big girl and can handle herself. My advice to you is to concentrate on your work and less on Sam. Ignore it. Don't let him bother you. You're a key player on this team, and I don't want to lose that."

"Ever notice how he ridicules this country?" Carl shifted the subject. "Okay—so I'm not exactly in love with the feds myself, but sometimes I feel like telling him to get the hell back to Arabia or wherever he belongs. I don't trust him."

"He belongs here," Peter defended him.

"I can't put my finger on it but I think Sam is—"

There was a knock on the door.

"Excuse me—gentlemen, this is Brent Harris," LaCroix announced. "He's from OTC, the Office of Technical Collection, at the CIA. We'll want to include him in all further mission reviews. Carries the biggest checkbook in Washington. He's already been briefed, so we're ready when you are. Be careful what you say; we haven't agreed on a price."

"Don't listen to him, Peter." Harris smiled and opened a laptop. "DIA really stands for 'delay it again.' "

A tall, gawky man with long, cranelike feet, Harris was a radio electronics expert specializing in photonics and imaging. Before joining the CIA, he had worked for QuadRange International, where he helped patent the first radar system to measure both backscatter intensity and Doppler velocity. A demanding scientist who lived in a workplace of black-and-white, yes-or-no, he thought his technical expertise was enough credentials to attain senior level ranking in the agency, but ran headlong into "kinder and gentler." He learned soon enough that one didn't encourage female staffers to use protection just so they could finish research. Some said he had unfairly lost out on the latest promotion to deputy director of science and technology for no other reason than physical appearance, but it was more his inability to recognize that people weren't robots.

Carl thumbed the door and mouthed his intent to leave.

Peter lowered the front room lights and started the overhead video. The scene opened to a bird's-eye view of the Anacostia Naval Station.

"How do you know you weren't tracked by one of the surrounding airport towers?" Harris asked.

"To be honest, we don't," LaCroix answered. "I thought we'd talk about that afterward."

"That the Douglass Bridge?" Harris stopped typing and wiped off his glasses.

Peter nodded and sharpened the picture.

The video played through the gang scene.

Harris raised an eyebrow. "Rerun that last segment, but this time with normal audio. I didn't hear your weapon discharge."

"I tried to tell you it was a quiet technology."

LaCroix grinned. He knew exactly what the OTC sector chief was thinking. With all the high-paid government resources on CIA's payroll—especially in the science and technology directorate—its own technicians couldn't compete with private companies who had to produce to survive. It was a perfect example of why free enterprise and competition would always outperform government-managed projects. It all came down to incentive.

Harris shook his head at the replay. "What's the range again?"

"Two hundred yards," Peter replied.

"No—I mean the effective range," Harris clarified. "How far before it loses—"

The same response came in unison from Peter and LaCroix.

Harris saw by their smug expressions that they were serious. He tapped out a long entry. "Fascinating. Our department might be very interested in this sort of ability."

LaCroix knew agency jargon when he heard it. "Peter and his team have a few more surveillance missions left, and the targets will get a lot tougher than a few gangbangers. I want you to be aware of it on your end."

Harris transmitted the report and noticed Peter ogling his laptop. "You know, it's funny. We can find nearly anyone and anything across the globe, but the bean counters in GSA asset verification are always in a perpetual quandary on how to track and manage computers. I ordered this one last month and received two. It's wireless with a plasma screen and voice recognition, with a battery that lasts up to sixty days without recharging. It's got all the software to interface nicely with your JWICS/JIVA platforms. I think it lists for around twenty thousand dollars. Why don't you let me send you one?"

The Joint Worldwide Intelligence Communications System—JWICS—was a secure, high-bandwidth system for full-motion video teleconferencing and data exchange among the major intelligence agencies. Joint Intelligence Virtual Architecture—JIVA—allowed analysts to interact and share modern databases from any location in the world

Peter shifted. "No, I couldn't possibly accept—"

"I insist. Leave everything to me," Harris said firmly. "Consider it a loan, if you feel uncomfortable. Return it anytime. I'll have it delivered. I don't suppose you'll let me see your machine?"

"*After* we're finished," LaCroix spoke up. "Then we'll start taking orders. And believe me, if we're successful, you'll be standing behind every service intelligence and police department in the country. This thing has that much potential."

"Great—but remember one thing. I just skipped in line . . . behind DIA, of course. Like you said about our checkbook? I'll wait to hear from you. Peter? Pleasure." Harris stretched his hand across the table and left.

"He's in, Peter . . . you sold him," LaCroix said confidently. "And you get a free laptop. He works for Jim Runyan, their new deputy director. That guy'll fill a truck with *Tigers* and deploy them tomorrow. He's absolutely desperate to make changes over there, and this could be the match that lights the fuse."

"They're apparently into bribes, too," Peter commented. "I didn't sell anything; the Simps did."

Who in their right mind would stand before some city council or finance committee and request a flying cop? Peter wondered. It was moving too fast. Pritchard was back from Europe and threatening to fly out. The last thing he needed was her nose poking around. Aerotech's board would run for cover if they knew their namesake was sailing through DC shooting at minorities like some airborne vigilante.

Capital Beltway

"Rich? This is Brent . . . get a pen. Contact the senior controllers at Dulles, Andrews, National, Baltimore-Washington, Leesburg, Potomac, Fort Bevoir, Hyde, Davison, and the Pentagon heliport and have them send us their radarscope reflections over the past forty-eight hours. Then pick four people from Imagery Analysis and meet me in my office in one hour. . . . I don't care what they're working on—tell them to drop it. I'll explain when I get in." He clicked off the secure cell phone and touched another number.

"White House Security, Mr. Turner's office," Barb Dwyer answered curtly.

"This is Brent Harris at CIA. . . . Is he available?"

"Let me check for you, Mr. Harris. . . . Please hold."

One of the last stalwarts of a regime fraught with accusations of intelligence mismanagement, the CIA director had recently been forced to resign. Two weeks later, the deputy director had done likewise, ostensibly for family reasons, but everyone knew he couldn't stomach the infrastructure and, with the DCI position vacant, got zero support from the president.

Turner was in his office reviewing personnel evaluations and hit the speakerphone. "Don't tell me you found somebody to run that agency for more than six months?"

"Not quite, but I'm still on the shortlist. Keeping busy with all those fence climbers?" Harris returned the sarcasm.

"How are you, Brent?"

"Good, John, but I'm pressed for time. We're doing some analysis of the surrounding air traffic centers and wondered if you'd send us your pictures over the last, say, forty-eight hours?"

Harmless as the request sounded, Turner felt a mild pain in his chest hearing that topic mentioned so casually over a cell phone with traffic noise in the background. The existence and placement of radar around the White House and the Mall was one of the best-kept secrets in the intelligence community. He also didn't take kindly to people thinking they were still buddy-buddy just because they'd served together on one interagency task force four years ago. CIA never acted this openly. "Something I should know about?"

"Just need some routine patterns."

Turner instantly translated the dodge into some petty turf battle for new technology funding. "How many directions?"

"All of them, if it's not too much trouble."

"I'll send someone over," Turner said reluctantly. "What else is new?"

"Working on a big shakeup. Appreciate the priority, John, but I've got to go. Keep in touch." He clicked off.

Turner sneered at the dial tone, but Harris was right. The CIA was in prepanic mode with the president's new Homeland Security restructuring plan. One version effectively called for complete retooling into organizations that actually had accountability. He buzzed the SCC. "I need a radar tape of the last two days strung together and hand-delivered to a Mr. Brent Harris at Langley. All five arrays."

"Forty-eight hours by five," Officer Adams repeated. "I'm going off in an hour and can run it over myself. What directorate and sector?"

"Science . . . Collection. I'll be there in a minute. Nothing leaves until I see it first," Turner ordered. He'd be damned if he'd give anything that sensitive to that intelligence agency without asking a few more questions. It was probably nothing, but a voice inside said this was one of those little details he preached about. The kind he demanded be pursued to full and satisfactory conclusion. CIA was so secretive that even its number of employees and funds were classified. A budget unchallenged by the public . . . he could only imagine all the pork.

Turner grabbed Paul Bristol's arm and turned him around in the hallway. The elevator doors to the SCC opened just as he finished the explanation.

"I can't believe the FBI's not involved," Bristol commented. "Why's CIA interested in domestic airspace anyway?"

"Good question. They won't say a thing unless you're in from the beginning. Harris gave me some song and dance about a routine analysis."

"How'd you ever get involved with him?" Bristol asked.

"He was on the CIA's analysis team during RADS implementation. We worked together for a few months. I think he's still in Technical Collection. Do me a favor and confirm that. He's not a bad guy, if you can handle the jargon. He's a stereotypical scientist through and through. He wears a white smock to bed."

"I've heard that about America's premiere spy lab." Bristol laughed. "Isn't that group run by . . . what's his name?"

"Runyan. Stephenson brought him in personally. Rumor says he did it as a final slap at the president."

"Yeah, that's him," Bristol acknowledged. "He's

a loose cannon. Got into a shouting match the other day with some congressional reps at a restaurant and wouldn't back down. Made the front page."

Turner shrugged. "Nothing wrong with standing up for what you believe. Cannon or not, Runyan has ruffled more than a few feathers at Langley, and not just in his own directorate. It's probably a good time to get noticed, with all the empty chairs over there. It wouldn't surprise me a bit to see him move up real quick. One thing's for sure: he's got Harris running his ass off." Turner chuckled. It was probably nothing but a grouse chase.

Special Operations post officer Linda Janis was finishing political sciences at Georgetown. If she chose to stay in the service, she was next in line for promotion. Turner had arranged the night-shift assignment to help her class schedule. Bristol owed him big-time for the transfer. She had excellent decision-making skills and was one of only five personnel authorized to act on a RADS kill alarm.

"Officer tae kwon do Janis," Turner sang. He remembered when he had enrolled in a refresher course and got kicked in the head so many times by the younger students that he had up and quit. Seemed that at a certain point in life, flexibility and age just went their separate ways.

Janis acknowledged Turner with a sharp nod. "It's been a hard four years but I still enjoy it. I test for my first black belt next month."

"Good luck," Turner offered. "You let me know

if you're ever interested in personal protection. I'm sure your boss would miss you, but I think you'd do well over there. You have something for me?"

"Yes, sir. We're making a copy now," Officer Adams answered.

"Anything unusual over the last several days, like close calls or strange images?" Bristol asked. He didn't have to inquire about outright zone penetrations; *everyone* knew about those.

"No, sir," Janis reported. "Nothing but in-line and routine traffic from National."

"What about George?" Turner asked.

"Nothing from any face."

Adams scrolled through an on-line log. "That's correct, sir. It's been a clear month, except for that Walk in the Park incident with the airplane ki—"

Turner covered the officer's mouth. "Don't you dare bring that up. Evans is still on my case about that."

DIA Center

Camden Yards was dedicated in April 1992 in a town that was serious about baseball. *Tiger* could fly from Bolling to Baltimore in minutes, but Peter decided it would be easier and safer to use the mobile control station to transport the UAV to a dark lift-off point close to the stadium. A review of the surrounding street detail confirmed that the targeting LaCroix proposed would be even more difficult than the entrance, with 48,500 sets of eyes in the area. Worse, ESPN planned to televise both games.

The intelligence rules for the exercise prohibited any member of the project team's traveling to Baltimore to study the site, surroundings, or layouts. Only photographs and maps were allowed—just like a live operation.

The penetration was set for the second game of a doubleheader between the Orioles and the Chicago White Sox. The first pitch was scheduled for 1800 hours. LaCroix warned Peter that Defense would deny any knowledge of the incident if *Tiger* was detected, but he did agree to conveniently leak a report that a U.S. Meteorological Service high-altitude weather balloon was in the area. He even had fake aluminum labels made that, if found, would point to some dead-end experiment—an elegant strategy to diffuse media attention if multiple witnesses caught the UAV in the open. By the time the false leads were investigated, the event would have died down—at least enough to quell the cable news commentary.

Peter gathered his team and distributed copies of the incursion plan.

Halfway through reading the material, CJ leaned across the conference table and bummed a cigarette from Sam's shirt pocket. She hadn't smoked in twenty days after quitting cold turkey. Born and raised in the state that led the United States in annual cigarette production, she'd found smoking a tough habit to break. Tobacco was a religion in Winston-Salem.

"What kind of a harebrained surveillance mission is this?" she asked. "I don't get the military significance at all. If D-one is so hot for a public simulation, why not target the tires on the president's limousine from two hundred yards?"

"And I thought I was into practical jokes." Sam laughed. "This must be one of your American, how do you say it, cowboy things? Maybe we could shoot pigeons off the scoreboard or eliminate the evil hot-dog vendors."

"Are you comedians done?" Peter asked. "There is no military significance, and that's the point. DIA wants to see us operate under different kinds of tactical situations. *Tiger*'s not always going to work the sky over some foreign country's chemical weapons site. Anyway, selection is not up to us. First, D-one already picked the targets, and that's that. Seven spotlights on the stadium roof. Second—and obviously—the firing setup, program, and sequence will be completed in simulation mode only, but we'll approach, sight, and exit live. If we're photographed, we'll all have to run for cover. What better way to prove your product than by targeting a focal point in a stadium? Comments?"

"Since I can't disagree with the entire plan, we'll need a high enough vantage point and free range and angle to the stadium," Sam said matter-of-factly. "We also need a safe place from which to target."

"Is this legal?" CJ asked pointedly. "If it's not, I'm resigning."

"Yes, and I'm glad you brought it up." Peter was prepared for such an ultimatum and spoke calmly. "DIA has special authority for this kind of work in the interest of national defense."

"Excuse me? What in the world does this have to do with national defense?"

"The U.S. civilian theater is one of the best places to test a top-secret surveillance device, especially now. Every think tank in the country says we're totally ill prepared to handle the next nine-eleven, which, by the way, is predicted to be ten times worse. If *Tiger* can perform under such visible conditions, it can certainly handle less conspicuous environments." Peter produced a set of aerial photographs of the stadium and surrounding structures. He remembered that LaCroix still owed him a copy of the Patriot legislation. "Okay, we need a high, safe position, preferably one with a back door if things go wrong. Ideas?"

The team studied the photos for several minutes.

"I don't see anything inside the park," Ricky observed. "There are too many remote cameras along the rooflines. That hotel to the north is way out of range."

"My thoughts exactly," Peter acknowledged. "Let's keep the outer boundary at half a mile."

"What's with the castle?" CJ observed.

Peter thumbed through his material and found the photo. "That's the Bromo Tower. You know, Bromo-Seltzer, the antacid."

"What's it do?"

"Settles your stomach."

"I know that; I mean the tower."

Peter read the detail. "Traditional landmark . . . 1911 . . . Isaac Emerson . . . antacid magnate . . . fourteen stories . . . three hundred and fifty-seven feet."

"Tall enough for the angle," Sam estimated. He laid a small ruler down. "I judge the distance at . . . one thousand. It's within omniview range."

"Anyone else?" Peter closed his folder. "Done. Mr. Bromo it is. I was going to ask for volunteers, but I've decided Sam and Ricky will take the lead. Three people in the van gets a little crowded. The rest of us will monitor the operation from here. I almost forgot . . . LaCroix is sending two Defense field agents to Camden. They'll be in the stadium without any knowledge of *Tiger* or its objective. Their official assignment is to have a nice time at the old ball game."

Chapter Sixteen

Oriole Park Target Simulation Flight

Maryland Stadium Authority journeyman electrician Kelvin Smith sat at a lunch table, bobbing his head back and forth like an impatient lizard. He was trying to make sense of the 3-D picture his daughter had bought for the drab electrical room in the lower level of the stadium. Frustrated, he rubbed his eyes to get clarity back.

"Damn—I can't see a thing. It's supposed to be a bunch of birds or something flying over mountains."

"Let me try. You need to expand your mind," his coworker Alonzo Hayes said. He stared at a point in the middle of the picture and waited, eyes frozen in a classic trance. The blurred designs mysteriously focused. "Look at that. Ain't it sweet. An American flag made of bald eagles. You were holding it too far away."

Smith pretended not to hear. "Yes, sir, one big crowd tonight. Where you want us to start, boss?"

Master electrician Reggie Mansfield was tracing a circuit route with his pipe stem and missed the question.

Hayes put the picture down and elbowed his partner. "Skyboxes. Big money don't get spent in the dark. There's a tribute tonight for Cal Ripken Jr. He'll be sitting in the Oriole dugout. How many runs you giving me?"

Smith was from Chicago and dreaded what was coming. "Here we go again. Do I have to put up with you all night?"

"Aw, c'mon—I know you miss Comiskey. Know why they call Chicago the Windy City?"

"Tall buildings and bad winters," Smith answered indifferently.

"Nope." Hayes pulled a tool belt tight around his waist. "They were the first city in the U.S. to reach a million people, and bragged about it so much that the rest of the country started calling them windy."

"You know how he gets when the Sox come in here." Mansfield chuckled. He checked his watch and rolled the prints. "Okay, men, let there be light. Just don't get windy in public."

The journeymen headed for the elegant skybox level, on sconce patrol of the interior decorative wall lighting. Mansfield reached the press level and opened the stadium's master control panel for a general condition test. He leaned out over the playing field, gratified that every one of the seventeen hundred sports lights mounted on rigid I-beam girders on the rooftop was working. Each sealed fifteen hundred–watt sodium-vapor bulb cost $140 and was rated for five seasons. A recent wave of outages had stretched his budget and the muscles in his electricians' legs. Replacing high tower lighting was such a hairy job that rotating the duty seemed to work best. Hayes would be damn glad, too. It was Smith's turn to change the next ten blackouts.

The incursion's liftoff point would take place from the far end of a freeway park-and-ride near heavy woods four miles west of the stadium. It was farther than Peter wanted, but the random shootings in the Washington area had placed vehicles with blackened windows parked near crowds under constant scrutiny.

The mobile control station was a hybrid cross between an oversize cargo van and a Hummer. LaCroix's technicians managed to cut the five-ton weight in half by removing the lead installed to shield occupants from radiation during a nuclear attack. Unassuming except for its bulk, the MCS carried enough electronics to operate the UAV with as much technical efficiency as would a fixed flight center.

The vehicle had two control chairs welded to the midsection. Sam occupied one, his eyes and hands trying to form a relationship with the new joystick.

Sitting cross-legged in the rear, Ricky had finished the preflight mechanical checks and disconnected the battery charger. He nudged the doors open with his feet and pointed the *Tiger*'s nose to the outside.

Sam clicked the startup sequence and the UAV floated out of Ricky's hands and silently rose to its entrance height of five hundred feet.

The flight path scenery looked strikingly similar to that of the Nicolet except for the easterly glow of Baltimore's city lights. Oriole Park was visible in the distance, and overflowing. The *Tiger* moved northeast at fifteen mph over suburban homes in hilly terrain that gradually flattened into Baltimore's infamous row housing in the poorest section of the city. The streets were alive with people.

The Bromo Tower came into view just north of the stadium.

Sam floated the UAV over it and lowered to a point three feet above its medieval crest. He took a visual bearing. At the DIA Center, the team was seeing the identical images. To the south the stadium was a bright hive of activity. To the north there was a glass skyscraper—a potential detection point, but even with binoculars, someone would have only a few seconds of visual identification time before the UAV dropped into its concrete nest and out of sight.

Sam focused the omniview on the pitcher's mound and brought the PTS scope lines together. Sweeping south across the stadium on the first base side of the infield, he noticed uniformed police officers at each dugout. Baltimore PD wasn't taking any chances of a repeat of the incident in Comiskey Park and the surprise fan attack.

During the first three innings, Sam manually calculated and recalculated measurements taken from prior aerial photographs—distances to bulbs, square inches of target points, flight line distance and speed, and firing intervals. CJ helped verify angles along the expected flight trajectory where each round would simulate its release.

By the end of the fourth inning, Sam had entered all the data. Based on the input, *Tiger*'s firing sequence would start by tailing downward from a point 485 feet above ground level in mid–center field, and end 3.5 seconds later 294 feet to the south. Distance to the first of seven target points was 440 feet—longer than anticipated but still an easy sequence. At that range, PTS could swat bugs off the roofline.

The fifth inning ended.

"Sam, come in. Do you read me? Over." Peter's voice was masked by static, probably from all the media electronics. "We are recording. This is Camden Yards aerial test one. Set and lock points for speed run. You make the call for the best exit height and hold south. When it's over, I want a nice, slow return. No rush. I don't want any unnecessary attention. Let's start this stealthy simu. . . ."

"We read you," Sam responded. "You're fading—over."

"Quiet," Ricky warned, peering through the rear window into the lot. "Police cruiser."

Sam immediately lowered the omniview screen brightness and froze.

Peter reached his arm over Carl's shoulder and clicked on wide angle. "We have the south roofline," he spoke into his mouthpiece. "Whenever you're ready. Target the bottom row—over and out."

"It's clear," Ricky announced, his voice confident. "We did this in college. Once my roommate and I flew a remote copter to peek into some dorm windows. We got some great video of fresh—"

"Do me a favor and check again."

"Relax, I said they're gone," Ricky replied. "What else you want me to do?"

"Nothing . . . just sit and be quiet. I've got everything covered." Sam swore to himself and clicked a miniflashlight. Vans always made cops suspicious.

Reluctant to trust Ricky's information, Sam made a final review of the calculations and program settings before bringing back the omniview. Double, even triple number and procedural checks were bursting from his head. That damn cruiser. He struggled to focus. He ran through one more mental checklist. Once started, he knew the autotargeting program would run to completion. It had to be correct.

It was.

Sam took a deep breath and clicked "Go" on the menu.

The operation started with the UAV rising from the tower to its designated height.

Tiger headed north—away from the stadium—to gain the 5.2 seconds necessary to reach sixty mph.

Satisfied there'd be no further interruption, Ricky slid into his chair and popped open a Coke. "You merged everything to simulation, right?"

The word *mistake* is defined as a deviation from right or truth; an error or blunder. The two men stared at each other. It was one of those moments. Seconds stretched longer than they should. Einstein had them. It was what started his time kick—mistake. This one was huge, and sure to turn Camden Yards from wonder to zoo to war zone after seven half-seconds—give or take a few after things sank in.

The autofire control menu ticked down.

It looked like a localized power outage methodically affecting each light in the tower. The velocity of the rounds penetrated the one-sixteenth-inch casings, and the resulting implosions made loud popping noises. Broken glass clanged onto the stadium's metal rooftop in a continuous shower. After eleven seconds, everyone on the playing field and every fan who could see or hear was church-silent, staring up at the sports lighting.

Mansfield was still in the press area and saw the last three expire. He couldn't believe his eyes. His first instinct suggested some weird but global failure in the park's system. There was no other logical or electrical explanation. He clicked his radio. "Alonzo? Kelvin? where are you?"

"Right under it. Kelvin's on his way to the breakers. What could it be?"

"I have no idea. . . . Can you climb?"

Wondering why he agreed so quickly, Hayes tightened his belt another notch and double-checked his tools.

There was ample lighting on the rest of the field, so the umpires ordered play to resume. No one complied.

Reaching the last rung on the support girder high above the stadium rooftop, Hayes clamped the end of his safety belt onto a rusted metal railing connected to the narrow catwalk that led to the bulbs. He glanced down and noticed that more fans were watching him than the players on the field. When he waved, loud applause came back. He reached for his radio. "I want a raise."

"Don't play up there," Mansfield said sternly. "Kelvin says everything's okay in the boxes. It's got to be your end."

Trying to ignore a slight sway in the girder, Hayes reached the first bulb and peered into the darkened shell. When he shone his flashlight further inside the casing and saw the quarter-inch hole pierced through the fixture's cast-metal backing, he didn't make the connection.

Then he saw the same hole in the next light.

Weak with panic, his legs gave out, sending him backpedaling over the railing and off the frame—

238

only his safety strap stopped the fall. The crowd gasped and shot to their feet. Dangling like a limp marionette, the electrician managed to pull himself back onto the catwalk. He lay facedown, trembling on the metal grates. The crowd cheered wildly.

An entourage of stadium security and Baltimore PD rushed to the tower.

Hayes closed his eyes and whimpered into his radio, "Reggie . . . help . . . I can't move."

"Alonzo, hold on—we're coming. Just hang on. We'll be right there, man."

"These lights been shot out! You hear me? There's somebody shootin' in here! Get my ass off this tower and call the goddamn po-lice!"

A chill ran through Mansfield's body.

Halfway up the tower rungs the rescuers froze and then started back down, stepping on one another's fingers and heads like circus clowns.

Stadium security poured onto the field—to the amazement of the crowd. One leaped on Cal Ripken's back as some kind of human shield. The confused superstar had no idea what was happening and started spinning around in circles trying to shake him off.

Mansfield raced back into the press box for a landline phone. Calls had already flooded 911. When the broadcast hit public radio, panic spread out into the stands faster than the wave. It was something no one ever wanted to hear again.

Sniper.

The UAV had reached a loiter position well off the stadium.

Peter stared at the omniview in disbelief. His facial expression was like that of a schoolboy after breaking a stern neighbor's window. "Did we do that?" he asked Carl.

"Holy *shit*! Did we do that?" Carl asked CJ.

Her mouth hanging open like a trout, she nodded once.

"Get outta there!" Peter screamed into his microphone. "We'll bring *Tiger* home from here."

Ricky burst through the frontal partitions and started the engine.

Sam was mesmerized at his monitor, watching people climb over seating and each other to get out of the open areas and into the safety of the stadium's interior. Officers with weapons drawn rushed to surround the northern and eastern perimeters, from where the shots presumably came. The noise produced by forty-some thousand mouths paled next to that of the sirens.

Peter ushered CJ into Sam's chair. "You're a better pilot than I am."

Sick to her stomach and fighting panic, she was trying to listen and click menu commands that would reroute flight control. "My Lord, what have we done?"

"We'll both get religious later. Take us to seven hundred and head west at best speed. Give me twenty minutes."

Peter had calculated an emergency escape route

240

out of Baltimore that ran forty miles west to the Potomac, then south following the contour of the river all the way back to the DIA Center. It just happened to require speed, height, and damned high confidence that the UAV really was too small to be detected by any major airport tower. In his heart, Peter believed that terminal control area radar would never detect his *Tiger*.

Faith had nothing to do with it.

Washington National Tower Control

The FAA defined the skies surrounding the busiest airports as Class B airspace. In addition to visual and instrument requirements, four main rules applied for access: preapproved clearance, radio contact, no students, and an altitude-equipped transponder.

As it flowed toward Washington, the Potomac made a series of twisting bends near Great Falls, Virginia, including a ten-mile stretch that paralleled Washington National's IFR departure and approach corridor, flight path 319—a no-brain lane for flying in and out of Washington's TRACON— Terminal Radar Approach CONtrol—airspace. The FAA set radar sensitivity to ignore anything less than three hundred pounds, but the airport's newest upgrade of Grumman's Airport Surveillance Radar, ASR-12, was tuned to track a six-inch hollow steel ball suspended from a weather balloon fifteen miles from the transmitter. Operators bragged that at maximum sensitivity, it could pick up a banded pigeon.

Local air-traffic controller Steve Kowalski's D-BRITE—Digital Bright Radar Indicator Tower Equipment—screen automatically labeled the object as unidentified based on the weak radar image and negative transponder signal. Kowalski had served four years in the navy on a *Ticonderoga*-class missile frigate with AEGIS radar so powerful it could detonate ammunition on nearby aircraft. He recognized that the object's speed was nowhere near that of ground-to-air weaponry. Missile or not, the object showed no altitude and was traveling at a hundred mph. That automatically ruled out a flock of geese from the tidal basin.

Something had appeared out of nowhere.

Dean Abrams, the tower supervisor, came running, expecting collision-level panic.

Kowalski calmly held up his hand. "There's not supposed to be anything in that vicinity for at least thirty minutes. It's ten miles out and heading straight for the zone. Approach Control never handed it off. What's it look like to you?"

Abrams concentrated on the faint image traveling down the telescoping corridor that kept pilots vectored on precise approach into National. The tower's anemometer showed winds calm at five mph. "Try and increase your—"

"Maxed out." Kowalski anticipated the question and had already checked the signal sensitivity.

"What about visual?"

"I've tried that, too; I can't see a thing."

Abrams cursed and lifted his own binoculars. "I've had it with these ultralights. If it's the last thing I do I'm going to fry this guy. Try and raise him."

"Raise him how? None of them ever talk."

"Then use the location. It's a long shot, but he might be listening. Try the NOTAM one-six-oh-nine frequencies." All aircraft operating near restricted or prohibited airspace were advised to listen on VHF 121.5 or UHF 243.0.

Kowalski adjusted his mouthpiece. "Pilot on eastbound three-nineteen . . . this is Washington National tower. You are entering prohibited airspace and are in FAA violation—over. . . ." No response.

Abrams pulled off Kowalski's headset. "Pilot, this is tower supervisor Abrams. You are not cleared for this airspace. Be advised . . . the military will use deadly force to protect this area from unauthorized incursion. We will scramble jets. This is a final warning—out."

Both men knew the threat was a bluff. Although they had the ability to literally lift a fiber hot line to Air Defense Command at Andrews AFB, there was no way either of them could or wanted to justify pushing a button that would close the airport and surrounding airspace, divert all inbound flights, and send DC into hard panic. Rationalization was a hell of a lot easier.

The mystery image was now barely registering, traveling at an improbable speed for something so small, and appeared incapable of following standard markers through the landing cone. Therefore, it was neither aircraft nor threat.

"It's either a ghost or clutter," Abrams concluded. He recently read an FAA advisory about controllers at O'Hare International seeing dozens of false radar images—ghosts—over the Lake Michigan triangle, forcing pilots to make sudden turns unnecessarily. He noticed the blips stacking up on Kowalski's screen. "Write it up for the incident file and ship it over to Flight Standards. American six-oh-two is running late and conflicts with United three-three-four. You'll have to hold one back."

"Clutter. Yes, sir." Kowalski nodded reluctantly. "Either that or somebody shot off the mother of all bottle rockets."

As the Potomac straightened to the south, both the *Tiger* and the river split from flight path 319. The image suddenly froze on the screen, and then made a distinct turn before disappearing completely.

Neither controller said another word.

Kowalski reset his alarm. *Definitely a ghost*, he thought. *Clutter doesn't stop in midair and change course.*

Chapter Seventeen

White House Security

It was the lead story across the nation.

An invisible shooter had methodically snuffed out seven overhead sports lights in front of a sellout baseball crowd in Baltimore. League stadiums proposed to triple their security forces, but the baseball union went on record anyway as saying that its members wanted hazard compensation. Hayes's high-wire act earned him dinner with the Ripkens.

Joe Grant sat on Turner's sofa with his feet on the coffee table. He was one of the few people allowed the luxury, but he still placed a magazine under his shoes. "Scary, isn't it? It's a wonder more people didn't get hurt. Thank God that stadium has wide exits. The paper said it took three hours to search everyone. Thirty K-9 teams worked the adjacent buildings and rooftops. Some witnesses in the stands are claiming it was aliens."

"I've tried to tell people there's UFOs in my forest," Turner joked. "Thirty dogs? That's more than we had at the Capitol. I can't imagine all those badges and not one bad guy? It's impossible. They missed something. Somebody in the stands had a scope, or maybe one of the groundskeepers was in on it. Selig's suspended all major league games until further notice. There's already a million-dollar reward."

"I heard they got the caliber figured out from the entry holes, but there's some controversy about the round makeup," Grant said between coffee sips. "They didn't find a single piece of lead anywhere. They think it's some kind of plastic. But what's really strange is that nobody heard anything."

Turner contemplated that for a moment. "He had to be on the roof."

"He? I don't think so. Each light had a single hole shot through it every half second. Twenty-two caliber. Pop, pop, pop—seven times in less than four seconds. One round in each light. Their sports cable camera above the scoreboard got the whole sequence. Some video expert on FOX News timed it down to thousandths. He said there's no way it could have come from a human. Think about it. Who could shoot like that all seven times?"

"Guess Lee Harvey Oswald's come back from the . . ." Turner paused. "Wait—say that again."

"I didn't think you were listening," Grant chided.

"I said they measured the time between each shot and it was *exactly* point five-zero-zero seconds. That's not human. I suppose it wouldn't hurt to step up our perimeter. Anyone who can shoot like that and vanish into thin air scares the hell out of an old-timer like me."

Turner glanced out his window and saw Jack Evans and his staff racing across the Executive Office Building parking lot for an emergency meeting with all personal protection. "Young-timers, too."

Capital Beltway

Finished with his shift and caught in the morning rush hour, Steve Kowalski was still thinking about the strange radar image when he heard the news on the radio. He never would have made the connection if it weren't for the unusual request the control tower had gotten recently. His first instinct was to contact Baltimore detectives. He had a brother-in-law at Langley who might be more interested.

Defense Directorate of Administration

Murphy considered offering DSS bodies to help with the investigation, but no military crimes had been committed, and he knew it was a jurisdictional headache to start meddling in civilian areas. He took his time finishing the article before flopping the newspaper onto his credenza. It never hurt to flaunt a little authority.

He buzzed the agents in.

"So what's your take on this Baltimore shooting?"

Agent Lange craned his neck at the headlines and boldly reached behind Murphy's desk. "I heard about it after class last night. Something about another sniper."

"Help yourself, son," Murphy offered, somewhat perturbed by the encroachment. "What class?"

"Fundamentalist terror," Lange said. "It's part of the curriculum Tom Marcus is coordinating. It's supposed to help us ID a new breed of deep cover. . . ." His voice trailed off into the print.

"It's all over the media," Beck noted. "I think there's a blackmail angle. Who benefits when nobody plays baseball?"

Murphy struggled with that for a moment, unable to think of anyone other than terrorists. *Interesting, but weak*, he thought. "Talk to me about our friends at Aerotech. What was that project's name again? Ah, yes . . . *Tiger*."

"Nothing extraordinary," Beck answered. "Some documentation out of place in one contractor's . . . Mr. Nasrabadi's home, but most of it was already declassified."

"He the Iranian?"

"He's not Irish."

Murphy smiled briefly. "Go on."

She lifted a set of files to her lap. "I'll start with families and spouses. . . ."

"Just the rankings," Murphy said, annoyed at Lange's preoccupation with the newspaper story.

"Fifty, twenty-five, twenty, and . . . Mr. Ricardo Benavides brings up the rear at five. He's a temporary hire, so we conducted his by phone. Squeaky clean. Nothing unusual there at all."

"Squeaky, huh?" Murphy smiled slyly. "Did you know that Mr. Benavides was arrested last year in Los Angeles for heckling the president's speech on medical funding cuts?"

How the hell did he find that out? she wondered. "That would be a misdemeanor. I'll take care of the update right away." Beck's foot kicked her partner's leg. Lange's face grimaced behind the newspaper.

"Who's the fifty . . . Nasrabadi?" Murphy asked.

She slid out the profile. "No, as a matter of fact it's Richter, Carl W. Born May 1948 to German immigrants. Father Arthur investigated for war crimes. It was a messy case, but he was eventually vindicated. Richter's clean on local and Interpol databases. White male, loner, expert with audio, video, cameras, and lenses. Personal interests"—her voice slowed—"marksmanship . . . scopes . . . profile fits potential snipe—"

Lange lowered the newspaper. "Jesus."

"Hold it right there," Murphy said firmly. "I'll admit the possibility is intriguing, but there is no evidence whatsoever of that team in Baltimore or its vicinity. Nobody breathes a word about this unless I clear it personally—understood? Who's the twenty-five?"

"Caroline Jennings." Beck retrieved the file. "We

uncovered some fairly troubling terror-drug link—"

"Good grief, you make her sound like she's working for al Qaeda, for Christ's sake." Murphy glanced at his watch. "What are the specifics?"

"Well . . . none, exactly. But her brother was convicted of—"

"Lower it." Murphy looked at his watch again. Beck caught the body English and nudged her partner. "Anyone who sees that wouldn't clear her for a janitor's job in a recruiting office. I'd like everything turned over to D-one by the end of the week. And tone down Richter's profile so no one assumes what we just did. You two did a nice job on this assignment, given the short turnaround. I appreciate it. You can close the door."

Murphy lifted his phone. He wanted Harold Floring.

CIA Office of Technical Collection

Rich Foley's phone rang just as someone yelled, "Breaking news" outside his office. Deciding to pass on the mad scramble for a position in front of the wall-mounted television monitor, Foley picked up.

"Rich? Steve. Hey—we had an incident last night. Can you talk?"

"Incident?" Foley asked warily. He shifted the phone so he could write.

"Uh-huh. We picked up something on one of our inbound corridors for roughly three minutes that was moving at a steady one-double-oh."

"Some*thing*?" Foley clarified. "That doesn't say much. You get an identification number?"

"There wasn't any," Kowalski said. "At first we thought it was an ultralight, but the signal was so weak we could barely keep it isolated, even on the surveillance band. I realize this sounds strange, but I watched it move with my own eyes. The thing came to a midair stop, then accelerated back to its previous speed in about twelve seconds. My boss figured it was clutter, but no way. It was airborne with a purpose. I've never seen anything like it. Whatever it was, it couldn't have weighed more than fifteen or twenty pounds, judging from the signature. With that stadium business, I figured the two events might be related. The time frame sure fits."

Foley knew he had to dance fast and slow at the same time. "Weird. Mind if I take a look? I'll make sure it stays under wraps, okay? I'll send someone over." It was the perfect CIA response, even to a relative—vague commitment to pursue with no accountability or admission of connected knowledge. If he had to, he could bury the source.

Harris appeared in the doorway. "I read your analysis. It's a shame. All those radar tapes and not one reflection out of the ordinary. You sure the White House sent us everything?"

Afraid to breathe, Foley carefully replaced the handset and took a moment to collect himself before sharing the information.

DIA Center

Floring was fingering through a desk drawer when his phone rang.

"Harold? That Aerotech project. Is that a local operation?"

Floring twisted the cap off a prescription bottle and popped two pills. They stuck to the roof of his mouth and he couldn't respond.

"Was the *Tiger* in Maryland last night?"

"Gavin—please, you know I can't—"

"Damn! Are you saying they actually had something to do with that baseball incident?"

"That's absurd. Where'd you get that?"

"Our contractor profiles. Specifically, that Richter fellow. What on earth are you people up to?"

"Gavin, you cannot repeat this to anyone," Floring warned. "We need to talk."

"You're right," Murphy agreed. "Especially if your flying camera is shooting more than pictures."

Floring slammed the phone down and raced down the corridor. Murphy had contacts throughout the entire law-enforcement community. It was a bad place for rumor.

"*Tiger*'s been leaked."

"Calm down, man. You smoke too much to run around here like that," LaCroix said. "What do you mean? How? To whom?"

"DSS. It's more than leaked; it's burst. Murphy even named one of Wescott's people as the stadium sniper."

"Please tell me you're joking." LaCroix reached for the phone.

"I am not, damn it. Somebody, somehow, has figured this out."

"Should we bring him in?" LaCroix asked.

"Murphy's not the source," Floring admitted. "But someone in his department has managed to stumble onto the targeting, and we have got to rein it in now."

"Goddammit—get Murphy up here," LaCroix said angrily. He checked his watch and dialed Peter's pager. "I'll handle the sniper issue."

DIA Center

Peter hung up the phone in his office and hurried into the flight control center. He gathered his team around a worktable. His face was ashen. "That was Ricky. His father had a massive stroke last night. He passed away early this morning."

CJ covered her mouth with both hands. "Oh, my God, he worshiped his father. Where is he?"

"On his way to the airport. He was so upset he couldn't talk. I don't know anything else, but I'll keep you informed." Peter exhaled a long breath. His eyes started to moisten. "I need all of you at the Camden Yards briefing in five minutes. There may be someone present who is not cleared for all aspects of this project. Do not mention one word about Baltimore, PTS capability, or even its existence—no matter what else is said. I'll do the talking. We ran a local test flight last night and nothing more. I don't know the details, but *Tiger* may have been seen, so you are to deny—or better yet, deflect to me—any lethality questions—understand? We'll take our detection lumps as they come. I apologize for the secrecy, but that's all I know; you'll have to trust me. That's all."

Peter held CJ back. Tears were streaming down her face, and he wished he had time to explain further. It was all he could do to keep himself together. He had to bring her around.

Unable to sleep after the Potomac flight, she was nursing a monster migraine. The throbbing in her head and neck was so painful she had to turn her whole body to look at him.

"Rough time last night?" Peter asked.

She pressed a tissue to her eyes and stared blankly at the wood grain of the tabletop. "Do you think what we did last night was right?"

"Define right."

She lifted her head. "You know what I mean. We put civilians in jeopardy, damaged property, and could have caused a lot of people to get hurt. Remember that soccer game in Belgium where all those people got crushed against a fence? What if we had caused something horrible like that?"

"But we didn't. It was an accident—an unfortunate accident, but one that will raise awareness." Peter edged his chair closer. "This may sound like rah-rah, but I'm beginning to agree with LaCroix that America needs the best intelligence capability possible. Instead of nuclear weapons superiority, think in terms of surveillance superiority. Defending against bad people and terror, whether foreign or domestic, is no longer just a top priority; it's the only priority. When you look at it that way, a few broken lights is a small price."

CJ lit a cigarette—taboo in the control center, but Peter let it go. "You've changed," she said. "You were always so cautious about everything. You never used to be a risk-taker. It seems you found an easier way to handle pressure. Now you're carefree, even daring."

Peter nodded at the observation. "I guess there's no one from corporate looking over my shoulder."

"I'm ready for a change, too. I could use a long walk on a beach."

"We'll all be home soon enough." Peter observed the pack of cigarettes. "Your mother'll be heartbroken you started again."

"I doubt it." She managed a painful laugh. "They practically own RJ Reynolds."

Peter saw LaCroix waving from the outer corridor. "We're late. Feel better?"

"Sure. Damn craving for nicotine started this headache. Poor Ricky." CJ slid her cigarette into an empty soda can. It sizzled briefly. "So who's the mystery guest?"

"Someone from DSS," Peter answered. "There may be others. We're getting popular."

LaCroix closed the conference room door. "Now that we're all here, you know Brent Harris from

CIA Collection, and Gavin Murphy from Support Services. Gavin's people certified your security clearances . . . which seem to have a major problem." Heads immediately started turning back and forth. "It appears that Mr. Murphy *and* the FAA believe that the *Tiger* was in the air last night, and was somehow responsible for that incident in Baltimore."

"We were," Peter readily admitted. "In the air, that is. I've personally spoken to everyone on the project and can assure you that no one breathed a word. And we certainly weren't followed."

"Then I suspect you'll appreciate this even more," Harris said. "Would you mind if I set him straight, Dan? We need to stop further damage."

LaCroix nodded.

"You were tracked," Harris said flatly, "on airport surveillance by tower controllers working the late shift at Reagan National."

The team sat stunned, no more than if Harris had stood on the table naked.

"I don't believe you; that's not possible. National could not have detected us," Sam turned to his boss. "Where's the proof? Their system is configured for mass ten times our size."

"Proof? You shadowed the Potomac and your speed was . . . one hundred, I believe? I watched the entire tape an hour ago. Because your flight happened just after that shooting, they also figured the image—your UAV—was somehow involved."

"I take full responsibility," Peter admitted. "We

did, in fact, attempt a test flight last night that might have strayed too close to National. Perhaps if we had some better technical support from—"

"Peter, it's not my place to teach Aviation one-oh-one. You should have done better research into the territory. Most airports deploy three types of radar tracking systems; terminal control, ground service, and IFR approach-and-departure surveillance. Control area systems radiate twenty miles out from the towers to first identify inbound flights. They're the major handoff points between controller networks. Ground service is self-explanatory . . . runway traffic, baggage and fuel vehicles, et cetera. But the IFR system is really the heart of modern air trafficking, and surveillance radar is the lifeblood. Every approach and departure corridor has its own fixed radar and you just happened to fly right into its search track. Let me give you a simple example." Harris's tone was softening. "If you had to sneak out of a locked department store after hours, you'd want to avoid roaming guards and alarms at the main floor exits. So you decide to ride the down escalator and get out through a basement window, never knowing the path you chose was monitored by its own camera. Now, if a fire started in sporting goods, who would you pick as a primary suspect?"

Peter drew himself up and took a deep breath. "I don't know what to say; I'm sorry if we caused any problems."

"It was really just plain bad luck," said Harris. "When the controller heard the news reports, he assumed the two events were related, and voilà, your little flying Tinkerbell gets caught."

Sam was ready to explode.

"Save it," Peter said softly. "This isn't the time or place. Besides, we were detected and it's a concern. Now, what's all this have to do with Baltimore?"

Murphy ran a finger inside his collar. He knew his agents had guessed that the UAV was in the area. He started to realize how weak the shooting assumption was. He wished he'd never brought it up. "Based on your team's . . . er. . . . Carl Richter's expertise with firearms, and the project's relationship to DIA, we concluded that there was a fairly good probability . . . um . . . that it was, well . . ."

"Firearms?" Peter cocked his head in surprise to one side. "Carl has nothing to do with any weapons."

"It's true, Gavin. He's a sensory technician. Heat, sound, imagery." Floring noticed LaCroix's mouth twitch. "How'd you arrive at your conclusions?"

"We speculated," Murphy readily admitted. "Badly, too. I suggest we forget it ever came up."

"You government investigators are all the same," Carl said disgustedly. "Just trying to make a fucking name for yourselves. Next you'll accuse me of trying to kill the president or some other trumped-up charge . . . just like you laid on my father." He lunged forward. Peter held him back.

"Hold it!" LaCroix shouted. "Can we please try to get control of this project? No more flights around National, or any other surveillance zones. I can't believe how these half-assed circumstances keep coming down on this team. It's like a curse. These events should never have fingered the UAV. Can you put a lid on your controller friends?"

Harris shrugged. "We don't have the original images, but they're convinced we're investigating. I think we can keep it quiet."

"What about your problem?" LaCroix asked Murphy.

"I can nip the source. It won't go any further."

"Okay—if those two ends are tied, *Tiger* should be tight again."

The briefing ended without any further discussion of targeting.

"Was that what I think it was?" CJ said after the door closed.

"Afraid so," Harris admitted. "We had to bring you in cold to make it believable. You did well."

"And the detection?" Sam asked.

"That was real. Surveillance corridors are a problem. Think Murphy bought it?"

"There's no guarantee, but believe me, the cost of wounding a little DSS pride is nothing compared to the liability and publicity damage to Defense if that ever got out—not to mention the fact that every service intelligence group would want to build its own machine. It'd be a mess." LaCroix wiped his forehead. "I'm sorry about your coworker's father. We're sending a memorial. Can you manage without him?"

Peter nodded. "Is there such a thing as a nice, easy exercise?"

"Perhaps we can accommodate that request," LaCroix answered.

"Let me guess . . . Mount Vernon?"

"Why in the world would you mention that?" Floring asked suspiciously.

"It's rated as a no-fly zone on the TAC charts," Peter observed. "What could possibly go on at that site that would cause it to be prohibited?"

"Take my advice and forget about that place. Anyway, I wouldn't consider asking this team to try to penetrate such a highly sensitive and secured area." LaCroix lifted his briefcase onto the table and unfolded another map. "My friends, I present you with the physical layout of Andrews Air Force Base."

Chapter Eighteen

I-295 Northbound

"Rita . . . this is Gavin. Find Agent Lange, please. I'll wait."

There was something about Carl Richter he couldn't put his finger on. Some latent vengeance. Maybe it was simply pent-up stress. Classified work had that effect on contractors sometimes.

"This is Jim."

"Have you discussed your sniper theory with anyone else?" Murphy asked.

"Absolutely not."

"Good. I want to personally inform you that the *Tiger* is operating in this area, but neither the team nor Carl Richter has anything to do with weaponry. In fact, there is no weaponry. It's strictly passive surveillance. I shared your assumptions with DIA just now and was made a laughingstock. File those clearances and end it. I want all further interest in that project dropped. I like the way you operate, son. You're a solid part of my team. Keep up the good work. And make sure Agent Beck gets the message, too. Clear?"

"Crystal. It's over," Lange replied, confident that he and the head of DSS had established a close working relationship.

That was exactly what Murphy wanted him to think.

Andrews Air Force Base Penetration

In addition to twenty-four thousand military and civilian personnel, the southern tip of Andrews housed a notable pair of VC-25A aircraft with 747 fuselage tail numbers 28000 and 29000 and rotating call signs of AFO—Air Force One—with the commander-in-chief on board.

The entrance over the beltway went smoothly. The moonless night provided an excellent backdrop for hovering. The UAV floated down to a deserted area of knee-high grass on the northern edge of the base, appropriately named North Perimeter Road.

There was no activity on the naval perimeter to the east except for routine mustering of vehicles at the base fire station. To the west, it was just the opposite.

AFO had already started to roll out of its maintenance and support hexahangar northward to a secured flight apron escorted by base security in eight air force police vehicles, a distance of 1.7 miles.

Carl outright laughed at the events unfolding on his monitor. "You really expect us to get close to that?"

"It's not that bad," Peter said. "If LaCroix's intelligence is accurate, at oh-four-forty they'll stop two hundred and ten feet east of the base operations building. Everything and everyone else will be cleared out of the area. The president and first family are scheduled to board at oh-seven-hundred for a brief family hiatus. We'll be long gone by then."

"How'd LaCroix manage to get such classified information about the itinerary?"

"No clue," Peter answered. "Something about fuel refill patterns. Another Mount Vernon answer."

CJ threw up her arms. "Do you know how utterly absurd and dangerous this is? What are we doing? This is the president we're spying on. If you really stop and think, there's nothing that says we're part of any authorized mission. No orders, clearance, or approvals for this or any other test. What if this is all just a huge setup? We get arrested for terror or espionage, DIA grabs the UAV and reverse engineers it in some desert in New Mexico, then denies that we ever existed. I don't trust them."

Sam rolled his eyes. "Will you please put a lid on the paranoia? It really pisses me off to hear you second-guess a mission while we're knee-deep in tactics. That's a great sense of timing, lady."

"I'm not paranoid. I just want reassurance that we're not being used, that's all. I haven't felt comfortable with any of these targeting missions. I know we signed on to the lethality specifications, but I never thought it would come to this. Some of us have decent reputations. In fact, this is more than reputations at stake; it's our future."

"Enough already. Can't you see they're stretching us?" Peter explained. "For your information, we're not going to get caught. This is our last hurrah, so do you mind if we push the surveillance envelope tonight as a team?"

"What was so hard about getting DIA to confirm—"

"The debate is over," Peter said sharply. "Sam—take us to twenty. That should keep us below the horizon and any silhouetting. Carl—bring up that plane. I want to see shadows."

The UAV rose to the designated height.

AFO and its surroundings filled the overhead screen. Ground control workers had unhooked the taxi-tractor from the puller arm and chocked all eighteen landing wheels. The escort vehicles had dispersed into the background. A squad of armed marines fanned out in a semicircle around the aircraft.

"There." Peter pointed. "The lights on the air terminal building. That shadow off the plane's tail. They've rolled out the black carpet."

"Same height?" Sam asked.

Peter paused to think. "No—hug the grass. But give me one more sweep of the southern perimeter from nine to three o'clock at rooftop level. I've got a feeling there are more eyes around."

Carl scanned the buildings to the east and back to the FAA tower. Unsure of exactly what they were looking for, the team finally spotted Secret Service Countersniper Unit—CSU—sharpshooters with night-vision gear on the rooftops of two naval hangars, the Maryland Aviation Division building and the fire training facility along the southeastern perimeter. A westerly scan showed bodies on top of the hexahangar, fire station, FAA, operations, and terminal buildings. The area was crawling with high security.

"They might see our heat," Sam warned.

"I doubt it, but if we're fired on, don't wait for me. Somebody spits in our direction and you get us off the ground, up and out. Northwest, then backtrack down the Potomac as low as possible."

Andrews's western runway stretched south for ten thousand feet. The UAV stopped once to reconnoiter at a lone maintenance hut near the middle of the airfield. It took another three minutes to reach the plane's tail shadow that extended from the aircraft to the edge of the interior field grass.

"Big sucker, huh?" Carl's eyes ran down the fuselage. "Amazing that thing even gets off the ground."

"A few hundred thousand pounds of thrust helps," Sam replied.

"What do you figure it weighs?"

"For takeoff and landing it has to reach at least a hundred and seventy knots, but that depends." Sam reached for a calculator. "With or without fuel?"

"Hellooo . . . are we here for surveillance or aviation trivia?" CJ asked.

Peter grimaced and hurried into his office rest room.

CJ's mouth hung open. "Now what?"

"You gotta go, you gotta go," Carl said matter-of-factly.

"I'm fully aware of nature's calling, but considering we're thirty feet away from the president's private aircraft you'd think it could wait. Must you be so gross?"

"Relax. We could sit out on this runway all day and nobody would notice. See for yourself." Carl opened the omniview lens and captured a wider angle of the surroundings. The marines were positioned on the boarding side of the aircraft, leaving the entire eastern flank unguarded. He zoomed in on a grouping of PPD agents huddled at the apron fence line. He could almost read their lips. "Secret Service doesn't look so secret now, huh?"

Sam frowned suspiciously at the monitor. "I think we've had enough of that. You know we're recording."

"Not anymore." Carl reset the video so the stunt wouldn't appear on tape.

Peter returned to the room and nodded to CJ. "Let's try to do it right this time. Simulation,

please—with a capital *S*. On my mark . . . set timing
. . . now."

Sam raised the *Tiger* four inches off the concrete
and eased forward, following the plane's tail shadow
all the way up to the rear stabilizer. The operation
continued with a devastating scenario—in simulation—to inflict massive damage to any aircraft. A
hidden timed explosive attached to the tail, remotely detonated at leisure posttakeoff.

The cub maneuver took less than a minute.

Carl indicated that he had a good recording.

"Okay, get us out of here and head southeast.
Let's take a tour," Peter ordered. "We've got an
hour before dawn. I want us home by then."

Sam lowered the UAV to the concrete and followed the shadow back to the grass that separated
the two main runways. South of the naval fighter
wings, he raised up to twenty feet above ground
level and tracked the center line of a single road
that encircled the base. The unrestricted access gave
precise positions of base communications, fuel re-
positories, parts depots, briefing centers, reserve
units, and personnel housing layouts. Even the
harmless tradition of displaying squadron identification across a flight hangar entrance in seemingly
impenetrable military bases could now provide an
enemy with unique intelligence.

"Let's take some souvenirs before we end this
project," Peter said mischievously. "Give me a fix
on those spotters."

The souvenirs he referred to would cause major

embarrassment to the Secret Service after the eastern row of CSU officers was "neutralized." There was little chance of causing small-caliber danger to the president from five thousand feet, so Peter decided to shorten the distance from the hexahangar. The ultimate security breakdown—eliminating rooftop protection—would place the flight apron within the PTS range.

After recording three target points on AFO's carpeted stair lift, the UAV rose to three hundred feet and headed west to the Potomac.

It reached the DIA Center flight balcony just as first light peeked over the eastern horizon.

Oakton

Turner finished his morning workout and clicked onto cable news.

A man in a blade-controlled hot-air balloon was hovering over a rock star's secluded estate videotaping a private outdoor wedding and transmitting the event over the Internet. LAPD air patrol helicopters had surrounded the trespasser but were essentially powerless, as were the bride and groom. The man claimed he had every right to perch in public airspace as long as no laws were being broken. The news commentators were actually joking with Balloon Man as he promoted his Web site.

Turner never cracked a smile.

TARGET ACQUIRED

Central Intelligence Agency
Directorate of Science and Technology (S&T)

With an annual budget exceeding $35 billion, the CIA's thirty-one sectors were overrun with fat-salaried government stereotypes devoid of technology and operational skills. Directorate costs kept increasing 10 percent annually, with no way to measure productivity or reconcile goals and accomplishments. Congress in particular viewed the agency as queen of the intelligence swine, with S&T fattest in the litter. It wasn't always that way. Some noteworthy accomplishments included design and operation of America's first spy satellites, the U-2 program, and advances in medical pacemakers. Then there were the disasters. In some twisted version of a McDonald's acronym, the MKULTRA drug experiments resulted in employee suicides. Exploding seashells and poisoned pens were designed in a futile attempt to assassinate Fidel Castro. Perhaps worst of all, the Acoustic Kitty project of 1966–1967 surgically altered a cat to implant control devices and a tail antenna in hopes of creating a Frankenstein-like mobile eavesdropper. The poor animal was tested unmercifully and, less than a minute into its first street assignment, was run over by a taxi.

When Winston Churchill defined a fanatic as "someone who can't change his mind and won't change the subject," he was speaking about a politics-be-damned cattle rancher from Wyoming. James Runyan had served two congressional terms and pulled more than his own weight on intelligence subcommittees. He was Scotch-Irish tight with a dollar; his first official act as S&T's new deputy director was to stubbornly keep his employees on the west side of Langley's original headquarters rather than move them into the expansion. And to solidify that statement, he tore out the dark paneling in his office—stained with nicotine from years of cigar smoke—and brought in used furniture. He refused to accept limousine or pool car service just to set an example—even at the cost of an occasional speeding ticket.

In charge of six agency sectors and four thousand employees, he took every opportunity to distance himself from the traditional spy legacy, a nearly impossible task in an organization that seemed to detest change. A voracious cost-cutter, with zero tolerance for poor performers, he was determined to prove that his latest brainchild, the 20/20 Vision Plan—20 percent personnel cuts this year and another 20 the next—would highlight his directorate as the model of change. Competitive success in his organization would certainly silence the Capitol Hill drumbeating. Runyan had admired LaCroix's UAV consolidation battles and had tried—unsuccessfully—to get him to shift agencies and roll double or nothing.

DIA Center

Master Sergeant Malcolm validated their identification and wave-saluted Runyan and Brent Harris through Bolling's front gate. LaCroix was waiting in DIAC's lobby at a security checkpoint.

"Hot damn, how the hell is Daniel LaCroix?" Runyan sang out. "I see you survived the lynching."

"Nice to see you, Jim." They pumped hands vigorously. LaCroix noticed Runyan's signature snakeskin footwear but refrained from comment. "I heard Director Stephenson's leaving."

"It's a damn shame," Runyan ventured. "He was one of those rare executives who still had some backbone left, even after the politicians finished gnawing on it. I suspect I was part of the decision."

LaCroix smiled. "Caused him that much grief, eh?"

Runyan nodded guiltily. "He bought most of my ideas but couldn't swallow the really big winners. Too much fallout."

"I've had my share of those culture battles, my friend." LaCroix swiped an access card through a reader. The elevator began to rise.

Runyan patted Harris's shoulder. "Our biggest problem at CIA is too many secret agents and not enough change agents. And speaking of that, when are you going to come work for me?"

LaCroix was flattered by the invitation but knew his time in government service was on the wane.

"Nothing personal, Jim, but I hear you're losing the war."

"That's why I'm desperate," Runyan admitted. "If my illustrious ex-colleagues in the dome would leave us alone long enough, we'd find some savings. And, by Jesus, the first thing I'd do is take an ax to the management layers. All eleven of them. When I took this job we had a strategic reorganization plan to build a strategic reorganization plan. We have entire workgroups who have no idea who they report to or what their purpose is. The geniuses who came up with the Clandestine Information Technology Office and National Imagery and Mapping Agency deserved their early retirement. CITO and NIMA. No wonder it failed. Sounded like some Italian magic act. You wouldn't believe the redundancies. Councils, staffs, support services, and especially systems. We've still got over nine thousand people reading maps. My wallet hurts thinking about it. This little gunslinger of yours as hot as it looks? I saw the gang shoot out at Anacostia. Heard it did quite a number on some lightbulbs, too."

The men entered the control center conference room. Peter was standing at a lectern.

"Today marks a milestone in the development and testing of our newest unmanned aerial vehicle, designed and built by Aerotech," LaCroix began. "*Tiger* has some unique capabilities for surveillance that I think S-and-T might find useful. We'll start with highlights of a surveillance exercise conducted last evening in the Washington area. The intelligence is about as fresh as you can get without real time. Project manager Peter Wescott will walk us through."

"Thank you, Colonel." Peter clicked the remote and turned to the overhead. "Our UAV infiltrated the physical interior of Andrews Air Force Base to gather random intelligence. Let's begin."

The room lighting dimmed. The video opened with the UAV moving over the beltway and descending near the first set of runway lights.

"I'm afraid I need help with location and speed," Runyan asked out of the darkness.

Peter paused the tape and apologized. "I-95 at two hundred feet. Speed is thirty miles per hour."

"I understand you caused a ruckus at National the other evening."

Peter hesitated, thinking LaCroix would respond. He didn't. "I guess you could say we misjudged a few things along the Potomac. But now we know to avoid certain radar areas via more direct routes like the southern leg of the beltway."

"You know where National's surveillance radar is but not all configurations in the area," Runyan said pointedly.

"Yes, that's correct," Peter admitted, caught in the generalization and taken aback by the senior executive's technical knowledge. He restarted the tape. "This is the northern tip of Andrews's western run—"

"Congratulations, son. You just committed two felonies. Prohibited flight in a no-fly zone, and infiltrating a federal military installation."

Peter cleared his throat. "This next segment shows a covert approach to AFO."

"Approach to *what*?"

The tape paused again.

"We approached Air Force One on its flight apron to perform a simulat—"

"Gawd almighty!" Runyan blurted.

LaCroix touched the lights. "I warned you, Jim. You haven't seen anything. This UAV gets close enough to watch the president eat his peanut snack."

Runyan twirled his finger at Peter. The lights dimmed.

"We used the plane's tail shadow as cover to skate ... crawl into position approximately four inches off the runway. You'll notice that the marine guards posted along this line"—Peter pointed out the crescent-shaped coverage—"face away from the aircraft, leaving the other side somewhat vulnerable, so to speak."

"I'd call it devoid of all security," Runyan clarified.

"A fair observation. Next, we simulated placing an explosive onto—"

The deputy director cracked up. "Brent, what in hell is happening here. Is this real?"

"Think this toy might turn a few heads in that agency of yours?" LaCroix suggested.

Runyan leaned back in his chair, trying to evaluate what he was witnessing. He quickly concluded it was nothing short of pure innovation. Radical breakthrough. The kind that could open up a whole new era in covert surveillance. He started the rapid fire. "What's the operating height?"

"Eight thousand," Peter answered. "High-endurance testing comes next."

"Range?"

"Three hundred miles, one way."

"Vision?"

"Standard zoom is one mile. Our next upgrade will reach five."

Runyan's eyes locked with Peter's. "Latitude-longitude capability?"

"Ultra-wideband positioning."

Runyan closed his eyes. "Accuracy?"

"Three inch—"

"Son of a bitch!" Runyan rubbed his hands together like some evil scientist. The folks in the National Photographic Interpretation Center and Central Imaging might as well start looking for hurricane forecasting jobs. His mind raced with the potential. Silent, undetectable flying monitors that could record and relay precise real-time intelligence day or night, in all weather conditions. He was particularly impressed with the UAV's ability to move forward and look in multiple directions.

Peter made a mental note to thank Carl for editing out the slack time during his nature break. "Our mission concludes with a general tour of the base and some interesting angles of the Secret Service personnel. I won't bore you with details; you'll get your own copy."

The lights turned on.

"Senate or House Select Committee on Intelligence know about *Tiger*?" Runyan wondered.

"There's a whole new appropriations crowd up there, so we used preapproved DARPA funding for the development," LaCroix answered. It was his way of implying that he didn't have to beg twice.

Harris leaned into his boss's ear. "DSS did the clearances but had no direct exposure to the machine. Nobody else is involved."

Runyan took a pen from his pocket. "One more question . . . how much per unit with bulk discount?"

"One-point-five million," Peter answered.

Runyan shook his head in disgust but not at the cost. "We plan for months to do surveillance intel on targets one-tenth as tough and you pull it off in, what . . . three days? Ever heard of Rocky Mountain oysters?"

"I believe I know what they are," Peter conceded warily.

"Be advised that the folks in personal protection would hang yours on the White House flagpole if they ever saw that tape. What's next?"

"To be honest, Andrews convinced me we're ready for production and deployment," LaCroix said. "I couldn't think of any other target that would give us more challenge."

Runyan took a huge gulp of bottled water and winked at Peter. "I want you gentlemen at my ranch tomorrow evening, eight o'clock sharp. Plan on an all-nighter."

Chapter Nineteen

CIA
Directorate of Science and Technology

After passing several security checks, each requiring ID and metal inspection, Peter and LaCroix entered the fourth-floor office. Harris stood over a large worktable piled with documents and maps, including a four-by-four overhead photograph of the Washington no-fly zone. Runyan was sitting in an easy chair, munching a vending-machine sandwich.

A White House penetration didn't shock anyone; it was a perfect intelligence target. Now part of an elite inner circle, Peter no longer worried or cared about consequences. It had all become nothing more than a scorecard of successful versus failed tests. A government game that surveillance agencies played all the time, he thought.

278

Harris waved to empty chairs and straightened himself. He wanted to be clear on this.

"Gentlemen. The first thing you need to know is that we're not talking about some darkened military base searching for fighter counts. This is a heavily guarded and secured zone of vital national security. *Tiger* cannot be armed with any lethality whatsoever, which means your PTS system must be disabled and emptied of all rounds. Secondly, neither the president, vice president, nor any member of their families will be in the complex. This is an intelligence-collection mission with the principle objective of penetrating frontline external security and observing the general operation of the grounds. Just like watching a baseball game."

Runyan finished his meal. "If you're successful, I intend to make *UAV* a household word in the U.S. intelligence community—all thirteen agencies. Worldwide deployment. Sign me up for two hundred."

Peter casually tried to calculate the sales revenue and lost track of zeroes.

"That's a helluva chunk of change, Jim," LaCroix noted. He had estimated half that for DIA and was actually jealous.

"Nah . . . only a couple hundred million or so in Aerotech's pocket for starters. Peanuts. That's less than ten percent of what the IRS can't collect each year from tax deadbeats. Now ask me about eliminating seventy-five percent of our existing collection technologies—just in S-and-T. Agencywide savings the first five years alone could top two billion. And if your machine doesn't take a bullet or run out of gas"—Runyan reached behind his ear and produced a toothpick—"the cowpokes on Capitol Hill can multiply that by thirteen."

"*Tiger* has a memory module that guarantees a return flight home, or at least back to its last control center," Peter assured him. "Instructions are sealed in a quasi–flight recorder that's almost indestructible. Certainly from anything at the White House."

"That a fact?" Harris asked smugly. He looked at his boss. Runyan nodded once. "Ever heard of HTA?"

"Hunter-Targeting? Our test facility uses that same technology," LaCroix said.

"Theirs is HTA/RADS—an advanced Rapid Air Defense System with an active killer module on its roof to defend against low aircraft. Guaranteed stopping certainty within two miles."

"Killer module? Stopping certainty? An air-defense system right in the heart of Washington? What about private carriers and pilot error?" Peter felt his head start to throb. His mind flashed back to the Bear Den and the sensor locks. Detection there had cost time, pride, and dinner. He wished he were back on the farm.

"They've got procedures to deal with all forms of real and accidental air attack, including fail-safe confirmations. The system's never been used because no threat has ever been labeled as certain deadly peril—at least not yet. Flight ninety-three on nine-eleven would've been the first because the vice president was on-site."

"But . . . what about that Cessna that crashed on the south lawn?" Peter wondered. "How come he wasn't—"

"Either you boys aren't listening, or you are and just don't get it." Runyan lifted the no-fly zone map onto an easel. "It's not the structure; it's the occupants. Certain deadly peril—CDP—is a condition that applies only to top protectees. The president and vice president were never in danger because they weren't there. Neither were their families."

"Damn—I heard rumors about that," LaCroix said.

"Believe me, that pilot came within a whisper of a Talon handshake, but there was simply no need for that severe a response."

"Talon?" Peter guessed by the name that it was something pointed and unpleasant.

"A three-foot, radar-guided surface-to-air missile so goddamned fast it's scary. An advanced Stinger upgrade that can't be fooled by heat flares or other countermeasures. We've tested them ourselves, and when they lock—boom, it's over." Harris lowered his voice theatrically. "We need to bring you up to speed on something that absolutely stays in this room."

"Enough of the compartmentalized secrets," LaCroix said. "We've all got top clearances."

"All right, then see if you can figure it out." Harris stood. "The Secret Service needed to find a way to identify and stop low-flying light aircraft that somehow managed to avoid airport radar and approach the White House—an attack that would most likely come from the south. To counter that possibility, they tested and deployed a roof-based system. It worked fine during trials but still allowed a low-flying plane to get too close to the building before detection. It drove their security director crazy. He wanted to identify anything entering the Mall at its outer edges."

Peter framed the perimeter in his head. "Outer edges . . . okay, that means monuments. Lincoln, Capitol, and Jefferson. Not a real big surprise. The whole southerly approach is open to low penetration."

"Exactly," Harris confirmed. "They needed two things: better vision and better tracking. And the best place to achieve vision was from the—"

"I don't believe it," LaCroix said, stunned. "Phased? How have you managed to hide the arrays all these years, even from Defense?"

"We wrestled with bringing DIA in on the configuration," Runyan admitted. "But we concluded it'd be suicide to allow the UAV to fly blindly into a radar system powerful enough to spot a hovering helicopter ten feet above the ocean's surface three hundred miles away. Besides, *Tiger*'s clearance level eliminated most of the concern."

Peter's face had a confused look. LaCroix dragged him to the overhead and pointed at the only thing tall enough.

"The Washington Monument? But where? There's no radar dish or antenna—"

"Not on—in," Harris explained. "Remember when the public could walk all those steps just about anytime the thing was open for tours? Not anymore. Under the guise of a maintenance overhaul, the Secret Service covered the first two hundred feet of the exterior and replaced sections of the upper block with special radar-dead face tiles that look exactly like the original stone. The arrays are stationary and flat-faced. The pads are fitted behind. It's all about steering."

"Steering?" Peter asked.

"Most conventional ground-based radar systems can only track a limited number of targets based on concentric sweeping. They're notoriously slow to react to moving targets. Phased radar allows us to align all the array elements into a single beam—in phase—and train its energy at a single point. There are four arrays in the monument, each with fifty-one hundred elements, any pair of which may form a single beam. A split of fifty element groups can generate one hundred separate beams and track one hundred different targets. They have the ability to literally focus a beam on anything that moves in that Mall. Humans, animals, and especially aircraft send high-resolution images to the Secret Service."

"What about clutter? That's always presented problems for moving target detection."

"That's the real beauty. When a target stops and starts again or moves erratically, no resolution technique works very well—even the Mall's system. You just can't get an accurate lock. But think it through . . . what aerial threat moves erratically?"

Peter shook his head. "And no one has ever suspected?"

"Even the DC Rangers and park police are part of the coverup, if you will."

"How can all those sources be trusted?" LaCroix scoffed. "Somebody would—"

"Slip? About what?" Harris asked. "A phased-array radar system or telephone equipment?"

Now LaCroix was confused.

"See the point?" Harris smiled thinly. "After it reopened, local law enforcement was told that the monument contained sensitive digital carrier systems in the locked equipment rooms. Anytime the arrays needs legitimate maintenance, it's done under a classified communications work order. About the only flaw in the whole configuration is the fact that some of the exterior tiles have discolored on all four sides. Next time you're there, check out the bleeding at a hundred and sixty feet. They've already scheduled another face-lift."

"Good old acid rain," Peter observed.

Runyan activated a laser-light pen. "Let's get back to tactics. Are we all in agreement on the south lawn?"

"What are the alternatives?" Peter asked.

"We hoped you'd provide some input," Harris said. "Pennsylvania offers concealment, but the risk of detection is much greater based on the security force positions and public openness. There are too many unobstructed windows along the northern face and constant street activity in the evening hours, not to mention the hotels. The southern exposure is just the opposite."

"Exactly what kind of surveillance are we talking about?" Peter wondered how CIA managed to have all this information at their fingertips, and concluded that S-and-T had played with the White House before.

"We need to see house security movements that are not plainly visible to the public. Think of it as gathering intelligence from a foreign embassy harboring terrorists."

"Precisely," Runyan chimed in. "All you have to do is prove your UAV can get in there and it'll sell my case. I can feel it." He was betting *Tiger* was his ticket to the beginning of real change at Langley but didn't want to waste the next two years testing, evaluating, and debating senior agency or congressional bureaucrats. He didn't have time. After 9/11, the CIA needed a win—a credibility win. They had completely missed the mark on the fall of the Soviets. China and France were defying test bans, and no one with any sense trusted North Korea or Iran, not to deploy their weapons. He also realized the risk and consequences of failure but figured it would shake enough people up to recognize the need for dramatic action.

"So if the east and west directions have no room

to maneuver, that defaults to south. Any thoughts on how?"

Peter focused on the map. His eyes lit up like a beacon. "There's a path."

Harris frowned at what appeared to be an outright poor idea. "Paths won't work. There's too much human and electronic security—"

"Through the trees."

The men stared at it. A hidden flight path above the treetops from the Lincoln Memorial all the way up to the White House.

"Damn . . . this boy's good," Runyan remarked to LaCroix. "But wait—the UAV's a turbine machine? What about your exhaust? Wouldn't someone notice the—"

Peter shook his head. "Batteries and fan blades. Trust me. We know how to fly through trees."

"Some reach forty feet," Harris noted, concerned with the monument's downward-scanning ability.

"Never pick us out of the background."

Runyan took all this in, then turned to Peter. "Mr. Wescott, you've convinced me that this incursion plan of yours is a theoretical possibility. Can it physically be done?"

Peter didn't need to look at LaCroix. "Yes."

"Without detection?"

"Yes." Peter knew his neck was sticking out a mile, but the very soul of his machine was at stake.

Runyan smiled mischievously. "You get me a tape of this mission and I'll kiss your UAV's ass."

Peter tried to envision that event. Did *Tiger* even

have an ass? "What exactly is our risk here from a criminal perspective? We're not CIA and have no proof whatsoever of any approved intelligence-gathering operation from either you or Defense."

"Whoa, partner," Runyan said. "What do you expect, a written authorization?"

"Well, maybe that's not such a bad—"

"Out of the question. You have my word that this is legitimate. Brent will be at your place the night of the operation to take care of any problems. Remember, your team has already, shall we say, bent a few air rules around here—not to mention turning out the lights at Camden Yards."

Peter couldn't tell if that was a veiled threat or just a friendly reminder. Either way, he didn't like where the conversation was headed and dropped it.

He was quiet the whole ride back to his office. His head was spinning. He closed his eyes, trying to reconcile what he just agreed to. *Think about cows*, he told himself. *This'll all be over in a few days.*

DIA Center

"The White House and Andrews are both government facilities that just happen to make excellent targets for surveillance collection. Don't get hung up on the residence factor." Peter tried to conceal his uneasiness. He was never very good at it.

"That's such a lame comparison," CJ argued. "This residence is the home of the president of the United States. We can't just drop in and take some spy-cam pictures for the Internet. Lord knows what kind of security they've got."

"It's nothing we haven't seen before." Peter figured he had just won the prize for the year's biggest understatement.

"Are there any conditions?" Sam asked.

"Two," Peter answered. "No weapons on our part, and the place'll be empty."

"The president won't be on the premises?" Sam clarified.

"Uh-huh. White House security has done this before to self-test their defenses. Both D-one and CIA will be observing. We'll be fine. There's one more thing." Peter took a deep breath.

"They've got a system in there to counter air threat. A hunter module with offensive capability. So we can't afford to bump into any kittycats. If they lock us, we can't light a firecracker and fly away."

Sam shifted in his chair after hearing the details. "You are telling me that the president's home— where he hosts parties and galas, plays games with his son, and entertains a multitude of rum-dum tourists every day—has a rocket launcher hidden on its rooftop?"

"One on each wing," Peter confirmed. "It's not unlike the Den's, only it can bite back hard for one mile. I'm afraid they also have a couple of strategically positioned radar units in the area."

After briefing his team on the information he had

learned about the Mall defenses, Peter spread out a contour map of the entrance.

"The road to the White House is paved in green . . . treetop green."

"What's our contingency plan for a hard detection?" CJ asked.

"We migrate south. CIA can deal with the rest. If it happens, I guarantee we'll be packing for the Nicolet. And screw DIA. It'll have gone way beyond that. The odds of a clean northern escape are practically zero. There's traffic and pedestrians out at all hours of the night on that stretch. We'd be spotted by a ton of witnesses."

"Is the cub in play?"

"No. This isn't about offense. Pictures only. We keep it locked down inside the fence. If we left anything on the grounds, it'd be a disaster."

Sam smiled at his boss. "Migrate south, huh? People say the Farsi language is confusing."

"What do you mean?"

"You don't believe their arsenal will attack us."

Peter nodded once. He figured he didn't have to tell them that no protectees on the premises meant no RADS retaliation. "That's what I'm betting."

National Mall

Peter and Sam left the Suburban near the Lincoln Memorial and started a walking tour of the Mall an hour before dark. They immediately came to the same conclusion: the entrance seemed too easy. The thick treetops formed a path up the northern edge of the reflecting pool all the way to the center of the Mall. The first open exposure would come at Constitution Avenue on the western edge of the Ellipse, the next from jumping across E Street into the White House tree line. Standing outside the south lawn fence, they noticed a distinct lack of human patrols and nothing suspicious about the rooftop. From ground level, the structures looked like routine HVAC housings.

Peter pressed his face between the iron fence bars as had so many awestruck tourists. "Seems like you could walk right in with no problem."

Sam focused a camera's telephoto lens on the roofline. "You probably could—for a few seconds. The radar is on the left. The face is too clean to be part of the building."

Peter lifted his binoculars. "That the antenna behind it?"

"Yes," Sam whispered, although there was no reason to.

Peter's eyes swept the lawn's perimeter and spotted several dark gray cabinets concealed in the foliage. "Monitors. Think any of those are tree-mounted?"

"Possible. For all the energy spent developing heat and sound alarms, a lowly motion sensor is still the most reliable detector. But we still have an advantage."

"Reassure me."

"If we move with the foliage, the motion sensors

are ineffective. They have no way to separate us from a swaying branch. Our vulnerability comes from open exposures between trees. That's a problem."

"You think we should fly near the ground?" Peter asked incredulously.

"No—too many cameras. And in this area, if security sees something suspicious, a rather unfriendly crowd will converge on the area. I prefer to remain in the air and take our chances accelerating from one position of safety to another."

"If we do set off a tree sensor, who says we're not just a bird?" Peter speculated. "That must happen all the time."

Sam nodded. "I wager there's a vigilant security staff monitoring this network. If a single sensor activates and nothing else, the intruder is feathered. But if it's consecutive sensors along a defined route, hell will break loose. That's a basic operative for this complex and a sure way to separate birds from UAVs, no?"

The logic was fascinating—almost as though Sam had somehow gone over this plan before, Peter thought. "So it still doesn't get us off the hook?"

"You want my honest opinion?"

Peter turned to his flight specialist. "I want the answer."

"This White House appears to have a distinct passion for optical and motion-based defenses, which place extreme demands on humans. Think what multiple UAVs approaching from multiple directions would do."

"Data overload and panic."

"Yes—and such a panic would be a major victory."

Peter frowned. "A victory for who? What kind of victory?"

"Inducing a reaction."

"I'm not following you," Peter admitted, frustrated at his tactical ignorance.

Sam mumbled something in Farsi. "Tell me how Israel, if they could detect it at all, would react to a large UAV like *Predator* crossing into their airspace?"

Peter thought for a moment. "If the signature were large enough they'd send a Pat-three or Arrow missile to knock it down."

Sam smiled. "How would they react to a micro-UAV carrying a present?"

Peter thought for a moment, then threw up his hands. "The same?"

"Precisely—a victory for the aggressor in two ways."

"Wait—that's the part I'm missing," Peter admitted. "Why is that a victory?"

"First, the economics. Compare the cost of fifty expensive missiles to fifty inexpensive drones, then think about the most overlooked advantage of unmanned flight."

Peter shook his head. "I have a fair amount of education, but I'm lost."

"Diversion," Sam said seductively. "A deadly tactic, and those who master it will always predict an enemy's response—a tremendous opportunity to hide true purpose."

It clicked. "Gottcha . . . White House security runs in circles on the ground while you spy on the Capitol from two hundred feet in the air."

Sam started back.

"Wait—bring this into perspective. What's it mean to us?"

"Well, as I see it, this complex is either well defended by the most elaborate and hidden mechanisms technology can devise, or it's vulnerable to UAV penetration and surveillance."

Peter paused in the middle of the sidewalk. Determined, he turned back to the south lawn fence and continued to study the grounds. Twenty minutes later he caught up.

Sam was leaning against the Suburban. He took a drag off a cigarette. "The Washington Monument is beautiful at night. Those spotlights make it look like some ancient god."

"I need to know," Peter said.

Sam exhaled a smoke ring that encircled the obelisk. "They are vulnerable."

Peter drove the Suburban north off Constitution Avenue for one more look at the White House perimeter.

"Isn't that the hotel you want to rip off?" Sam asked innocently. Peter cut a corner too closely and bumped the curb. "CJ mentioned a painting of cows that helps you sleep."

"I can't seem to convince them to sell it," Peter admitted sheepishly. "They won't even negotiate."

Sam smiled and reclined his seat. "You're the one who needs a diversion. Take the damn thing and replace it with another painting. Housekeeping, guests, maintenance workers come and go all the time. No one would notice for weeks. By the time it's discovered, you're far away."

"I'm just not that daring. Besides, it'd be a problem for my conscience."

"I'll get your cows for you," Sam promised. "And don't worry if you don't understand Middle Eastern engagements. Iranian strategy is a little different. Sorry if I confused you. The Pat-three radar system should provide enough fire-control data to identify the size of the intruder and use patrol aircraft with spray weaponry—and never panic at the diversion. Unfortunately, most Americans can't understand the principles and invariably, shall I say, fall for the ploy. See you upstairs."

Peter decided to walk down to the Potomac's shoreline and watch the approaches at National. He wondered what kind of diversion could put cows into a briefcase.

Chapter Twenty

DIA Center

LaCroix hung up the phone. "Intelligence says there are no protests, marches, or mass sleep-ins happening in the Mall tonight. The usual number of street people, but DSS has been rousting them away from the flight path. Other than a late thunderstorm, wind should be ten to thirty by early morning."

"Wind is good," Peter said. "Do you really think we can run an operation like this and conceal it? Why would the CIA take such a risk?"

Harris entered the room and overheard the remark. "I'll tell you why. Runyan. There've been rumors about a radical faction intent on changing the perception of the whole agency—including people and their abilities. The younger workers view Runyan as the leader of that faction. Employees in virtually every department are buying into his philosophy and vision of change. This certainly would be a catalyst. Where can I go to stay out of trouble?"

Peter pointed to empty chairs in the back of the room with a clear view of the overhead screen. "All right, people—listen up. Things could get a little dicey tonight. Hopefully this will be our last test flight together under these rather stressful circumstances. To be honest, I'll miss the teamwork but not the pressure, so let's do it right, okay? I need to get back to the farm."

Sam clicked the commands that started the *Tiger*'s motor. The UAV floated off its maintenance pedestal through the balcony doors and gently lowered to the ground. As it crossed the Potomac's shoreline, the machine's airflow and movement formed a triangular wave as it glided over the calm water toward a steel railroad bridge, the first of four structures it would pass under.

Monitoring river traffic for alcohol violators, DC Police Harbor Patrol boat fourteen was wedged between the wooden pilings of the George Mason Bridge near the west shoreline.

Officer Tommy Deal untied the mooring ropes and started the ignition in the twenty-foot gray runabout. "Let's try downriver. I saw five pontoon boats headed to Jarhead Jerry's sandbar. We might as well check it out. Are you done?"

"In a minute," Officer Sharita Marks replied. She

lifted her binoculars and gave the river one more lazy scan to the south. Along the eastern shoreline, a lone mercury bulb cast just enough light over the water to expose a soft, rippled wake. She followed it to the source. "Shut off those engines."

"What is it . . . a Jet Ski?" Deal asked.

"Not sure. Something on the surface . . . port side . . . about a hundred yards. Damn, I lost it. . . . No, wait—there it is!" She stiffened her legs as her body rotated to the left.

Deal tried to judge her line of sight and swept his glasses back and forth. "I need a reference point. Where will it be in twenty seconds?"

"Far right side of the Arlington."

Deal groped blindly for the ignition key, trying to keep his vision focused. Fighting the urge to scan south, he fixed a bearing on the stone bison's face in the center of the bridge's arch and waited. It was probably a seagull gliding close to the surface, and he tried to think up some catchy bird phrase that rhymed with *Sharita*. His discipline paid off as the object came into view with help from the overhead streetlights. "I'll be damned . . . that ain't no bird."

"It stopped," Marks said without lowering her glasses. "Underneath the bridge."

Sam raised the UAV up to the cement ceiling and panned the western steps of the Lincoln Memorial.

"Damn—I didn't want all that light," Peter said. "We need to cross that somehow. How's our tail?"

Carl opened the rear omniview. Locked in a battle with summer allergies, he dried his watery eyes and pronounced everything clear.

Emerging from underneath the bridge arch, the UAV accelerated over the riverbank and up the memorial's steps. It disappeared behind the north face.

"Holy Jesus!" Deal shouted. "Did you see that?"

"I'm not sure what I saw." Marks finally sat down. "And don't give me any bird talk. We both know it wasn't—unless they don't have to flap wings anymore."

Deal reached for the marine radio. "Dispatch—this is fourteen . . . over."

"Fourteen—go ahead," a female voice crackled.

"We're at the Arlington. Um . . . we've got a small . . . um . . . unidentified flying thing that—"

"Fourteen—say again."

"We saw something flying on the river . . . I mean above the river . . . without flapping its wings. It didn't have real wings, because we don't think it was an animal. It just sort of moved on top of the water, then flew up to the Lincoln Memor—"

"So it's a flying fish, huh? Or maybe a mermaid. Did she throw you a kiss, too?" said the male voice of Lieutenant Miles, the shift supervisor. There was raucous laughter in the background. "You and Sharita got a bottle out there?"

"I wish," Deal answered without depressing the transmit button.

Marks grabbed the squawker. "Lieutenant, we both saw something glide, fly, skim—whatever you want to call it—over the river. I haven't had a drop and neither has Tommy. Do you copy? The thing didn't touch the water."

Miles told the others to quiet down. "Okay—now *you* copy. If you want land backup, say the word. Otherwise, write it up while it's fresh and I'll give it to watch command. Carry on—out." He figured that his officers had seen something unusual, but he couldn't raise it to any priority higher than ticketing some misguided pelican. Alerting the U.S. Secret Service was the farthest thing from his mind.

The UAV reached the first line of Mall treetops. A tight mass of thermal signatures appeared near the middle of the Vietnam memorial.

"We've got heat and sound to the northeast," Carl reported. "I think I hear . . . singing."

"Confirm that. I hear it, too." Sam cocked his head at the lyrics. "Who's Kevin?"

"Huh?" CJ turned to Carl. "What's he talking about?"

"Don't ask. He's mumbling again."

Sam heard the insult and removed his headphones. "I'm just asking a question. My hearing is fine. Kevin. Knocking on Kevin's door. Who is Kevin?"

"*Heaven*, you jackass. Even I know that," Carl said.

The UAV continued east at three mph. Its fanblade airflow created movement in the branches but blended in with the increase in prestorm wind. At the center of the Mall, Sam banked north with the natural pattern of the foliage toward the Ellipse along Seventeenth Street. Using the Organization of American States Building as a guide, the *Tiger* crossed Constitution Avenue at a point that kept a row of trees between its tail and the obelisk. With a short burst of speed, it glided across E Street and into the western tree line of the White House complex.

Oakton

"No—go lie down," Turner ordered from under his pillow.

Prayerlike, Tress lifted both paws to the bed and whimpered.

Turner tossed off his sheet. He couldn't sleep anyway for thinking about Camden Yards. He slid open the patio door. The dog scampered outside.

Turner picked up the remote and clicked the TV from all the way across the living room. The news came on. *Where would people be without these damn little black boxes?* he mused. *Somebody should invent one that opens a door so a dog can go outside by itself. Or how about an automatic poop scooper or lawn mower?* He shook his head. *They already have those. Jesus, how lazy can people get? Sit in a lawn chair with a martini and operate a machine clear across the yard by remote* control. *Remote control!*

The Internet high-speed on-line search drew 88,600 hits.

Turner scrolled through the Web site information on remote-control machines until his printer ran out of paper. Most were aircraft.

White House Complex

Joe Grant couldn't explain the strange feeling he had that his shift would see action. Summer storms were a welcome break from the heat but tended to trigger street violence. Extended calm only meant something was ready to bust. There hadn't been a murder in the District in three nights—the longest streak in years. He had a full shift of internal-sector patrols, but was short two officers assigned to the Mall.

"I'm losing audio clarity," Carl warned. "You're too close to the treetops."

"Do you want to fly?" Sam snapped back. "If not, then tell me where I should be."

"Anywhere but scraping the underbelly on branches. We've got company sixty yards northeast, but I can't focus and I can't hear." Carl increased the omniview zoom that showed a K-9 handler and his dog posted near the portico stairs. The Belgian was staring directly at the lens.

"That's all we need." Peter groaned. "Tell me the second they move."

Sam raised the *Tiger* one foot higher in the treetops and continued forward movement all the way up to the famous magnolia Andrew Jackson had planted in the early 1800s. He settled into a comfortable loiter thirty feet from the White House, with an unobstructed view of the west wing and the Rose Garden. To the east, audio picked up clicking toenails.

"Stop!" Carl cried out. "We've lost everything. I'm not detecting any sensors. Our link must be down."

"*Carl!*" Peter said sharply. "Did you verify?"

"It'll take a few minutes to run the diagnostic."

"Then do it, for God's sake, and lower your voice. You scared the hell out of me."

Sam raised the UAV even higher above the top branches. The current zoom setting made the building's exterior seem just inches away. He downgraded it while they waited.

"You won't believe this, but everything's working," Carl announced. "There are no sensors. They must have turned them off for the dogs."

Light appeared in a third-story window. A dresser and bed were visible through the curtains.

"Who would be up at this hour?" CJ wondered.

Peter glared at Harris. "It had better be security. Everyone else is supposed to be gone."

CJ bolted upright in her chair. "It's the first lady!"

The woman bent over her son and placed a hand on his forehead.

"We've got a situation here," Peter shouted to the back of the room.

LaCroix conferred with Harris before responding. "The intelligence was short. Continue the operation. It's going fine."

"Short my ass," Peter swore under his breath.

Sweating profusely, Sam was having difficulty maintaining a firm grip on the joystick. He reached for a towel.

"Cover! She's looking!" CJ shouted loudly enough to be heard through the control center's floor. The woman was trying to open the window, prevented from seeing the UAV only by her own reflection. Sam quickly probed *Tiger* downward between the foliage to get out of direct view.

There was a distant rumble of thunder. Satisfied it would be another quiet night, Grant decided to thin the dog patrols for the rest of the shift. In the SCC, Linda Janis touched three switches and reactivated all motion, pressure, and optical sensors across the complex. The magnolia tree was immediately crisscrossed with thin red lines.

Tiger cut one in half.

Sensing a tickle, Carl drew a tissue to his nose. Four seconds passed before his eyes refocused on his monitor. He registered the scene with a terrific blast. "*O, mein Gott!* Sensors! They're everywhere. Do you hear me? You broke light! Get out. Peter! Tell him to get out!"

Sam was frozen in position like some helpless deer that had just been shined.

Carl scrambled around his station and lunged for the joystick. The thermal display screen showed multiple heat signatures approaching the area.

Peter reached the flight station and pushed Carl aside. He grabbed Sam squarely by the shoulders.

"Get us out of this jungle and into free space!"

The UAV continued downward, bumping its wings against the tree limbs.

Sam twisted the joystick and finally managed to push through to the middle of the circular drive. The movement set off an IDU hidden near the portico.

"Give me rpms!" Peter screamed at CJ.

She dragged the rotation speed bar to seventeen thousand.

I-sector officers rounded the corner of the building. Floodlights illuminated the complex.

Peter wheeled toward Sam once more. *"Now!"*

The system responded at once.

Within three seconds, *Tiger* reached thirty mph and launched skyward at a forty-five degree angle over the south lawn.

The moment it cleared the E Street fence, the western-rooftop RADS-battery doors flew open on an aerial target lock. Four hinged sides of a small, unassuming white closet collapsed as hydraulic lifters pushed eight pug-nosed Talon rockets into view, angling the group toward the UAV's calculated flight trajectory.

The scene looked like a mini–nuclear launch sequence from some silo in Nebraska.

White House SCC

A wild scramble ensued as the HTA killer module alarm gave out a loud two-tone clang that signaled an airborne threat. Janis flew to the RADS radar station where the red light of a CERTAIN DEADLY PERIL warning message flashed, begging for confirmation. She raised her right arm at the intruder's image, knowing that whatever was outbound in the Washington night sky was about to make history—guaranteed.

She spoke a single word, took another second to confirm, and pounded her fist down onto the console.

With flawless execution, she hit the "No-kill" release that canceled the RADS alert and retracted the launcher.

On the roof, the hinged doors immediately rose back up, clamped tightly together, and reformed into a harmless four-sided air-conditioning unit.

The climb angle put *Tiger* into the center of the Mall in twenty-eight seconds. Speed at the Potomac reached ninety mph. Janis continued to watch the luckiest target on earth—whatever it was—cross the western RADS boundary and disappear off her scope.

Oakton

Aerial short-threat penetration.

Turner jumped up from his computer. "Where?" he demanded.

"South portico," Grant's voice answered. "We think he was in the trees."

Turner had one leg in his trousers and slipped

on papers trying to talk while stuffing the other leg in. "Trees? A climber? I thought you said short—"

Grant interrupted. "No, sir. A flyer. . . . John? Hello?"

Turner was already out the door redialing his cell phone for a Virginia State Patrol escort on I-66.

The sixteen-mile hop took nine minutes.

DIA Center

Peter judged that White House security wouldn't have time to make an informed decision about the penetration if the UAV had to make a rapid exit. His calculated gamble-guess was right, but for the wrong reasons. With Secret Service protectees on-premises, all decision making on what was or was not certain deadly peril came down to one of three training words: sidebound, outbound, and inbound. As with sidebound, the one Janis spoke tonight identified an airborne intruder considered incapable of threat. If the UAV had been traveling toward the White House, she would have spoken "Inbound" and hit the "Kill" release on her console. The execution was flawless, and in this case, just saved thirty million dollars and more than a few careers.

Peter stared through the glass doors on the flight balcony, somehow trying to hurry the UAV home. "You have my word this is a legitimate operation," he said to his reflection. His eyes passed through the image and out into the Washington sky. "James

Runyan, you need to stop this before things get any uglier, if that's possible."

"He won't," CJ spoke up. "You watch. They'll cut this whole project loose. We'll have to ride it out."

Peter turned to confront Harris with that suggestion, but noticed that both he and LaCroix had left the facility without saying a word to anyone. "Ride it out? By morning there'll be a new word in America's vocabulary. Can you spell *Tigergate*?"

"She's here . . . get the doors," Sam interrupted. "There's no way this will ever get out to the media. The Secret Service has no choice but to keep it quiet. I suggest we shut things down for now. Let DIA handle any damage control."

Peter was beginning to understand why people didn't give a damn about consequences. They just didn't have as much to lose. Earlier, he thought he had seen LaCroix and Harris actually congratulating each other on the penetration. He knew it was time to stop.

"Okay, that's *exactly* what we're going to do. I want this place closed down immediately," Peter ordered. He turned out one set of lights.

"I'll lock up," Carl offered. "It'll only take me a few—"

Peter rapped his knuckles on a table. "I said out. Nobody, but *nobody* works in here anymore. Tomorrow as well. Aerotech doesn't exist, this project doesn't exist, and you don't exist. Effective immediately, you're all tourists here to enjoy the sights.

Do what they do. Take in the zoo or rent a Wave Runner on the Potomac. Planes at National land twenty feet over your head. Just get out. Low profiles and keep your mouths shut." The room went silent. He turned to Sam. "No speeding tickets."

The control room had been dark for nearly two hours when the lock on the door clicked open. The timing carried a huge advantage: the White House had detected the UAV closer to the ground than in the trees. With all the human movement, sensors would be disabled. It was a perfect time to return.

Potomac River

Officer Marks secured the docking rope to a shore-line anchor post while her partner walked up to the Lincoln Memorial's rear steps, attempting to retrace the object's path from memory.

The UAV nearly stumbled into them and had to alter its course to the south face. Hovering below the southwestern corner of the monument's roof, the craft angled its nose down toward the river.

The first ceron round hit Marks's left shoulder, spinning her into the port rail. The second hit her right shoulder, rendering both arms useless. She plopped into the water, kicking frantically to stay afloat.

Officer Deal heard the gurgling screams between breaths and flew down the steps headlong into the river. Reaching his partner with one arm and the boat's side-step handles with the other, he pushed her body onto the rear deck. Arms limp at her sides, she slipped into shock.

Scope lines found a target point on the back of Deal's head, but faded off the omniview as the PTS subsystem closed.

The UAV turned east for the Mall tree line.

White House South Portico

The first lady sat on a marble bench outside on the portico wearing only a bathrobe. She had ordered her complement of PPD agents to stand fast inside the diplomatic room so she could finish a private conversation. They threatened to invoke overriding protection authority, but relented after hearing whom she was arguing with.

"My son needs rest and I will not listen to any more talk about moving him out of his own room in his own home," she said angrily. "What kind of security do you call this, John? I expect you to capture and punish anyone who trespasses on this property."

"Ma'am, I know he's not feeling well, but you don't understand. Something's out there that can fly just about anywhere it wants. It was spotted on the premises near this very balcony. For all we know there might even be more than one. You have to vacate—now. You shouldn't even be sitting—"

"Stop ordering me!" she said on a sob.

Turner knew when to back off and figured Evans

could deal with it later. "Very well, ma'am. But you need to under—"

"No—you need to understand that we have private lives, too. Do your job so we can live in peace like normal citizens."

Listless and still burning up, Aaron pushed open the large French doors and shuffled toward his mother. She cradled his head. Turner started down the portico steps.

The PTS crosshairs found a target point and locked on his temple. The trigger clicked but nothing happened. The load sequence had never initiated. The menus came up.

Turner's eyes moved over the spot where the intruder had tripped the light sensor. He looked the magnolia up and down, turned away, then felt it again. Something was there. A soft waving of the top branches. His forest grouse. He reached for his radio.

The *Tiger*'s audio picked up the code word. *How predictable.*

With the first family safely inside, Turner and attending PPD charged off the portico. Seconds later, Grant and twelve uniformed officers reached the position and surrounded the tree. Nothing.

"John!" Grant pointed to the south. One by one, the four majestic spotlights and each bank of base lighting units encircling the Washington Monument were mysteriously being snuffed out, turning the center of the Mall black. "It's him. It's our sniper."

Turner clenched his teeth but couldn't stop his body from shivering. The sporadic blinking of the monument's beacons spoke to him. Crosshairs centered on his right eye.

The range from the top of the obelisk measured thirty-five hundred feet, so the aim would have to compensate for distance drop. The ceron would enter his skull and shatter into burning fragments, but such marksmanship would only confirm presence and ability.

Not clean.

The UAV dived down the western face of the monument. A homeless trio saw the exhaust wave lines in the reflecting pool and stumbled into the water in a hapless attempt to catch the object. *Tiger* arched high over the Lincoln's roof and feigned traveling upriver before dropping down to the waterline and reversing course—south to the DIA Center—skimming low to avoid National's surveillance radar. There was no need to reset the battery fuel timer to hide the unauthorized flight. Procedures no longer mattered, only the mission.

The monument's western phased array lost the UAV, but Janis had its track on tape.

"Where'd it go?" Turner radioed.

"North," she replied.

Chapter Twenty-one

"It's definitely being operated remotely, but if there's a terror angle, tell me why and by whom?" Turner ranted to his shift supervisors. "Some Unabomber pilot sitting in his basement? I don't buy it. We know he's fast, can see and hear, and maneuvers in and out of tight places. It's like we're chasing a flying robot. That's all we need is some avenging game bird that shoots back. I can see it already: 'Secret Service helpless as president killed by remote-control turkey.'"

"Has anyone else tracked this thing besides us?" Bristol asked. "What about the local traffic centers?"

Grant shook his head. "With all the commotion, nobody's actually seen it."

"Doesn't surprise me. There's no way the air-ports could spot something that small unless he flew through the wrong . . ." Turner's voice trailed off.

"Damn, John—thank God he had no way of knowing the president extended one more day. He likes to sit outside before a storm."

"Don't even think that. The whole country would be in panic right now. Jack's already there."

"Maybe one of the civilian agencies got a pic-ture?" Bristol wondered.

"It doesn't make sense," Grant said, frustrated. "If it is the Camden Yards shooter, why let the world see your capability? Terrorists never act that way."

Turner's face lit up. "What did you say?"

"I said terrorists never act—"

"Not you." Turner turned to Bristol. "What did you say before about pictures?"

Bristol straightened. "I just wondered if some other radar in the area might have picked him up. You know, some strange pictures or images that no one could expl—"

"You scientist son of a bitch!" Turner shouted.

"Who me?"

Turner never answered. He raced across the room for his directory and punched up a number. He'd bet somebody was working late.

Harris picked up on the first ring.

"Get your ass over here," Turner ordered. "I know about your remote-control flying sniper."

DIA *Center*

Peter arrived at his office the next day exhausted from a three-hour walking tour of the National Air and Space Museum. His feet felt like molten lava. He sprawled out in a chair and kicked off his shoes. His phone buzzed.

"Hi, it's me," CJ's voice said. "I'm almost afraid to ask, but has anybody said anything? Did we make the newspapers?"

"Not a peep. And to tell you the truth, I really don't care. LaCroix said he'd handle the repercussions . . . so be it. I'm not going to worry. Where are you?"

"A mall in Tyson's Corners. This place is huge. Where's everyone else?"

Peter glanced at the control center door. His CLOSED UNTIL FURTHER NOTICE sign was still there. "You tell me. I just got in."

"Carl said something about that engraving tour where they print money. I called him a nerd. I think he's ticked."

Peter chuckled.

"Sam's out on his motorcycle, where else? Are we allowed back in the building?"

Peter yawned. "Uh-huh, but don't rush. I'm beat. Think I'll take a nap. Let's plan on reviewing the video in an hour or so."

"We were all pretty upset last night," CJ admitted. "I'll bet no one set up the charger. It was Ricky's job. You hear anything from him?"

"Not a word. I've left messages, but he's probably got a lot to handle with the arrangements and all. I'll take care of the battery. See you in a bit."

Peter walked into the control center and flipped on the lights. What he saw looked like a blast zone. Every PC screen and drive was smashed. The electronics and circuit board faceplates were stripped off and the wiring was torn out. The overhead projection screen dangled in pieces. Peter unconsciously reached for a phone but couldn't remember a single number to dial, or why he had even picked it up in the first place. His eyes turned to the maintenance pedestal. The *Tiger* was gone.

"Peter?" LaCroix shouted from the doorway. Floring was with him. "Who besides your team had access?"

Unresponsive, Peter knelt on the floor, trying to reassemble pieces of the flight station joystick.

"Do not touch anything," Floring ordered. "We need to sterilize the area."

LaCroix heard the elevator and raised his hand.

Carl appeared in the doorway. "What the hell!"

"Where are they?" LaCroix asked sternly.

"Who?"

"Your coworkers."

"I . . . I don't know," Carl stammered. "CJ and I split hours ago. I don't know anything."

"But you were with her?" LaCroix questioned.

Carl nodded. "I didn't want to spend all day shopping, so I—"

"All right, that's enough." LaCroix dialed Bolling's main security. "This is Colonel LaCroix at the DIA Center. We've had a level-one breach . . . seventh floor. I want an alert. Do you have an exit record of Sam Nasrabadi? No, he's a contractor."

A piercing, intermittent alarm filled the building.

The elevator chimed again. Brent Harris approached with a stranger.

"Very well, keep me posted." LaCroix replaced the handset. "They're backtracking through the gate records now. Who the hell are you?"

"Someone who's gonna send your ass to jail," Turner snapped savagely.

"What? Now you hold on, fella. Do you know who you're talk—"

Turner wanted to clock him but kicked a chair across the room instead. "Shut your mouth before I do. I don't care if you're General fucking Patton. You and your people have broken every federal law on the books: mayhem, damage to property, reckless endangerment, military espionage, and a shitload of aviation felonies—not to mention conspiracy to assassinate a U.S. president! Jesus—you're all wacko! Whoever convinced you to do all this? I thought the days of Hitler's SS were gone. I'll put every one of you away for fifty years."

Peter lifted his head. "Sir, calm down. We're independent contractors from Wisconsin working under special surveillance authority of the Patriot Act."

LaCroix closed his eyes.

"Wisconsin? The what?" Turner asked incredulously. "You should have stayed there, you dumb shoeless farmer. Get up off your ass."

Sergeant Malcolm and a squad of armed MPs entered the control center. "Colonel, sir? Your mobile command vehicle exited the base at fourteen hundred."

"It's got to be him," LaCroix ventured.

Malcolm nodded a little. He didn't think it necessary to mention that one of his men thought the driver had a ponytail.

Peter rose to his feet and lifted a phone. Turner snatched it away and dialed a Secret Service access line on board Air Force One.

"Jack—it's an Iranian male. He's mobile and headed your way. Better go to short-threat. There are people here who can brief us on the machine, but I'd rather run it from the complex. From what I've heard, you've got to convince the president to avoid Andrews. It's suicide."

"What is going on here?" Peter shouted. "I have a right to know."

Turner covered the mouthpiece. "I'll get to your rights in a minute. Your flight specialist shot a Metro police officer last night before returning to the White House to kill the president. You're goddamned lucky he decided to delay an extra day or we'd all be taking orders from the VP. Can Nasrabadi operate this assassination machine from that mobile unit all by himself?" No one responded. They could hear Evans screaming on the line. Turner pounded his fist into the wall. "Answer me!"

"From a hundred miles away," Peter said in a squeak.

Turner digested that for a moment. "Oh, that's just friggin' great. Jack? He can do it alone . . . from anywhere he damn well wants."

"Is there anything we can do?" Peter asked.

Turner slammed the phone. "Okay, Shoeless Joe . . . I want you at the White House. The rest of you stay here and keep this line open. We'll need to know what we're up against if we expect to stop this crazy bastard."

Carl started sifting through the damaged equipment, figuring he might be able to rig a parallel controller feed from what was left of the wideband receiver. It might give them a location bearing.

Peter collected his shoes and glanced at the time. It wasn't like CJ to be this late. She hated to shop.

White House Command Center

In just thirteen minutes, contingents of DC law enforcement and military units had mobilized in the surrounding counties and issued a combination APB/shoot-to-kill alert to locate and stop a presidential assassination set to occur on the Andrews approach in less than two hours. Having previously vowed publicly to the nation never to run from terror, the president refused to reroute. Evans placed the District on Platinum alert status, and grounded air traffic within a hundred-mile radius so TRACON, Washington Monument, and White House radar sweeps could reach their highest sensitivities. Turner tried to explain the UAV's operational capabilities to his officers, but needed Peter to lend credence to the speed, lethality, and silence they found so hard to believe. Metro police sealed off a ten-block perimeter as patrols swarmed through the surrounding neighborhoods for the MCS. Turner ordered the SCC to engage any airborne target. Evans made the obvious decision—if they ever got the president on the ground at Andrews—that helicopter transport to the White House was out of the question. Although the actual flying time to the south lawn lasted just under seven minutes, the potential for UAV collision into the chopper's titanium blades was too great.

Air force and naval security personnel formed human skirmish lines combing the runways at Andrews within two hundred yards of the plane's approach. Evans posted CSU sharpshooters in double pairs on top of structures on both sides of the airfield. They were covered in Kevlar and stood back-to-back with night-vision equipment. If they could just get the president into his limousine, only an armor-piercing tank shell could penetrate that. After learning the UAV's speed, acceleration, and maximum altitude, Evans was certain Sam would try to strike from the air by vectoring to the 747's rather lazy approach and exploit a number of vulnerable positions.

Metro police detained Peter's Suburban on Twelfth Street until Turner personally radioed clearance into White House reserved parking. Uniformed officers ushered him into a briefing room hastily set up in the west wing near the press office. Bristol had arranged a three-way communications link with Andrews and AFO.

"What are *Tiger*'s weaknesses?" Evans's voice asked.

Peter struggled to find one. "It's not something from *Star Wars*, but it was designed specifically for stealthy approach. It does release a small infrared signature, but we . . . er . . . Sam knows that, too."

"What else?"

The word came to him. "Surveillance—it's susceptible to surveillance radar. That's how National detected one of our test flights. Of course, it can't compare with what you have in the Mall."

The inhabitants in the room collectively stiffened. Turner rose off his chair. "What did you say?"

Peter swallowed hard. "Um, Brent Harris gave us a little insight."

"That motherless son of a . . . I'm gonna personally beat the living—"

"John, do you mind if we deal with our slight emergency up here?" Evans sang out from the speaker.

"Mr. Wescott . . . if you were flying the machine, what would you do?" another voice spoke up from Andrews.

Peter paused for a moment, considering how to professionally express destroying the leader of the free world. He was too tired for eloquence and simply blurted his thoughts. "I'd do one of two things: ram the exposed hydraulics or intakes causing massive power loss; or pace the aircraft and lock the cub onto the exterior . . . preferably something in the rear. Either way, it's good-bye, Mr. President."

There was muffled conversation in the speaker's background. "Cub? Lock onto the exterior? What's that mean, sir?"

"I wonder what kind of woman she was," Peter mused to himself. "Anybody here know Margaret Reudi?" Conversation around the table abruptly stopped.

"Who?" Turner asked.

"She was an artist. She painted beautiful Holsteins. Did I ever tell you that cows affect me like sleeping pills? I need to look at cows to get a good night's sleep. There's one of her paintings at the Hay-Adams. I don't know why, but they absolutely refuse to part with it. I'm certainly not a thief but I'd give my right arm to—"

"Peter, stay with us here," Turner pleaded. "I'll buy you a hundred cow paintings, but we don't have time for this. What is a cub?"

Peter yawned deeply and perked up with the inflow of new oxygen. "*Tiger*'s got great eyesight for wide-sweep identification. It can sit undetected and scan the ground or sky in multiple directions. The cub is a secondary independent drone that can carry an explosive charge. It can literally stick to a target and detonate remotely."

"He's got to fucking divert, Jack!" Grant shouted

into the speakerphone. It was obvious their decision to halt air traffic had done nothing but give the UAV a clear line of attack.

"It ain't gonna happen—dammit. The president won't consider it. He will not run the country from a position of fear, or something like that," Evans answered, disgusted at the man's political stubbornness.

Peter shared more of the UAV's specifications and small-caliber targeting capabilities. Confident in their own military prowess, some of the brass at Andrews downplayed the lethality because of its size. They suggested that deploying some handhelds should be enough to dispose of the little pest.

The plan was way off base.

White House Reserved Parking

The *Tiger* cautiously emerged from beneath Peter's Suburban.

The omniview lens panned the surroundings and spotted a trimmed hedge on the south exterior wall of the Oval Office. Shadow lines from surrounding trees pointed toward cover. The UAV reached the hedge and tucked itself backward underneath the foliage, retaining a clear view of the complex. Dark was good.

George Washington University

DSS Agent Jim Lange caught himself nodding off to Dr. Sydney Krohn's lecture on radical Islamic culture. He'd heard Krohn speak before on mind-over-matter feats by Australian aboriginal tribes and it nearly bored him to death. Tonight's subject, the 1979 Iranian revolution, wasn't much better. Instigated by the Shia sect of Islam, its followers had sworn holy and violent allegiance to their deceased religious leader, the Ayatollah Ruholla Khomeini. Lange thought about his own religion and prayed he'd stay awake through the next portion of the lecture: slides. Fighting another yawn, he noticed Agent Beck waving at him through the hall door.

"What're you doing here?" he whispered when she came in. "I thought you had a day off."

"We're in trouble," she whispered back, and sat next to him. "What a boring instructor."

"Tell me about it. We're old friends," Lange said. "What kind of trouble?"

"I just talked to Murphy. You won't believe what's happened."

Lange straightened with newfound energy. "Try me while my eyes are still open."

"Remember Sam Nasrabadi . . . the guy we interviewed outside Chicago?"

"The Ace of the Flyboys?"

Beck nodded, impressed with her partner's memory. "Uh-huh. He drove off Bolling with that secret flying machine. They think he's on his way to Andrews."

"The *Tiger*? Are you serious?" Lange spoke in his normal voice.

Krohn glared at the two agents and clicked the next slide.

"I heard it was responsible for that Baltimore incident after all. Four counties are on high alert."

"See . . . I knew that thing carried a weapon. Why Andrews?"

"An assassination. Murphy said the president's due back in DC sometime tonight. I guess he refuses to change his schedule or something."

"Jesus—that's incredible. Who would have ever thought?" Lange paused. His eyes widened. "We're in trouble."

"Bingo, but there's more. Caroline Jennings, that female technician from North Carolina, is missing, too. I wonder if they're both involved?"

"Great. That means we'd be two for two. Where's Murphy now . . . Andrews?" Lange was distracted by the next slide on the overhead—a list of Islamic titles.

"These ten agents are some of the most specialized in the Western world," Krohn explained. "Some were recruited as children, and some later in life. All exist for no other reason than to carry out final requests from their beloved Ayatollah—and they will never stop. This particular information is declassified and came to us courtesy of the Israeli Mossad. We are indeed fortunate to have it."

Beck gathered her purse and keys. Lange was riveted to the list on the screen.

FARSI	**TRANSLATION**
SHIER-EH SHAH	LION OF THE KING
KOSHANDEH-EH SEPAHAN	MURDERER OF THE ARMIES
AZ BAIN BARANDEH SHAHRHA	DESTROYER OF THE CITIES
QAATEL-EH ZABAN	ASSASSIN OF THE TONGUE
SADAYE KHODA	HE WHO DIES FOR KHODA
PESSAREH AYATOLLAH	SON OF THE AYATOLLAH
PANAHANDEH SHAITANAT	PROTECTOR FROM ALL EVIL
TANBIH KONANDEH-EH SHAITAN	PUNISHER OF GREAT SATAN
QAATEL-EH BACHEH AVVAL	ASSASSIN OF THE FIRSTBORN
DEFA KONANDEH-EH ZA-EEF	DEFENDER OF THE WEAK

Krohn continued. "Notice in the first translation the term *shah* for *king*—a title bestowed upon all Iranian royalty, such as Reza Pahlavi. The fourth agent was a pleasant fellow given the honor of fulfilling a holy mission ordered by Khomeini in 1988 to assassinate Salman Rushdie for writing *The Satanic Verses*." Krohn clicked the next slide.

Beck rose from her chair. "I'm going in."

Lange saw something. "I'm sorry. Yeah, thanks for stopping in."

Irritated at his rudeness, she poked him. "I said I'm going in. You should, too."

He stopped her. "Did you see that?"

"See what?"

"That translation . . . on the last slide."

"What translation? I have no idea what you're even talking about. Salman Rush—"

"Excuse me—would you bring up that previous slide?" Lange interrupted the class.

Krohn fumbled with the remote. The list came back up.

Lange stood. His pen and notebook dropped to the floor. "Oh, my God."

Beck hid her face from the stares. "Will you sit down!"

"His family," Lange said.

"Jim—what's wrong? You're scaring me."

"Where's his family?"

"Whose family?"

"The president's! Are they on the plane?"

Beck paused. "Yes . . . no . . . I don't think so."

Lange climbed over the seating for the exit. "They'll never stop it."

"Jim—wait . . . what is it? Jennings?"

He was gone. Several students rose to their feet as if someone had shouted "Fire." Krohn thought the young man was either ill or drunk.

Beck unbuttoned the trigger strap on her weapon and slowly started to read the translations on the overhead. A flurry of presidential assassination horrors raced through her mind. "Excuse me . . . did Khomeini have a son?" she inquired of the class.

"What on earth are you talking about, ma'am?" Krohn asked. "Will you please take your seat so we can continue?"

"I don't think so . . . there's nothing on record," a woman answered from two rows away. "I did a paper on him."

"Do you remember how old he was when he died?"

"Not exactly, but I think late seventies."

"Eighties," Krohn chirped.

Sam could be his son. The age sort of fit, but why did that spook Lange the way it did? Beck wondered. Something was missing. She turned back to the slide. *Protector from All Evil . . . Punisher of Great Satan . . . Assassin of the Firstborn . . .* She stopped. It was there. She spoke it again, slowly. With her eyes closed, her memory stretched across the country to Chicago and the interview. A water tower. Hanover Park. A flying trophy. First place. Firstborn. A pilot's call sign. Ace of the Flyboys.

The initials!

The hair on her arms bristled as she forced herself to move, screaming to clear a path after her partner.

Chapter Twenty-two

Potomac River
Roosevelt Island Nature Preserve

The public parking lot outside the preserve was empty except for a Pontiac Trans-Am with steamy windows. When the hulking MCS rudely parked next to them, the couple decided to leave. A steady stream of police vehicles raced along the George Washington Memorial Parkway toward the city.

Qaatel-eh Bacheh Avval neatly clipped the padlock on the steel gate that guarded the island entrance and drove across the pedestrian footbridge onto a dark nature trail that led to the Theodore Roosevelt Memorial. He parked next to a service shed—safe at least until morning. If all went well, he would easily escape out of the territory before anyone could suspect his objective. The fate of the

UAV was of no consequence now; it was merely a tool. He knew this was his best opportunity.

Born in Qom, a leading Shiite center, Qaatel's parents had pledged undying allegiance to the holy quest that would bring Iran back to the pure teaching of the Koran, long abandoned by Shah Reza Pahlavi's government. By 1964, tensions between the two cultures reached full-blown revolution that saw Khomeini exiled to neighboring Iraq for fourteen years. Under religious pressure, Khomeini fled to France, where he continued verbal agitation for the overthrow of the shah. It was there on student hiatus that Qaatel rejoined his beloved leader, received his sacred name and charge, and renewed his vow to bring pain and suffering upon the leader of the Great Satan. Having no timetable other than within his lifetime, Qaatel established residence in the United States, and devised a plan to complete his holy mission. Flying and gambling be damned. His only calling in life was to assassinate the first-born child of an incumbent U.S. president.

White House Complex

Ignoring the danger, the first lady demanded to be taken to Andrews. Aaron was still too sick to attend, and had used the opportunity to slip through the Rose Garden unnoticed. Fascinated at all the excitement, he lay quietly in his hiding place in the hedgerow. The cool ground soothed his overheated body. He closed his swollen eyes and rested his head on a Baltimore Oriole blanket.

Qaatel cursed at how perfect the opportunity was in the magnolia tree, when he had the child's temple in his crosshairs. He would have been out of the country before anyone suspected. His plan had now degraded into something crude and desperate. He clicked on a retrieval file for the boy's thermal signature, recorded the night before. He'd find the match in the complex even if it meant entering the house's interior.

Bound for holy glory, the Assassin of the Firstborn eased the *Tiger* forward.

White House communications relayed the message to the SCC, who tracked Bristol down, still on the conference. The caller claimed he was from DSS. When Bristol heard the word *Tiger*, he passed the phone to Turner.

"Sir—you've got to stop the attack!" Agent Lange shouted.

"Who is this?" Turner asked suspiciously, uncomfortable with the person and the conversation.

"Sam . . . Aaron . . . dammit—I mean Lange. My name is Jim Lange and I work for Gavin Murphy. You've got to stop him . . . Sam Nasrabadi. But it's not his real name . . . well, it is, sort of. He's an assassin. But he's not after—"

"Jim—slow down, we've got it covered," Turner assured him. "There's an army of security at Andrews—"

"A holy mission. He's going to use the *Tiger* to kill the president's son!"

It hit like a bomb.

Turner slammed the phone down. "Joe, bring everybody inside the fence. I want response team reinforcements on the roof. You come with me."

The entourage raced through the west wing to a stairway that led up to the president's living quarters. PPD agents were already standing in the child's empty bedroom. Within minutes Metro and White House officers and agents tightened the perimeter and were combing the house and grounds for the boy. In a brief moment of security carelessness, questions arose about whether the child had somehow gone unnoticed to Andrews. After an embarrassing call, Turner confirmed he wasn't there.

Through the omniview, Qaatel saw officers approaching and quickly slipped the UAV deeper under the hedge, content to let the patrols work themselves into a feeling of control. He smiled to himself. They all kept scanning the sky. When agents stopped at the corner of the Oval Office not six feet away, he remembered to activate the thermal sensors. The system came up. A message box flashed TARGET ACQUIRED. Somehow destiny was stretched out on the ground just twelve feet away.

Smiling at the good fortune Khoda had given him, Qaatel rotated the UAV and tried to poke through the shrubbery, but was stopped by thick base roots. Growing impatient, he thought about blind pattern fire, but decided against leaving anything to chance—not after getting this close. He moved the UAV into clear space, but was immediately forced up into the foliage of a nearby tree. Two officers paused on the footpath below. Their dogs sniffed the air.

Qaatel fixed a target point on an ERT sergeant three hundred feet away at the E Street fence line. Giving no directional warning, the shot purposely glanced off his helmet. With shots fired, the officers below the tree immediately responded. The diversion worked.

Alone again, Qaatel angled the UAV down from the branches to the top of the hedge, directly above his sleeping target. Now only five feet away, he decided to shoot freehand rather than waste another precious second fixing a target point. Khoda would guide his aim. He carefully aligned the PTS crosshairs onto the center of the boy's forehead and began to squeeze the flight trigger. He would see it penetrate. Mercifully, the child would not suffer. His mission was finished. Praise to the Ayatollah and almighty Khoda, who struck such a blow to the Great Satan, the United States. Praise to the Assassin of the Firstborn, Qaatel-eh Bacheh Avval!

A moment before the boy's certain death from the ceron round, Qaatel's targeting eye noticed something from a lateral omniview lens. Movement. It was coming from the background against an Oval Office porch column. He squinted through the darkness, steadily increasing the frame's resolution until the blurred object came into focus. His eyes widened.

The black muzzle of a Remington shotgun.

As the two lines of vision met, one from a red-beaded sight, the other from a video monitor two miles away, Turner fired first, unleashing a stream of double-aught buckshot screaming across the Rose Garden at sixteen hundred feet per second. The full-choke magnum load ripped into the *Tiger*'s lower and left sides, blowing out all but one video lens and tearing through the airflow housing on the underbelly.

The UAV cartwheeled across the lawn like some metallic boomerang.

Thanks to its thin profile, the damage wasn't fatal. The Oval Office wasn't as lucky. Stray pellets left a pockmarked swath on the building's exterior.

Qaatel howled with rage as he caught a fuzzy, inverted glimpse of the boy running across the lawn into the arms of Turner's uniformed officers.

On its back, the *Tiger* spun its fan blades violently.

"I'm gonna end this," Turner said, pumping another shell into the chamber.

"John—no!" Peter forced his way through a circle of officers and pushed the shotgun aside. He turned the UAV on its belly and into a vertical take-off position. It briefly lurched into the air. The PTS barrel was poking out of its casing. "The memory module is trying to absorb and dissipate the shock wave. It wants to fly."

Turner slithered his necktie off. He took a flashlight and jury-rigged both items to a jagged piece of metal hanging below the *Tiger*'s tail.

The officers stepped back and watched the battered UAV slowly rise into the air and float westward like a helium balloon caught in the wind, the bright beacon dangling beneath it.

Turner lifted his radio for the SCC. "You seeing this?"

"Affirmative," Janis replied.

"Let it go," Turner said. He turned to Peter. "Will he know we're coming?"

Peter tossed his keys. "Not if we stay far enough behind. He's got a rear view."

"The rest of you secure for the president," Turner ordered. "We're going hunting."

George Washington Memorial Parkway

The UAV leveled off at 150 feet on a flight path that ran parallel to the Theodore Roosevelt Bridge across the Potomac, maintaining a northwesterly course to the Roosevelt Island preserve.

Devastated in the mobile unit, Qaatel sat contemplating his own death. He had failed in his holy mission and weighed his options to save face for Khoda and Iran. There weren't many. He prayed for a second chance. That was it. He would pray to his Ayatollah—prayers his parents taught him at such an early age. It was what they had died for. His beloved . . . MOM! He had completely forgotten about the damned module that would bring the UAV and its pursuers right to him. He needed to get out of the area quickly.

Peter's cell phone chirped. "Thank God I got you," Carl's voice said. "I'm not sure, but I think we can override the flight controller. The omniview's got one working lens. What happened?"

Peter covered the phone. "It's my team; they can get control back."

"Can *Tiger* still shoot?" Turner asked.

Peter relayed the question, relieved to hear CJ's voice answer from the background. "Don't do anything to upset the flight path." Peter nodded at Turner. "We can target."

The swaying flashlight slowed to a hover in the center of the island.

Turner continued north on the parkway, straining to see through heavy brush along the roadside. A motorcycle screamed down the nature trail, across the footbridge, and raced into oncoming traffic in the southbound lanes.

Turner gave Peter his handgun and floored the Suburban. "I hope you know how to use that. I've never been in a police chase."

"I've got a better idea." Peter passed the phone.

Turner shifted it to his shoulder. "This is John Turner of the U.S. Secret Serv—Oh, screw that. We need your help; you're all we've got. I'm going to ask you to do something that—"

"I understand," CJ responded. "What AGL?"

"AGL?" Turner repeated, not understanding the acronym for "above ground level."

Peter snatched the phone. "You won't have much choice. As low as you can and best speed. How's your vision?"

"Bad . . . everything looks like it's in a tunnel," she answered. "Wait—there's water."

"That's the Potomac," Peter confirmed. "Fly northwest. It's your only chance."

CJ clicked the commands. Peter saw the *Tiger* respond. With only one working fan blade, it had no speed. The only advantage was the angled flight path. The Suburban couldn't gain ground because of the construction—the southbound lanes were even worse.

"I see him!" CJ shouted. The elation was short-lived as Carl announced that the battery load timer showed sixty seconds of flight time left.

From the air, Qaatel's faint heat pattern barely registered as the image dodged back and forth underneath the parkway's foliage. He had to slow for more barricades, giving *Tiger* four more seconds to catch up. The timer showed twenty seconds.

There was open straightaway in the distance. The motorcycle nearly lost control through a turn.

CJ centered the crosshairs and locked a target point.

At thirteen seconds she tried to roll the mouse pointer to the PTS firing control menu, but there was no response. The ball was stuck! Knowing manual keystrokes would take forever, she turned it upside down and frantically blew into the base while trying to thumb it free.

At six seconds, fan blade power stopped completely; the UAV started to fall.

A tiny piece of grit broke loose and the cursor arrow reached the command menu. The PTS barrel had just enough instruction memory to swivel. The screen's thermal image faded to black as CJ touched the joystick's trigger.

Qaatel's body arched violently from the ceron round, and then slumped onto the handlebars.

Forward momentum kept the cycle upright as it veered across the boulevard and rammed headlong over the curb, careening down the steep, rocky shoreline of the Potomac.

Powerless, the *Tiger* glided down onto the southbound lanes and skidded to a stop on the grassy median, the flashlight clanking behind like some metallic rat tail.

A veritable frenzy of intelligence personnel neatly sanitized the area. The incident quickly morphed into a routine traffic accident, leaving no trace of any flying machine. Only then were park police called in to recover the body. Someone on a motorcycle had simply lost control.

"Well, I think the lions are about finished feeding on their kill." Turner leaned into the Suburban's window and woke Peter from a mild sleep. "Sorry if I was a little rough on you back at DIA. Guess I owe you an apology. Hell, I'm a Wisconsinite myself for a few weeks every year."

Peter managed a tired nod. "You like animals too, huh?"

"Why don't you head back?" Turner suggested. "You can't do anything else here."

Peter pressed moisture from his eyes. "My *Tiger* almost killed that boy. How'd you know he was in those bushes?"

Turner grinned. "Hank Aaron once showed me the way."

Peter smiled back. "I like baseball."

DIA Center

Peter collected his briefcase and took one last look at the control center before turning out the lights. He glanced down the corridor and saw a well-dressed figure walking out of Floring's office.

"You're even starting to look like a consultant." Peter smiled. "I'm glad you passed on Israel."

"The Defense Department bought me out. I figured I might as well fill one of these empty chairs," Dutch Miller said sheepishly. "I heard it's official. Aerotech and DIA are now long-term partners in the production phase of *Tiger*-class UAVs. The initial orders have topped five hundred machines. God help us. The damn things'll be buzzing all over the place. Upgrade testing has been restricted to D-one personnel only. Looks like you got a new boss, too. Someone from Teledyne-Ryan. He's on a speakerphone with LaCroix right now, discussing transition and system passwords. They're already planning phase two. Sounds like a real fireball. I wonder why none of your team signed on? What about you?" The elevator doors opened.

Peter shrugged. "Family reunion. Think I'll spend some time on a farm."

Miller smiled and massaged Peter's shoulder. "Farming's a good thing. See the fish on Floring's wall? Missed Ohio's state record by two ounces. We're planning a trip in the spring, if you're interested. Need a lift?"

"Thanks, my ride's over there." Peter thumbed the opposite direction. "Guess I still owe you a meal. Don't let all this technical power go to your head. It's easy to do. Call me sometime—we'll plan a trip of our own. And I'll make the shore lunch."

"Double or nothing on Packers-Bears?" Miller asked.

Peter extended his hand.

The Bolling shuttle dropped Peter at the adjoining naval station heliport for the ride to Andrews and the flight home. Sergeant Malcolm's base-security Jeep raced down Laboratory Road and pulled onto the transport service drive. There was a package under his arm.

"Mr. Wescott? This was just delivered to our front gate, sir. Priority mail."

The helicopter rose over I-295 and headed southeast.

The morning traffic on the beltway seemed to

pause briefly, retightening its grip on the city like some motorized constrictor. Peter gave the Washington Monument a dutiful smile as it faded out of sight. He wondered when he'd see it again from his next unmanned aerial vehicle.

The package was unmarked except for the word *fragile*. Finally—his new laptop. A bittersweet gift, Peter thought. Now he'd have to answer e-mail from the farm.

He set it aside and closed his eyes. He'd open it later. Inside, unseen, a cryptic note taped to the glass pane over Margaret's contented Holstein cows said, *Pleasant Dreams.*